**Praise for *Chuck Steak***

"Unfortunately, it's not quite what I'm looking for."

"I just didn't connect with the story."

"Unfortunately, upon review, I just do not feel confident in my ability to represent this work and place it with a publishing partner in this competitive environment. With regret, I must step aside."

"It's simply too far from what my list demands, but I have to tell you, I loved it anyway! Good luck with this one, and please keep me posted on your success."

"Unfortunately…"

"While you are a very good writer and I do think that you have a very good story here, I'm sorry to say that I'm unable to offer you representation at this time."

"You should take that chapter out."

"…sorry…"

"I don't think you can say that."

"Best of luck getting this published somewhere else."

# Also by Casper Pearl

# Chuck Steak

## Something Something LLC

*Casper Pearl*

**Badass Cover Art**
*by J. Caleb Clark*
www.jcalebdesign.com

# Slab of Innards

# SATURDAY

Thank you, **Dad**. If it weren't for your fandom and constant belief in a bat-shit crazy idea, I wouldn't have rewritten this story or had the inspiration to publish it. I basically did this for you, so now we're even for having to raise a semi-difficult child.

**J**, you're terribly missed. You always asked about my writing, when I'd be publishing my first novel. Here it is, Brother.

# FRIDAY

## Chapter 1
## Bill

Chuck soars downhill inside the car he commandeered. It's rust-colored. The make and model are up for debate. The owner sits dazed in the middle of the road nearly two miles back with a goose egg rising on his forehead.

The jalopy rattles violently at 72mph due to a bent rim. The peeled paneling and half-attached passenger seat and unclamped hood don't help matters, either.

But Chuck will make it. He always does.

His radio bounces around the backseat. He spots it in the rearview mirror for a fraction of a second before it disappears and clangs against the window. It tumbles and flips and tries to yell above the noise, "Steak, goddamn it, where are you?" That's his lieutenant speaking—Lieutenant Anderson. Lieutenant Anderson is a man packed full of treats. His mustache is a skirt of hair which conceals his entire mouth even when he's screaming. "Goddamn it, you should be at the hostage situation by now! Goddamn it to Hell!"

Chuck hits a bump and goes airborne. The jalopy lands in a heap of sparks. The tire with the bent rim pops off like a cork and flies into an alleyway. Despite this setback, Chuck pushes 60mph.

1

He grinds through the street. To the few he passes who are out and about, he is a giant nail on a chalkboard.

Chuck peels a hand from the wheel and flips his wrist. He's wearing a brand-new chrome watch. Despite its sleek, futuristic appearance, Chuck's still ashamed to wear it. In some sense, it's comparable to having a big, juicy piece of spinach stuck between his top central incisors. Or ratty toilet paper stuck to the bottom of his boot. Or a mustard stain on the thigh of his white-washed jeans.

Fact is, who wears a watch nowadays? Not somebody anybody wants to associate with. *Irregardless*, Chuck has been stripped of his choices, so he checks in with the expiring timer. Under two minutes left. Okay, so it's going to be a close one, but he'll make it.

"Goddamn it, Chuck!" The radio is juggled from side to side. "Now it's on the news! Every goddamn channel, even the shitty one! The maniac's got some poor lady out on the ledge!" Anderson shouts and hollers everything he says. "She's screaming, for the love of everything, that she's got kids, Chuck! Five to be exact! FIVE!"

Chuck smashes the steering wheel with a meaty fist. It snaps right off. He tries to fit the oblong wheel back on, but it doesn't work like that. The jalopy smacks a parked truck and gets spun around in circles.

"Goddamn it, Chuck, her name's Sally, and she works for a nonprofit organization!"

The jalopy punts a mailbox.

"When she's not chiseling out time to spend with her family," the radio yells, "Sally can be found at the local homeless shelter!"

There goes a telephone pole along with the street's power.

"Jesus H. Christ, Chuck, she's also a pastor!"

Since he's not strapped in, Chuck's head jackhammers the roof. It takes nineteen thumps to turn the jalopy into a convertible. Nineteen thumps to knock Chuck Steak senseless.

He awakens in a puff of smoke to this:

"Sally's being nudged, Chuck! Do you hear me? A devoted wife, a beloved pastor, a selfless mother of five, a patron saint of community service—this female Swiss Army knife of everything good and decent in the world is being nudged off a thirty-story ledge!"

The door has already been torn off, so Chuck stumbles out of the car. The engine's caught fire. It's the only source of light for blocks. Everything's a bit hazy due to the concussion, but when his double vision merges together, he confronts the timer.

Twenty seconds left.

He's arrived at the correct address with a busted nose and two fractured ribs. There's no woman trapped on a ledge. There is, however, a blackened bank with an entrance barricaded in thick, steel bars.

The timer strikes 00:00, but where's the crime that's supposed to take place? Chuck wonders if the thieves are hitting the bank from underground, but then the radio cries out from inside the smoking car, "She's dead, Chuck! Flattened! It's horrible! If you were here, you'd be able to see for yourself! Since you're not, just flip on any ole goddamn TV to any ole goddamn channel!"

The neon blue zeroes flash on and off. Zeroes. Zeroes. Zeroes. But there's no crime. Save for the crackling fire, there's not a single peep to be heard at this dead intersection. Chuck rushes over and grips two of the bank's fat bars. He pulls with everything he's got, but not even the mighty Chuck Steak can budge steel.

He throws a frustrated punch and busts every knuckle minus the thumb (because according to the laws of physics, that would be impossible) on his right hand. "I barely felt that," he mumbles while desperately scanning the area. There's an elderly man clinging to a walker trying to cross the street. Chuck catches him halfway and asks if he's seen any suspicious activity.

The old, pale, spotted, bald, stick-figure man barges by.

"You hear me, Sir?"

3

"Piss off."

Chuck's taken back. "Excuse me?"

"*Piss…off.*" He talks with his hunched back turned. "And get your hearing checked."

"You best watch your dentures."

"Or what, ya knucklehead? Are ya gonna whoop an old man?"

"I'm a cop."

"Are ya gonna shoot me in cold-blood even though I pose no threat?"

"Listen, old man, this conversation is veering off course."

"You listen, Meathead McGee, I've got orders. Now unless you're gonna ask me out on a date, piss off."

The radio cries out, the plastic melting, the distorted voice drowning in flames, "And now Bruce is dead! If you're just tuning in, Chuck, he's the gentleman who erects wells in third world countries to give poor people fresh drinking water! He also owns and operates the local animal shelter!"

Chuck spins. There's no fucking crime anywhere. But then an idea bores inside his thick skull. What if?

*Yes?*

What if it's the old man?

*Preposterous!*

"Hey, old man!" Chuck jogs toward him.

"The name's Bill, and piss off yet again."

"Freeze!" Bill stabs at the street with his walker and drags his body closer to the curb. Chuck places a hand on his shoulder, engulfing it, and says, "You're jaywalking."

"Get your lousy mitten off of me." Bill tries to bat at it with his chin of hanging flesh.

"Come on," Chuck says, slowing every action in order to work delicately, "I don't want any—"

It's swift. Maybe the concussion made it so, but Chuck feels each tooth slide out of his neck. He feels the lines of blood rush down his bulging deltoid and soak into his shirt's collar. He feels the numbness rapidly spreading and stumbles backwards.

Bill cranes his neck and smiles red. After spitting out his vampiric dentures, he's all gums.

"All right," Chuck says, pausing to feel his body sway, "pappy," his lips have become bricks, "I'm going to," his head slumps to the left, "knock you," he strains to lift it to no avail, "into—"

"Let me guess," Bill's gummy hole says, "next week?"

"Eeeeeeeeeeeeeeeerrrrrrrn't!" It's the sound Chuck believes erupts when a contestant on a game show answers incorrectly. "A nursing home."

"Been there, done that." Bill stabs at the asphalt with his walker and drags his body forward. Stab and drag. About ten more stab and drags and he'll have completed the crime, at which point Chuck's girlfriend will be executed.

Chuck figures a smack upside the back of Bill's head will apply enough force to knock the stubborn man out for good. But after waddling into position, Chuck's right arm feels anchored.

Stab and drag.

The numbness has bitten into Chuck's right ankle. He finds out the hard way when he puts all of his weight on it, rolls it and takes a dramatic, flailing side-fall to the ground.

Stab and drag.

Chuck tries to speak, but his lips won't allow it. Just as his tree-trunk neck won't grant his head movement, forcing his chiseled face to lie there horizontally.

Stab and drag.

A numbing agent has knocked half of Chuck's body out of commission. With his workable half, he reaches for his weapon. It's not a standard issue tube of pepper spray. Not a standard issue taser. Not even a standard issue pistol. Chuck Steak only deals in customs, so he takes hold of his trusty, illegal hand cannon and tries to steady the heavy chunk of metal in his weak hand. But the sights frantically hop from target to target. From Bill's poor, shriveled head to Bill's barely beating heart.

Chuck can't kill this man. Not only is he a senior citizen, but Anderson specifically yelled in Chuck's good ear, "Goddamn it, no more casualties, you hear?"

The cannon sways with the wind. It's a split-second decision to pull the trigger. After a deafening eruption, it takes a moment for the discharged gust of smoke to clear. Chuck squints and assesses the damage. He's taken out one of Bill's legs. Not one of his actual legs—one of the walker's. It's slowed Bill a hair but hasn't ceased his jaywalking.

Stab and drag.

Chuck fires again with henchman-like accuracy and misses by a mile.

"Faaaosoooookkkkkkksssssssssqqqquuueeeee," Chuck slurs, which translates to, "Fuck me."

"Sssoaoaoosoafaskfoksfowjkiojfaekfjsjfowfskfs," the melted blob of radio cries from inside the inferno, which translates to, "There goes Jennifer Davies! She was the valedictorian of her graduating class! She had a full ride to M.I.T.! Did you hear me, Chuck? M.I.T.!" Even though M.I.T. isn't what it used to be, it's still M.I.T.

Stab and drag.

Chuck fires another wild shot that splits the walker in two. Bill takes a nasty face plant which gives him rubble for teeth. He then goes on to whine that at least half of his body has been broken. Then he goes on a tangent about police brutality—how he wishes he didn't hate technology so he could record their event to share with the world so they'd see the injustice suffered here today.

Chuck slurs, "Bbbbbbbbbbbbbbbbbbbbbbbbb," which, if finished, would translate to, "You deserved it, you baked potato bastard."

But the baked potato bastard isn't broken enough, because he reaches forward and fits his fingers inside a pothole to pull himself closer to victory.

Of course O.D.O.T. didn't repair this highly-traveled street after the bat-shit-crazy winter the city just endured. Why would they?

Bill has become a zombie. He sticks out his tongue and tries to lick the curb, but he's still a good three feet away.

If the radio inside the car wasn't already smelted into black liquid, and if Bill was the next victim nudged out onto the ledge, Anderson would probably scream, "Goddamn, Jesus H Christ, Holy Shitballs! This is Bill Flannigan, Chuck! He's a vet from every war imaginable! He's also a cancer vet, having beaten stage four brain cancer twice in his lifetime! Back in the 90s, he was wrongfully convicted of a murder he didn't commit and sentenced to life in prison! He wouldn't be released until twenty-two years later only to discover that every member of his family tree had died off! How goddamn sad is that, Chuck? Bill Flannigan is a goddamn survivor if I've ever heard of one, but he couldn't save a single person he cared about. Goddamn it, goddamn it right to Hell!"

Bill swipes with his tongue again, strike two.

Chuck aims but can't fire, because at this angle, he'd plug a bullet right into Bill's anus.

Bill uses another pothole to pull himself within licking distance.

There's no other option than to fire and give the old man a lethal enema.

Chuck musters forth the power to steady his cannon for just a moment, and in this moment, he fires a perfectly aimed shot that blows off the fire hydrant's bonnet. The desired effect was for a gushing line of water to strike Bill in the chest and roll him up the street, but what transpires is this: the fire hydrant has lost its head, and it vomits a funnel of water into the sky. The funnel eventually peeks and casts a torrential downpour upon the street below. Bill laughs at the audacity. He's not stupid—he has, in fact, been kickin' for ninety-two long years. He knows there's nothing left to stop him from completing the crime at hand. Well, except for the flood of water building in the storm gutter, and that storm gutter is located right in front of Bill's face.

The flood rises abruptly due to the uneven foundation. Thanks O.D.O.T. The taxpayers should demand a refund. But that is neither here nor there, because Bill is suddenly drowning. He is up to his eyeballs in a raging river, and every gasp forces an elevator of fluids down his throat.

"Yaaayayayaaaaaakaaakaaammmmmm," Chuck spits and sputters, meaning, "You've gotta be kidding me."

There's no timer for this one, but Chuck's sure the geezer doesn't have long. He abandons the cannon and stretches his reach for the first pothole. This feels like the equivalent of performing yoga, and Chuck Steak doesn't like yoga. He's not a fool—he knows its purpose. In fact, he knows the very definition:

*A means to create strength, awareness and harmony in both the mind and body.*

Chuck Steak is also not color blind. He respects pink and knows it has a place in the world. That doesn't mean he's going to wear it. He prefers his clothing and actions to portray his true feelings. That's why Chuck Steak wears black in abundance, like his current tee-shirt, and why he allows himself to have bitchy-resting-face—because he's always angry about something, whether it be tailgaters on the freeway during severe weather conditions, or jackasses aiming guns at his forehead and threatening to blow his brains out the backend.

After dragging all of his two-hundred-and-fifty-pounds through another pothole, Chuck stretches his reach one last time and latches onto Bill's black tube sock. The thing comes right off to reveal a stank-ass foot. The yellowed, cracked nails seem to have gone untrimmed for at least a decade. But Chuck must take hold. He pinches the old man's big toe and tugs…and dislocates it. The toe now feels like a testicle, but Chuck yanks on it anyway and pulls Bill back far enough so he can grip the man's tender ankle and pull him back even further. Chuck's then able to reach Bill's thigh. This is the awkward yet necessary part to drag Bill's soggy face out of the river, so Chuck Steak sets aside his dignity and wraps his paw around an old man's mushy thigh and heaves with everything he has left.

Bill is now beached. After some moments pass them by, Chuck realizes he's dead.

Not knowing exactly how much time has passed, but knowing brain damage occurs after two-and-a-half minutes without oxygen, Chuck thinks back to that resuscitation class Anderson enrolled him in. He thinks a little bit more, but nothing comes to mind. Then he realizes why—he had excused himself to pee then proceeded to exit the building. He signed the little book ahead of time so he'd get credit for the course, and it worked.

"Fuuuuugggggggkkkkkk." There's still quite a bit of slur left on Chuck's tongue. And half of his body is still pinned, so he grips Bill by the beltline of his khakis and pulls him down further. Then he grips Bill's breast pocket and pulls, but it tears right off. He squeezes a clump of Bill's plaid shirt inside his fist and pulls, only to rip that clean off, too. There's nothing left to grip except the bush of white fuzz on Bill's chest. Chuck retches as he takes hold and pulls, this time gently, causing some of the fuzz to tear like a 92-year-old Band-Aid. He pulls with tender care, whispering, "Cooooommme ooooooon baaaabaaay." And like that, Bill and Chuck have come head to head.

"Coooma unnnn Brillllll," Chucks says, raising his hand high, "drrrrooooon't youuuuuuu drrrrrrrrrry beeeeecauseeeee aaaaaaa meeeeeee!" He bitch-slaps Bill's Rhomboid major. That doesn't work so he bitch-slaps Bill's Rhomboid minor. That doesn't work so he searches his limited view for any peeping Toms. Then he grips Bill by the back of the head and turns him around. Now they are face to face. Chuck retches one last time before reeling Bill in and engulfing the man's withered, stale lips with his own. They won't open, so Chuck makes a crowbar out of his tongue and pries them apart. He has to hurry, because the vomit is building in his throat, so Chuck blows and blows and blows. He feels a draft rush out of Bill's flaring nostrils, so Chuck pinches them shut and blows some more.

It takes a few more blows before Bill convulses back to life and regurgitates what amounts to a cup of water. Once the seriousness of the situation settles, the two nestle into the street. Chuck lies there curled with his left cheek pressed flat against the asphalt. And Bill lies there spread eagle with his arms thrown up haphazardly above his head. Bill's pruney hands are caught in the river's flow. They sway left.

Bill stares up at the bright stars in the sky. He thanks whoever's up there looking down over him.

Chuck stares straight across at the weird patches of white bushes rising and falling on Bill's chest. A melted gumdrop is trapped inside one, fused with the hair. He curses whoever Bill's thanking which Chuck believes, a fraction of a second later, prompts the next event to unfold in this absurdly ridiculous chain of reactions.

The jalopy explodes. It was supposed to wait until Chuck regained feeling in his body. Wait until the badass motherfucker stood tall, patted himself off, punched Bill in the face for all the trouble, then walked away, slowly. Then, and only then, was it supposed to spit a hot-air-balloon-sized flame ball into the night.

But of course the jalopy works on its own timetable—a timetable comprised entirely of appalling inconveniences. For the previous owner, still sitting dazed and confused in the middle of the street miles back, who's still awaiting any sort of assistance, he's probably head over heels about some dumbass relieving him of the source of all his problems.

But that is neither here nor there, because the unnamed owner has no further role in whatever transpires from this point forward, so onto the massive flame ball, and onto the way it's belched into the sky. The hues, the brightness, the swirls of orange and red and yellow are, for a moment, breathtaking. But flame balls are highly dangerous, especially when they eat through telephone poles. One poor telephone pole in particular gets torched right to the bone. The bone snaps, and the cord above snaps with it. That cord spills to the ground and slices across the river, zapping the water with a surge of electricity. It flows upstream and shocks Bill's pruney hands ferociously. It seems like old times again with Bill dead and everything.

Chuck can't believe this bullshit. To think, if it weren't for the shady call that came through on the mysterious phone which had to have been eased into Chuck's back pocket when he wasn't looking, maybe he was chowing down on a bacon-double cheeseburger, if it weren't for the preprogramed name which appeared on the plastic-looking screen stating *Killer calling...*, if it weren't for the guy on the other end who said all deep, raspy and robotically, "Hey, Chuck, I've got remote-access to the bomb inside your girlfriend's liver," and if it weren't for Chuck hanging up but hanging onto the phone (which came with two accessories, both of which were left on his stoop's unwelcome mat—a used, once-ivory-now-yellowed wedding planner, and a futuristic watch), if it weren't for Chuck going, "Huh, what if?" and wandering over to Mia's apartment since they don't live together even though they've been dating for forever now, if it weren't for Chuck arriving, Mia asking, "What's the matter?" and him going, "Um, never mind—that's preposterous," and if it weren't for the unknown phone ringing again, at which *Killer calling...* said, "Listen carefully," and if it weren't for Chuck listening carefully and hearing a beep inside his girlfriend, her going, "What's that?", him passing it off as, "You farted," and leaving abruptly, if it weren't for Chuck putting the phone to his ear and listening to the madman's diabolical plan of, "Having coaxed some poor schmuck into committing a crime," Chuck would surely just let Bill pass violently into the night. The guy has, in fact, almost lived a century. He has probably done everything imaginable except lived a full century.

But for all intents and purposes, Bill is yet another victim in this villain's twisted game.

With the wire hopped up on the curb, dancing from slab to slab, Chuck's able to yank Bill's arms from the water. Then he French-kisses Bill again, blowing to no avail. Then he burps out globs of bacon and meat and cheese all glued together by grease. It oozes down Bill's neck and appears as though he's wearing a vomit turtleneck.

*Hell no,* Chuck thinks to some more French-kissing. This time he pounds each bush of fuzz on Bill's chest like it's an arcade fighting game. After a few rounds of this horseshit, Bill shoots upright, gasps, and yells, "Whaaaaaat?"

Chuck hasn't even come close to sniffing real action, yet he finds himself completely spent. Upon reflection, he concludes that saving one measly life is light-years harder than taking out a drove of bad guys.

And like that, Bill's on the move again. The old man swivels and has the nerve to get back to crawling on his belly. He swipes with his brittle tongue to complete the crime.

*You son-of-a-bitch,* Chuck thinks as he latches onto Bill's left pant leg, pulls, splits the thing from seam to seam, pulls some more, tears the khakis completely off, then latches onto Bill's grey tighty-whities and pulls, revealing Bill's crater-filled moon, but still pulling until they are again face to face. Before Bill can whine about being let go, Chuck pulverizes him in the face with a fed-up haymaker. If the old man still had any teeth left, they would've been knocked a block over yonder.

By the time a squad car finally shows up, Chuck has regained most of the feeling in his body. He's able to stand and hold a corded radio which stretches from the inside of the car to Chuck's outreached hand and say to Anderson, "Shit, my bad," after of course Anderson says to him, "Goddamn it, Chuck, are you even kidding me right now? You mean that for the first time in forever, you've finally listened to one of my orders? You saved a man from certain death not once but twice? Chuck, goddamn it right to Hell, Bill is a serial child molester who's been on the loose for over twenty years! If there's one goddamn person in the entire world you *should've* killed, it's him! Goddamn you, Chuck! Goddamn you straight up and down!"

Chuck drops the radio and plucks the ringing cell out of his pocket to answer accordingly: "You're dead."

"Of course, of course, but not in chapter one, Chucky. Don't be silly."

"Don't call me Chucky."

"Don't look down."

Chuck looks down, there's nothing there.

"Made you look."

"Bastard."

"You know my fiancée used to do that to me all the time. She'd tell me I had a stain on my shirt, and when I'd look down, she'd flick me in the nose with her finger. She got me good every single time."

"Dumbass."

"That's not nice, Chuck. I told you my fiancée was killed by a man in uniform such as yourself."

"I wear tee-shirts, boots and jeans, Asshole."

"Stop striving for cleverness."

"It comes naturally."

"Good, because I'm going to put that to the test in the next chapter."

Another car on the other side of the street which was struck preciously three minutes ago by the downed, snapping power line, has since caught fire. It has since turned into another inferno.

This car has great timing. It has always been reliable for its owner. It is a foreign car. They're built well.

"Welcome," the killer says, "to the greatest action story ever told."

Click.

Dial tone.

The foreign car explodes.

# Chuck Steak

# SATURDAY

## Chapter 2
## Grace

The doorbell rings, so Chuck holsters his oven mitts and rushes to answer. In the hallway, he jogs past a standard living room on the right, a great room on the left, the formal dining room on the right, a bathroom on the left, and Chuck's memorabilia room on the final right—the previous owners used this space as an office.

The memorabilia room is filled with shelves made of glass and desks made of cocobolo. There are two reclining, leather chairs aimed at it all. And the walls have been painted Peach Tickle. Chuck hand-picked and self-applied this special color. He likes to plop down, kick his feet up, kick his boots off, pour a mountain of baby powder into the palm of his hand, reach down and slap it against his undercarriage, rub it around so it's all smooth-sailings, then peruse the plethora of framed pictures and magazine articles and newspaper clippings of every ass-whoopin' he's ever dealt. And then he likes to meditate.

Why Peach Tickle?

Well, back in the early '90s, little Chuck would rush home from school to get a jumpstart on livening up whatever drab apartment his mother had relocated him to. She hated the instability. Often, she'd sit little Chuck down and say, "Do you think I'm a terrible mother?" He'd wrap her up fast with a strong hug, a strength unbefitting his stick-like frame, and whisper, "No, Mom—Hell no!" She'd reprimand him for the language and explain that even though the world wasn't decent, that didn't give them the right to be indecent. Then she'd squeeze him back and say, "I love you so."

To prove his love, to grant her some sort of relief, Chuck would dive into renovations while his mother worked tirelessly to keep their only source of income, a self-owned convenient store, afloat.

Chuck would patch holes in the walls with colorful pictures he'd drawn at school. He'd trace unwanted bugs back to their cracks and crevices and destroy their nests. Spiders were okay in his book. In fact, he considered himself and arachnids partners in crime.

Chuck would also fix leaky pipes and polish rusty metal and chisel off black continents of mold.

His mother would stumble home exhausted, riddled with body aches. It'd take a bit for her to notice a loose bannister retightened, or a dead outlet rewired, but when she did, she'd stumble right into Chuck's bedroom, wake him from his peaceful slumber, and she'd profess her love for him, and she'd gush and praise about all the improvements, about how thoughtful and skillful they were, and then she'd get that tear in her eye, the one which rolled around the bottom of her lid—the one signifying that she had bad news to break—that she had been robbed at gunpoint yet again, so they were going to have to downgrade into an even shittier apartment.

Near the end, the two were living in the convenient store's office which turned out to be the most inconvenient place yet.

Chuck's dream of becoming a home improvement guru died the same night he watched his mother shot execution-style by a German capitalist and then lit ablaze.

He didn't want to be soft anymore.

He didn't want to be puny.

Helpless.

Gentle.

Loving.

Kind.

Polite.

He didn't want to continue to fix things which the next person to come along would just ruin or let fall to shit.

So he became hard.

And angry.

And developed a nasty temper.

And a thirst for vengeance.

And also a thirst for fist-pummeling wrong-doers. And cocky pricks. And inconsiderate douche bags.

This information would help Lieutenant Anderson understand how it is Chuck can nonchalantly destroy half of the city on a consistent basis.

But Chuck refuses to talk about B.C.S. (Before Chuck Steak), because that kid was a fucking pussy who let his mother die, so let's honor his decision and cease immediately, at least for the time being.

Chuck was sure his girlfriend Mia would be the first to arrive so she could deal with her own parents. But as Chuck opens the door, it's like there's a string attached to the knob and her father's hand. Suddenly, the rough paw is in Chuck's face. It bobs. A deep, confident, snooty voice plays. The father, Orpheus, is wide-eyed as he nods at his outgoing hand and says, "The lord is great, Chuck."

This man is not an idiot. He's a repeat customer of the nightly news. He likes to be in-the-know about the current issues plaguing the world. He likes to figure out ways he and his lord can repair things back to their collective image of how things should be. To Orpheus, Chuck Steak is a problem in dire need of fixing.

"Thanks for coming," Chuck says, caving on the handshake.

The two fists bob strong. "The lord's great." Just in case it went unheard.

"Yeah, got it." He turns to hug the mother, Henriette. "You look lovely this evening."

Orpheus sidesteps into the hug and squeezes Chuck tight and leans in and whispers into his ear, "Lord...great."

This is not the main reason Chuck has yet to propose to Mia, although it's a goddamn fantastic one.

Chuck brings his lips next to Orpheus' ear and whispers, "Oh...kay."

"See!" Orpheus pops off and claps and swings around to face his wife and says, "I knew there was some hope for this one. I just knew it."

Chuck is Orpheus' ticket into Heaven. He has imagined himself on numerous occasions standing at the pearly white gates, and the gatekeeper instantly recognizing Orpheus' name and shouting, "Hey, everybody, get over here quick! It's the guy who converted the unconvertible Chuck Steak! Sweet Jesus." And the gatekeeper would glance over his shoulder at Jesus in the distance, who, without a doubt, had heard him, and mumble, "Sorry, Jesus." He'd shake it off and continue, "You're like really famous up here, Man."

Tis Orpheus' pig-in-shit dream. But even so, that doesn't mean he wants his daughter anywhere near Chuck. In fact, if Orpheus could break down and rebuild the mighty Chuck Steak according to his and his lord's specific blueprint, the once-demonic cop still wouldn't be good enough for his precious baby.

"And what is this I'm looking at, Chuck?" Orpheus has never been welcome inside Chuck's condo, so the memorabilia room is a flashy, new thing to him.

"Oh, just past accomplishments."

"No, Chuck. No, no, no." Orpheus is too close. His panting fogs the French doors' glass. "Those are sins."

Orpheus is lucky there's a bomb lodged in his daughter's liver, and that some mysterious madman concocted a list of chores for

Chuck to complete in the allotted time to prevent said bomb from detonating, or else...

Chuck tries to unload the parents into the formal dining room, at the fancily-prepared table with its vibrant white, unwrinkled table cloth, its shimmering and perfectly set dinnerware, the bleeding candles. But Orpheus can't be chained and contained. He puts a stubborn finger up and says, "Chuck, a word?"

They step, man to man, inside the bathroom. The door's pulled shut, softly. Orpheus flicks the fan on to drown out their voices. He examines the mint green color-scheme. The fluffy, hanging bath towels. The shag throw. The glass jug filled with mouthwash, and next to it, a stack of plastic, black, one-use cups.

"Are you gay, Chuck? Is that what this is all about? Is that why you're stringing my daughter along? Why you pretend to be the toughest man in the world? Because secretly you're gay, and you know it's terribly wrong, and you think if someone finds out, you'll go straight to Hell?" Orpheus has the nerve to poke Chuck in the chest. He does it repeatedly, each word annunciated by a poke. "Newsflash, Chuck, the lord already knows. He knows everything. He's always everywhere. He sees and hears everything."

*Then he's fucking nosy.* With one simple flick to the nuts, Chuck could bring Orpheus whimpering to his knees. He would snap a picture and get it blown-up for his memorabilia room's wall. It'd be the focal point.

Tis Chuck's pig-in-shit dream.

"I'm not gay," Chuck says, "I actually want to propose to Mia, and I'd like..." He clears his throat. "...your blessing."

"So that's why you dragged us all over here." Orpheus chuckles. "Even if you weren't gay, why would I ever, in a million, trillion years, consent to such blasphemy?"

The doorbell rings again. That's Mia's slightly younger brother, Chet. Chet's a closet homosexual. He has never, even once, thought about coming clean to his parents. When the father eventually passes, he'll let the entire world know. But until then, he has a reputation to uphold.

"I bet that's Chet," Orpheus says, grinning. "Now there's a real, straight man, Chuck. You should take notes." He winks and turns to leave.

"Wait."

"I think we've kept my wife on hold long enough, don't you think, Chuck?"

Why does this man insist on using a person's name over and over again? It gets repetitive. Doesn't he realize once a name's announced for the record, it no longer needs to be stated?

Chuck consults the brand-new chrome watch handcuffed around his wrist. "Come on," he says, "work with me on this."

What Orpheus does is chortles his way out into the hallway. He chortles all the way to the front door where he helps himself to the knob and the right to not only answer, but to grant access to a residence he holds no stake in.

"Chet!" Orpheus goes in for a hug, like usual, and Chet throws up a flaccid hand, like usual, and reminds his father with a long, overdrawn sigh, "Come on, Pops, hugs are gay. How many times I gotta tell ya?"

Orpheus turns, and he and Chuck shoot stares across the seemingly endless hallway. It represents a gap which will remain between them always and forever. "See, Chuck, this here is a real man."

Chuck would love none other than to effortlessly snap off Orpheus' thumb, which he confidently bobs at his blatantly gay son, but the problem is this:

If Chuck can't successfully check every chore off his list, which includes becoming engaged to Mia *and* getting her father's blessing amongst others, then in roughly forty-two minutes, there won't be any Mia left.

"That doesn't make any sense," Chuck said to the lunatic earlier on the phone. "What do you get out of me marrying her?"

"It's not what *I'll* get out of it, Chuck. Think about the audience. Why should anyone care about you in your current state? You've been in a relationship with a sweet girl for over a decade, and you've yet to tie the knot. You're scared of commitment, and nobody will appreciate that. If you're going to be the hero of this story, then everybody needs to like you."

Orpheus leads Chet into the formal dining room. He tells his son to take a seat, to take a load off, but Chet waves him away, says he doesn't listen to orders—he'd rather stand like a man.

When Chuck floats in to unload a silver, lidded, steaming platter, Orpheus nods at his son and says, "See, this here's a real man. Won't hug. Won't sit. Won't listen. One-hundred-percent man." The blasphemy kills Chuck, but after he deposits the entrée, he tucks his head and scurries away. He is, in fact, sporting two plaid mittens along with a knee-low, beige apron reading, *I'm grilling a witness*. Even though it's a clever, fitting message, nothing changes the fact that Chuck's befitted in such feminine attire. But this is the only place in the world where he's allowed himself to undress his vulnerabilities. That's why he never proposed to Mia—he never wanted her life involved in the stakes. After his mother was shot execution-style and lit ablaze before his ten-year-old-eyes, Chuck let his love plateau, because he knew the greater the love, the greater the loss. And he didn't want to feel the immensity of such pain ever again, even though it's meant lying to the world about his true feelings.

By the time Chuck returns with a steaming bowl in either mitten filled with stuffing and lobster risotto, his beloved Mia has arrived unannounced. She goes in for a hug with Orpheus who's seated at the head of the table, and after they pat each other's backs and pull away, he says, "Why didn't you ring? I would've let you in."

"Dad, I have a key."

"Right, of course you do. Why wouldn't you, Mia?"

She shakes her head, because she's not an idiot, either—she knows this little get-together probably isn't going to end well. Which prompts her to utter, while leaning in to place a neat, secretive kiss on the side of Chuck's rough, square chin, "I sure hope you know what you're doing."

He nods.

"Because I'm nervous, and you know me—I seldom get nervous."

Chuck hurries into the kitchen and flips his wrist. Twenty-one minutes remain. He's gotta hurry this along. He was going to toss a salad, but there's no time for that shit. When Chuck turns around to get the ball rolling, he bumps into Chet.

"Sup, Dawg?" Chet bobs his bald head. "You gots yourself like a maid or something?"

"No." Not only is Chet a closet homosexual in his dad's presence, but he's also a closet gentleman. Chet is a sophisticated man who frowns upon such language. Chuck's had drinks with him and Mia countless times, and every question he's ever asked has ended with *please*. "No maid, no butler. Now can we all just sit down and eat?"

"Damn, yo, it look like a bitch live here."

"Chet!" Mia blurts.

Orpheus is hunched over in his master throne, laughing whilst slapping his knee. "That's my boy," he chants repeatedly.

Chet gives Chuck a slight shrug coupled with a nervous wink.

Everyone finally takes their seats with 19:12 to go.

Everyone makes tents out of their hands and puts them on display. Chuck's is barely visible, so the head of the table, the new alpha male known as Orpheus, clears the snot from his nasal cavities and says, "Come on now, Chuck, don't be shy. Put your elbows up."

Chuck lugs his elbows onto the table.

"There ya go, Chuck."

The table might as well be a sauna. Everything steams. Chuck feels the loss of mass. His face melts off.

"Dear Lord," Orpheus says with shut eyes, "thank you for another day of life. You're too kind, honestly. Truly. Wholeheartedly. And thank you for—"

"Ahem."

Everyone looks at Chuck. He mumbles.

"What, Chuck?" Orpheus says as he cups his ear. "Speak up, Chuck."

"I'd like to lead grace." Of course this is a blatant lie. Everybody knows, especially Mia.

"But you hate grace," Mia whispers.

He's always hated grace, even before Orpheus randomly called on him one Thanksgiving.

*"I think we'd all finally like to hear you lead grace for once," Orpheus announced, "Chuck."*

*Chuck panicked and drew a blank. Seconds earlier, he had been reliving an event from the previous day where he thwarted a villain who called himself The Gardener. The event had made Chuck giggle, so this was Orpheus' revenge:*

*"Come on, Hotshot, it's only grace," Orpheus had said.*

*The entire length of the table stared at Chuck. There must have been thirty-some Johnsons there.*

*"Hello?" Orpheus knocked. "Earth to Chuck Steak! Yoo-hoo! Over here!"*

*In his mind, Chuck was still stuck with The Gardener. The guy wore an aluminum bucket on his head, a bright yellow, plastic raincoat, and matching rain boots. What sort of crimes did The Gardener commit? Well, he snuck into citizens' professionally landscaped yards to plant goutweed, periwinkle, poor man's mustard, English ivy, and dog-strangling vine amongst many others. Over time, The Gardener wreaked havoc upon lawns. Over time, The Gardener ruined peoples' perception of perfection.*

Chuck had long since forgotten about that dreadful Thanksgiving where he never mustered forth the strength to give grace its due diligence.

"Hello?" Orpheus knocks on the table. "Earth to Chuck Steak!" Déjà vu.

Chuck's trapped in time.

*The Gardener would venture back to the scene of his crimes. He'd catch his victims on all fours, lost in foliage, hacking at the land with their weeding hoes, trying to undo all his hard-earned work of weed-planting. Angered and confused and feeling a sense of entitlement, The Gardener would use bricks to beat the homeowners in the back of their sweaty heads. When the victims eventually came to, they found themselves blinded by the blistering sun. Their mouths were stuffed with leaves and bound by vines. And worst of all, they couldn't move a muscle, for they were planted, neck-deep, in the soil. Seven out of The Gardener's nine victims succumbed to heat exhaustion. One went by way of vengeful sewer rats driven by their ancestors' brutal and unjust demises. And the last, such an unlucky S.O.B., went by way of their significant other. The significant other, a wife, had peeked out into the yard, seen the weeds still plaguing her garden, yelled for her husband, his name was Ben, and when Ben didn't answer, she became annoyed, because she had told poor Ben to whack the weeds at least sixteen times that very day. Maddened, she set off to complete this chore herself. Thus, poor Ben was soon taken out by his own wife's atrocious weed-whacking abilities.*

"Well," says Orpheus, "this is downright embarrassing."

*One would logically assume Chuck Steak got ahold of The Gardener in the nick of time before attacking a tenth victim and successfully planted the maniac in the ground to give him a dose of his own medicine, but this was not the case.*

"I'm sorry, Lord," Orpheus shuts his eyes again and chuckles, "but some things never change. And sometimes, Lord, certain people just don't belong. They're out of place. They need to hit the road and never come back."

*Chuck Steak yelled, "Freeze!"*

*The Gardener dropped his steel, handheld spade and fat, hemp bag. The spade speared the ground. The bag burst open and spilled seeds. The Gardener swiveled around mannequin-like, the plastic coat making weird rubbery noises as he did. With his hands held behind his head, The Gardener frowned and said, "Didn't see this coming."*

*"Me either." Chuck lowered his firearm, a cannon, a notch. "I never thought I'd yell* freeze. *This sucks."*

*Some time passed. It was awfully boring.*

*"Well, what's going on here? My arms are getting tired. Are you arresting me or not?"*

*Chuck shrugged.*

*"You wanted to blow my head off, didn't ya?"*

*The answer was obvious, so Chuck did something more beneficial—he looked around. He nodded at a toolshed located at the yard's furthermost corner.*

*"What about it?"*

*Chuck nodded again.*

*"I don't like this. Tell me what you mean."*

*Chuck aimed his gun at the shed.*

*"Ah, I get it." The Gardener took off in a full sprint. His boots squished with each step, because it had just rained. His boots became hairier with each step, because the homeowner had just mowed the lawn. He reached the shed first and flung the door open. Inside, he found an arsenal of backyard weaponry. The door closed and locked. It had become a changing room of sorts.*

*Chuck skidded and squished to a halt. He waited patiently, yet eagerly, in a puddle of muck. He had dropped his cannon yards back and bent over to pick up The Gardener's handheld spade instead. Thus why he finished second. And he would've wanted it no other way, for he had previously envisioned this encounter as an epic story which would be handed down throughout the ages from one action lover to the next.*

*The shed door popped open.*

*The Gardener stood slumped with a leaf blower slipping from his limp, gloved grip.*

*"Really?" Chuck said. He looked back over his shoulder and spotted the homeowner crouched and peeking out a second-story window. The homeowner had a cell pressed into the side of her face, and her lips were paused, waiting anxiously to spit out, in great detail, exactly what was about to transpire between the two rivaling forces.*

*"There's nothing else in there?" Chuck whelled. Whelled is what occurs when one attempts to yell and whisper at the same time.*

*The Gardener let the leaf blower drop as he rummaged around for a few more seconds. This time he clutched a chainsaw which lacked an actual chain.*

*"Whatever," Chuck said, "just fire it up." He figured the homeowner wouldn't know the difference.*

*But the chainsaw only sputtered.*

*"It's outta gas."*

*"In addition to murdering people, can you do other stuff, like make noises?"*

*The Gardener's chainsaw impression sounded like a ripping fart.*

*"Well shit," Chuck noticed the homeowner blabbing away, "quick, grab something and come at me already. And make sure it's sharp!"*

*"Got it!" The Gardener hit the grass running and slipped. He lunged forward as if flying. He had a death grip on his choice of weapon, but unfortunately, he had ignored the cardinal rule of keeping all blades face-down. Was it so surprising that a serial killer had chosen to break every rule imaginable? No. But what was surprising, especially to Chuck, was when The Gardener broke the fall with a pitchfork through the face. Close-up, The Gardener was absurdly dead. From a distance, depending on the angle and whether or not the homeowner had any sight impairments, The Gardener could've very well still been alive and kickin'.*

*Chuck took hold of The Gardener's hanging wrists. He raised them into plain sight. Then he began smacking himself across the face with the dead palms. The pitchfork impalement kept getting in the way, so Chuck used the hands to pluck it free—nothing looked natural—then he palmed the pitchfork and speared it through his own shoulder. Both men collapsed.*

*This went on for some time.*

*It played out like a crossover event of* Fight Club *meets* Weekend at Bernie's.

*It ended with Chuck, shirtless, bleeding profusely from the face, driving away from a cornfield on a tractor at 5mph. The cornfield was on fire. Chuck hoped it would explode, but it did no such thing. With the homeowner still blabbing away on the phone, he did the next best thing—he hit the shed head-on—actually, he bumped into it and came to a peaceful stop—and then he flung himself off to complete a half flip before belly-flopping onto the soggy ground.*

*He peeled his face from the mud, and glancing at the homeowner, gave her a thumb up.*

"Hold on, Dad," Mia says. She leans into Chuck and, staring down at the napkin on his lap which has been scribbled all over, whispers, "why are you acting so strange?"

Because Chuck must give an awkwardly prepared grace.

Because he must serve her parents a delicious smörgåsbord of food they can't eat.

Because he must break the news that Chet's gay.

Because he must slap Henriette on the ass, get Orpheus' blessing, and then propose to Mia and have her say yes.

It's never going to work.

Chuck secretly checks the ticking, blue digits and discovers it's T-minus 13:01 until failure.

"Can I finish this grace already?" Orpheus says. He looks at each individual as he says, "Mia? Chuck? Henriette?" She doesn't talk—not because she can't, but because she chooses her words very wisely. She is not, in essence, a hot-air balloon like her husband. "Chet?"

Chet leans back in his frail chair, bending the poled legs, and says, "I don't see why not, Nigga."

"See, that's funny," Orpheus smiles big, putting his bleached-white teeth on display, "because it's something only a black person can say."

Great, now race is suddenly involved.

"As I was saying, Lord—"

"No, as *I* was saying," Chuck says.

"Excuse me?" Orpheus does a double-take.

"I didn't get to finish grace."

"You're about ten years too late, wouldn't you say, Chuck?"

Chet laughs hysterically. Nobody joins him, so the laugh ends abruptly.

Chuck flattens the napkin on his lap. He drips sweat profusely, dotting and blurring words at random. He clears his throat, and with 11:14 remaining, says, "Dear Zen Aee…Aees…"

The looks he's getting.

"Zen Aeesho'po!" Success at last. "You are—"

"Hold on a second, Chuck." Orpheus' ring-riddled hand has requested a timeout. "Who or what is this Zen Aee…Aees—"

"Zen Aeesho'po," Chet says.

"Knew I could count on you, Pal." He faces Chuck. "Well?"

"Will you just let him finish?" Mia says, and to Chuck, "I'm begging you."

Chuck hasn't looked up once. He stares at the napkin and realizes he has to start from scratch with 10:09 left. "Dear Zen Aeesho'po, the true creator of human life—"

"Whoa, whoa, whoa." Orpheus' hands are already en route to fetch the mini Bible from his breast pocket.

"—you created us through an experiment in your mother's…" the word *basement* has been altered by the sweat, "*butt.*"

Everyone gasps.

"It's obvious we are…" Another distorted word appears at random, this one *failures*, "fuck…fuckers?"

Mia latches onto the napkin because she's determined to get to the bottom of this, but Chuck's too quick. He latches onto the other end. An intense tug-of-war rages on as Orpheus finally manages to pluck his mini Bible free. It flops onto the table. He pins the thing down and furiously thumbs through the worn pages.

With 8:32 to go, Orpheus pinpoints a paragraph and says, "Ah hah, right here, on page 232, it says, and I'm repeating this verbatim—"

"Does it say, 'Orpheus, for the love of God, show some respect and let Chuck Steak finish his grace'?"

Orpheus checks.

Chuck wins tug-of-war. "Zen Aeesho'po, you tossed us into the Milky Way to avoid getting in trouble, because mother said, 'Look here, Dumbass, no more experimenting, you hear?'"

Chet keeps his mouth covered with hands to hide a flood of giggles.

"You didn't hear, because…" He reads ahead and turns bright red. "No way." He shakes his head in disgust.

Mia squeezes his arm—it's like squeezing the stump of a tree. "Did you get another concussion at work?"

"I'm not doing it." He crumbles the napkin, and with 7:54 to go, a loud beep steals the room's attention. It sounded like a smoke detector.

It beeps again, and suddenly everybody has made it their mission to quietly search for the source.

"You need to change the batteries occasionally, Chuck," Orpheus says, figuring he's easily solved the case, "*you* of all people should know this."

Mia feels over her bubbled stomach. "I think that was me."

"Come again? You beeped?"

Embarrassed, Mia doesn't make eye-contact whilst saying, "I think I passed gas."

"And that's the noise you make?"

"Lately, I think so."

"You need to see a doctor, because that's not normal, Mia. Why haven't you gotten her in somewhere, Chuck? This is no longer funny, Chet."

The napkin has been ironed out flat over Chuck's knee. "You didn't hear, because you wanted to create the best Mother's Day gift ever."

Henriette thinks that's thoughtful.

"So you..." Chuck coughs. "...made a bunch of sex slaves to pleasure her." He gags. "We are your mother's failed sex toys."

Henriette thinks that's repulsive. Orpheus even more so as he pushes his chair back and shoots to a stand. "I've had enough. We're leaving, and I believe I speak for everyone." Henriette is fine with this decision. She stands alongside her man in silence.

Chet is on the fence.

"Hold on, that's it." Chuck balls the napkin and chucks it over his shoulder. "I'm done with grace. We can finally eat." With 6:46 to go.

Orpheus lifts one of the silver lids and releases a blast of the shredded, succulent beef basking in a glazed puddle of red wine and onion juices. "Really, Chuck?" Just a year ago, this was Orpheus' absolute favorite dish. "You do know I'm a vegetarian now, don't you?" The alpha male proceeds to lift the remaining lids, one by one, until all is revealed. "And I'm also gluten free, Chuck. I can't eat any of this. Either can Henriette. We found out she's allergic to gluten recently, and I'm very supportive. That's why I'm gluten free, too, Chuck, to show my support."

"Why are you a vegan?"

"Why am I a vegan?" Orpheus laughs as he scans the crowd. "Because it's Lent, Chuck. I gave up the one food I love the most, meat."

Mia has already begun digging in. She pretends she's alone in her apartment and slaps three portions of stuffing onto her plate.

"So this is reason you've been packing on the pounds, huh, Mia?" Orpheus stares hawk-like at her every move.

"Excuse me?" She stops mid-dip in the lobster risotto.

"I don't mean to come across as accusatory, my dear. I know it's not your fault. You've been blinded by this man." He motions at Chuck. "He's been coercing you into obscene amounts of food in order to decrease your value to other mates, thus ensuring he always has some sort of sick and twisted hold over you."

Mia pushes back and shoots to her heels. "How dare you!"

Chet lifts himself up, because he doesn't want to be the odd man out.

With under six minutes to go, Chuck has to face the shit storm head-on. He grips his steak knife and bangs the handle against the table, rattling what sounds like a China cabinet's worth of glass.

He gets all the looks, but he only wants Mia's hands, so he takes them and says to her belly, "You don't look a pound heavier than the day I met you."

Orpheus forces out an exaggerated cough, and somewhere hidden within the phlegm was the word *Wrong*.

"And it doesn't even matter, Mia, because I can't stand those run-of-the-mill, easily breakable girls out there now-a-days. They're all unhealthy. They're all gonna fall apart at some point, and nobody's gonna want to put them back together. It's just too much work." He sighs. "They just don't make 'em like they used to. It's not even about looks. You're the most beautiful woman in the world, but that's not the reason I love you."

3:16 left.

"I love you because you're a smart, independent businesswoman. You don't talk just to hear your own voice—you take after your lovely mother, so you do everything by the book, and you work hard even if things aren't fair, and you do what needs to be done because that's that good, ole-fashioned American work ethic everybody seems to have forgotten about."

Mia can tell by his shaky voice something big's on the horizon. She begins to shake, too, so Chuck squeezes her hands tighter, and they both tear up.

2:26 remain.

"I love you because you always smell like a tangerine, even after getting all sweaty from stuff like, well, like, whatever."

She snorts. Chet giggles. Orpheus does not see the humor in any of this.

"You changed my life from the moment I met you, Mia, and the only reason I haven't done this sooner," he sneaks one hand into his back pocket, "is because the one thing I'd never be able to overcome is if anything ever happened to you." He lowers himself onto one knee with 1:48 to go and brings a shiny, platinum ring with a single pea-sized diamond to her ring finger's nail. "I'm ready for the joys, and I'm more than ready to keep you safe for the rest of eternity. So will you, Mia Johnson—"

"Yes!" she blurts, guiding her trembling finger through the hole.

She saved him five extra seconds, leaving precisely 53 to go.

After a snappy kiss, Chuck's on his feet, strategically maneuvering himself around the table to where the alpha male stands tall and stubborn.

"Orpheus, can I please get your blessing?" Orpheus smirks. "For the love of God, Man, come on. I'd do anything for your daughter."

"You know, Chuck," Orpheus has raised a lesson-teaching finger, "when I was your age…"

With under thirty seconds to go, Mia's as good as dead. There's simply no time to finish the rest of the chores. Hell, it seems like Chuck could go an eternity without getting a single blessing from Orpheus.

"Whoa, hold on!" Chuck blurts with 13 seconds remaining. "Can I at least get your blessing for the food?"

"Hmmm, I guess so."

10, 9…

"Well???"

"Lord, bless this terrible food." Orpheus waves his hand around magically. "There, Chuck, you happy, Chuck?"

4.

"Like you couldn't believe." 3. Chuck gives Henriette's rump a mighty smack. 2. "Chet's gay!" 1.

No explosion.

Well, except for the entire room, which erupts into chaos.

# Chapter 3
# Chase

Chuck's been rehearsing an apology for the past twenty minutes. He hopes it sounds as good as it does inside his thick skull.

The condo's front door is unlocked, so he enters. He'd call out her name, but some crazy Slipknot song's rocking the basement. He creeps down the stairs to the constant refrain of, "PEOPLE EQUAL SHIT!" She spots him halfway and lets her barbell filled with over 300lbs. of weights drop from thigh-level. The plates rattle, adding to the chaos. Mia sports her giant, purple onesie. It's drenched in the sweat which bleeds from her sour face.

Chuck asks if she'd mind killing the music. She grabs her boom box and hurls it at his face. He ducks, and it shatters against the brick wall. Pieces rain down upon him. Before he can collect his thoughts, her baby-powder-covered, throbbing hands are latched onto his shirt's collar. She tugs, meaning to throw him further into her makeshift workout space, but the shirt tears clean off his body. He snorts. She hooks an exercise band around his neck and slingshots him across the floor, but not before tripping him so it's done by tumbles.

Chuck shields himself with a bench as Mia comes at him with 30lb. dumbbells in each hand. Those one-on-one personal training lessons really did her wonders. She swings wildly, at one point spinning herself dizzy. Okay, maybe she should have seen the lessons through, but who has that type of motivation now-a-days?

As the dumbbells whisk by his head, Mia hunches over to catch her breath.

This seems like the perfect opportunity to apologize.

A dehumidifier smashes to bits at his boots. Okay, maybe not.

Mia hops onto Chuck, wrapping her legs around his thighs and her arms around his upper torso. They fall onto the sweaty mat and roll. Once on top, Mia readies her balled fists. Chuck pries his hands free but lets them fall to his sides. She deserves this. He did, in theory, just blow her family up.

The punches come out the gate with tremendous force but quickly lose steam, then give up. Gee, she's giving up on everything lately.

"Keep going," Chuck encourages.

She pants. "I'm not even hurting you."

"Of course you are!" He squints and hisses and massages his ribs. "The guy who trained you really did wonders."

She socks him good, slicing his cheek. At least she's still wearing the ring.

"Seriously," he rotates his jaw in large, slow circles, "that—" He shoots an alarmed look slightly over her.

"Let me guess," she says, "I have something on my face? Ha, ha." Actually, she has a tiny red dot hovering above her head, directly outside the basement window. The fuzzy light sways left and right.

"Enough with the jokes, Chuck. What you did tonight isn't funny. You broke my family, and if you expect us to move forward and eventually get married, you need to fix it."

The light abruptly switches off, revealing the faint outline of a hooded figure.

"Please tell me you're listening."

His eyes grow wide.

"Why do I even bother?"

"Mia, listen to me—don't turn around."

She whispers, "Is it a spider?"

"Act normal."

"Is it a spider?" she shouts.

"Throw that water bottle at me."

She hops off, swipes the bottle and pitches it, but it falls short and bounces off the ground because it's plastic and empty. Even still, Chuck uses this as a diversion to roll out of the stranger's view.

"Someone's crouched outside your window."

"What're they doing?"

He shrugs while tip-toeing toward the stairs. "I'm about to find out."

"Chuck, I swear to God, if it's some deranged murderer…"

"Shhh!"

She throws a boxed set of workout DVDs at him.

"Everything's going to work out in the end," he plants his right foot on the first, rickety step, "I swear." He enters a runner's stance as seen on the boxed set's now-bent cover. "It always does." And off he goes! Not before tripping and face-planting. Mia spins around and spots the hooded figure scampering away, clawing at her lawn. She's quick to grab a 10lb. plate and fling it through the window, striking the figure, making them yelp in that all-too-familiar, robotic voice, "Ooooooouch!"

*The killer!*

Chuck barrels up the stairs, into the living room. There's a large window overlooking the ten-foot patch of grass before the sidewalk. There'll be enough landing to break his fall. He wraps a quilt from Mia's sofa around his upper body, then sprints across the room. At the last possible second, he hurls himself through the window. He sticks the landing on the curb, vaulting himself onto the hood of a neighbor's car, denting it badly. As he rolls off, peels the sticky quilt from his person and plucks shards of glass from his sliced-open arms, the killer darts into traffic, the headlights of an oncoming vehicle illuminating their ankle-length, tattered, black, baggy, Trick-or-Treat robe. The killer waves his gloved hands as if apologizing for the vehicle having to slam on its breaks. Then he cuts the corner.

In retrospect, Chuck should have exited the front door like a normal person. Next time, perhaps.

As Chuck hobbles around the corner, he finds the killer paused a few streetlamps away.

*He's tying his goddamn sneakers!*

Chuck takes off.

*Jesus Christ, now he's double-knotting them!*

Separated by the gap of two streetlamps, the killer runs away. Chuck gains streetlamps. The killer twists his head, straining to see through the circle of mesh concealing his face. He starts to flail, as if swimming frantically away from a shark. Chuck reaches forward, feels a piece of flimsy fabric tickle his palm, so he squeezes tight, but the fabric snaps forward.

There's a robotic laugh as the killer starts to pull away. Half a street lamp. One full street lamp. Then two. Hot damn he's fast, is this guy a track star or something? And then the killer disappears into none other than an alley. Fifteen seconds too late, Chuck follows suit and slips on a hundred marbles and gets laid out flat on his back. Directly above, the killer finishes hoisting the escape ladder into a locked position. From there, he hangs over the rusty railing, staring down at Chuck.

"Can you believe it, I'm actually faster than you?"

"Race me again when I'm not bleeding profusely."

"Heck no, I'm officially retiring as the champ! I'll never race again, not even if my life depends on it."

"You know I'm going to find you—"

"And pummel me, and choke me, and cut my arms and legs off, and drown me, and revive me, and yadda, yadda, yadda? You won't. You have no idea who I am. You never have." He wags a finger. "Nice try, I see what you're doing. No more hints for you. I'm leaving now. Bye!"

# Chapter 4
## Cheeky Fellow

Outside the cell, two officers lose their minds, and not because of how late it is. They go on and on about how Chuck shouldn't be here, and how this will ruin their case, and, like the killer said, yadda, yadda, yadda.

Chuck pries his jeans down and over his rump and clamps his ass cheeks around Bill's fat nose, then lets a long, bubbly fart rip. Bill jerks back and swats at the air. Chuck thrusts his buttocks backward, smothering Bill with cheeks and crack.

"Better talk, Bill," Chuck says, his fists clenched, his teeth gritting, "else your night is about to get real shitty!" His butt retracts, gives Bill a chance to breathe some fresh air, but when Chuck peeks back at him, Bill's clutching his chest with both spotted hands and slumping into the bench.

"You're not fooling me this time."

Bill gasps as his wrinkled face turns bright blue. Chuck fumbles the keys out of his pocket and unlocks the cell. One officer rushes in as the other ducks away to make a call.

"He's gone," the assisting officer says.

"He's not dead," Chuck says, "he already played that card. Just sock him in the gut or suck face."

"Look at him, Chuck," they both look at the stiff and crinkled skeleton smothered in a tan jumpsuit, "he had a massive heart attack."

"Speaking of heart attacks," in waltzes the other officer, "Anderson would like a word." He holds out an iPhone. The center of Anderson's mammoth face appears through FaceTime.

"Really, Chuck, you couldn't murder this rapist outside of police custody???"

"No, no, no, this one's not on me—he died of natural causes!"

"Oh right, then I guess you're not on video wiping your ass with a prisoner's nose?"

"Excuse me, Sir," the iPhone holder says, "but we've been experiencing technical difficulties with our surveillance system."

"You don't goddamn say? What kind of 'difficulties'?"

"Ted. He was doing a nice thing, Sir. He dropped by with two carriers of premium coffee. He approached Graham in the surveillance room first and tripped on some untied shoelaces. One of the carriers doused and fried the entire system. The other he managed to salvage. There were four coffees left. He gave Graham one, me one, Dustin here one, and he even donated the coffee meant for himself to Bill, the undeserving child molester. It sounds so very wrong the way I'm describing it, but I promise you it was a special moment filled with sincerity."

Chuck grins. "Never thought I'd say this, but Ted actually saved the day."

"Sa-sa-saved the day?" Anderson stutters. "This isn't th-th-the early goddamn 2000s, Chuck! Today's society demands answers, and if we don't have any? Well sh-sh-sh-shit!"

Chuck shrugs.

Anderson's left eye twitches.

Chuck adjusts himself.

"YOU'RE FIRED!!!" Anderson squeals, but then the skin in his face tightens, turning his cheeks into boulders, and his eyes explode and pause mid-blast, and Anderson cranks the phone backward to display part of his other hand which is clawing at his chest.

"Bill had a heart attack," the iPhone officer spouts, "and now Lieutenant Anderson is, too! Oh my gooooooooooooooooooooooooooooooooooooood!"

# SUNDAY

## Chapter 5
## Take Thy Hand

Chuck jolts upright. It's as bright as a motherfucker out, so he throws a beefy forearm over his eyes. The mystery cell goes ballistic on his nightstand. He lets it ring for sixteen straight seconds, and during this time, Chuck reminds himself how paramedics had gotten to Anderson in time, and after being rushed to the hospital to undergo bypass surgery, doctors discovered not a single clogged artery. In fact, internally-speaking, Anderson was said to be in perfect health. Turned out he had been suffering from an undiagnosed condition which caused massive weight gain.

"Good morning!" the killer's robotic voice yaps.

Chuck grunts.

"I've gotten fired, too, you know? For—"

"I wasn't fired. He threatens that all the time, it means nothing. Plus it's too early for this bullshit."

"Hush already, I'm giving you a clue!" The killer smacks his tinny gums. "For being *different*."

"Could you be any vaguer?"

"Probably not, tee-hee."

"Why're you so annoyingly cheerful?"

41

"I'm simply ecstatic about today's lesson is all."

"Is that what this is all about? You want me to get my GED?"

"We're not teaching you, Chuck—we're teaching them."

"Great, now we're playing the pronoun game."

"I'm referring to the world, of course. Our future audience, of course."

"Of course."

"Our capitalistic society will eventually turn our story into a mass media frenzy—movies, books, merchandise, you name it."

"You're gonna bore me with the details. Seriously, every villain does it, and I always fall asleep."

"Good heroes make tough decisions in the heat of the moment. But what exactly constitutes a 'good' tough decision you're probably wondering?"

"I've laid back down and placed my face on the cool side of the pillow."

"Well I'll tell you: one where there are no wrong choices."

"Now I'm closing my eyes."

"And don't even get me started with the stakes, for they should continue to remain extremely high."

"Oh no, I'm starting to drift."

"To ensure this, the storyteller must force the hero into a game of would you rather?"

Chuck mumbles gibberish. He's doing a great job of conveying his fake grogginess rather than telling. In a way, he gets today's lesson. Either that, or he's a natural.

"Meadowlands, room 512."

Chuck jolts upright, again.

"You fucking touch her…"

"Calm down, your Nana's safe…for now. As long as you—"

"Complete some ridiculous tasks by some random time?" He *is* a natural! "I'm onto your fucking schtick."

The killer sighs. "Soon, all of the pieces will be in play. Then, *then*, the plot can unfold organically."

"Did you forget about the seven-day timer you set? Isn't that the main plot?"

"Sorry, come again? I was too busy waving bye-bye to Nana."

Click.

Click.

No boom.

There's a process to this.

Chuck first sprints over to Avis.

He consults with Bernard. Bernard works there 24/7. He's Avis's bitch, but he doesn't seem to mind. He's a down-to-earth, red-bearded gentleman who always opens with the same song and dance: a shrug, a sigh, puckered lips, and, "Whelp, it's me again—your favorite overworked and underpaid attendant."

Chuck always goes in with a raised, flexed arm. When the two lock hands over the counter, it appears as though they've begun a midair arm-wrestling match. They squeeze their fists hard, and while smirking at each other, they watch (out of their peripheral vision) as their muscles expand and their veins bulge.

"Bernard, you son-of-a-bitch. You've bulked up quite a bit"

They smirk harder.

And harder.

And then Chuck winces. And then he snaps his hand back and examines his fingertips. They've got a blue tint to them. Maybe it's the lighting in here, which doesn't explain the slight numbness creeping up into his palm.

"Have I finally overtaken your strength?"

"What? No. It's this goddamn watch." The silver band digs into Chuck's skin. He turns his wrist from side to side, each pass shedding seconds from the countdown, but can't seem to find the clasp. How'd he even get this thing on in the first place? Didn't he slide his hand in and clamp it shut like a handcuff?

"Earth to Chuck."

Whatever, he'll figure it out later. He always does.

"Wanna know my secret?"

They both lean into each other, almost touching foreheads, even though there's no one else in the building.

"I've been pulling the cars up curbside for customers."

"That's not much of a secret."

"Yeah, but beforehand, I deadlift the frontends."

Chuck's genuinely shocked.

"Only the electric and European cars, of course."

"I knew there was a catch."

Bernard shakes his computer mouse violently while saying, "Come on already," to bring his old, dusty monitor back to life. Finally, after the screen blasts his face with a vibrant shade of green, he says, squinting hard, "Okay, so what'll it be today?"

Today the details don't matter. Chuck only has two stops to make, so today he makes his selection based purely on his nana's personal tastes. Today he chooses a pearl white PT Cruiser.

Chuck nods when asked if it's for business, so Bernard punches it in. While handing over the keys, he says, "Bringing this one back?"

"Maybe."

They both wink. This is their inside joke, but it's not really a joke. Plus the public has heard the rumors regarding Chuck Steak totaling most, if not all, of the vehicles he rents under the department's name.

They pound out a hug before Chuck leaves. Luckily they're alone, because it'd be a complicated task explaining to a random stranger the logic surrounding the city's most active, fast-paced cop being best friends (or the closest to it) with the city's most active, stationary Avis attendant.

In the slight crack of the door, Chuck whispers, "Best get working on those delts."

"You—" Bernard says, realizing Chuck's gotten in the last word yet again, "—son-of-a-bitch." He smiles, because seeing his brother rejuvenates his day. He compares the encounter, in his mind, to the euphoric satisfaction of swallowing a Danish.

Perhaps tomorrow, Bernard thinks, he'll finally remember to get the last word in. "Ha!" he remarks, knowing that's about as likely as him ever seeing the pearl white PT Cruiser again.

Next Chuck drives all the way across town to the Meadowlands. The bitter attendant, Chaz, such a frail thing, squawks, "Sign in, will ya?"

Chuck does so with a smirk. "You're not gonna sell this autograph or any—"

"Very funny," Chaz says to his fingernails as he files them down, down, down, "just so you know, she's been having a lot of listening problems lately."

"She has Dementia."

"Pssst." He waves Chuck off with a manicured finger, not the bad one, and slips in there, *whatever.*

Chaz is an appetizer of sorts. He's masterful at setting the depressing tone for Chuck before he opens the door and sees the back of her white head. He calls out her name multiple times, each "Cynthia" progressively louder to capture her attention. She turns slowly, doll-like. Her chair is always set so the armrests kiss the windowsill. The blinds are always blown open. She can see everything below. She's the busybody of their building, and the world is her television. Every time she turns away to look at him, he knows she's still stuck wondering what's going to happen next in her self-produced programs. Even when they lock eyes, hers fading to the color of the PT Cruiser parked outside, he knows it'll take a few moments for her to snap back to reality.

It'll be precisely long enough for a meaningful flashback.

*Following his mother's death, Chuck Steak had deteriorated into a little shit. The process took years, but Chuck had become exceptionally multi-talented in the following (but not limited to): thievery, breaking and entering, unlawful residency, littering, public urination, defecation, vandalism, disorderly conduct and pyramid schemes.*

Why not? *Chuck reasoned. Why should he be the only fool abiding by the rules? Such a mindset had, in theory, churned him into a homeless orphan.*

*Things weren't going to change much. Even when Chuck had pried his way in through Cynthia's basement window. He located her purse upstairs in the kitchen where she confronted him.*

*Chuck was too old for a lecture—he was, in fact, thirteen. He turned to leave, but Cynthia called out, "Wait, I'm not mad at you."*

*Chuck didn't care.*

*"How much do you need?"*

*And like that, his interest was piqued, because what sort of person could remain intact in such a pathetically broken world?*

*Cynthia paid him to listen.*

*Each week, Chuck would stop by. A little, green triangle would be sticking out of her purse on the kitchen table. Some days it was a real $20. On others, it was a Monopoly $20. Cynthia would be seated next to the purse, a chair across from her always pulled out. Chuck would plop down, act as though he were enduring a chore, yet he'd listen intently.*

*Over the weeks, he learned the entirety of her sad and depressing tale. With breaks excluded (all the times she paused to cook him dinner or let him bathe or challenged him to a game of Rummikub), it went a little something like this:*

*Several months prior to Chuck robbing her, Cynthia had found herself in a similar situation when a gang of punks sporting loud attire and done-up from head to toe in vicious tattoos robbed her first. She had been on a walk with her* son, Timothy. *The two were en route to a round of miniature golf. Along the way, the gang in question reached out and sucked them into an alleyway. They demanded Cynthia's purse and Timothy's wallet. The mother and son handed them over willingly. In fact, they seemed gracious to fork over their hard-earned money and be done with the encounter. But the punks weren't really in it for the cash, especially with the way Timothy trembled—they came to realize there was something much more valuable at stake, and that something was pride. So they forced Timothy out of his clothes. He begged for his life right down to nudeness. Cynthia joined in on the begging, but all it did was get the gang off.*

*Wanting more of a climax, the gang began a verbal lashing, calling Timothy a plain-looking pussy, a saggy-skinned skank, a pale, putrid, puke body, and of course, dinky dicky doodles. Cynthia and son were brought to tears. The gang ultimately came. Afterwards, there wasn't much else to do except get out of there. But Timothy looked so pathetic. They didn't want to leave him in such a state. In their eyes, that wasn't much of a life to keep leading, so they yanked off Cynthia's wig and hacked it apart with their pocket blades. They turned it into a reputable Mohawk. Then they circled around poor Timothy and carved tattoos into his skin. They wiped his body clean with the Mohawk, painting it blood red. By their standards, it looked badass. They placed the makeshift crown atop Timothy's head and nailed it into place with a single switchblade. Timothy might have died before the impalement, nobody could truly remember—but afterwards, the punks propped him against a dumpster in a way which made his corpse look laid-back yet confident.*

*Before the punks scattered, they said a few parting words. Mostly they called Timothy a "faggot" and reasoned with Cynthia about how lucky she was their paths had crossed, because the punks ensured her son died a real man.*

Cynthia finally snaps to this world. Her pupils grow with recognition. It brings her much joy to say to Chuck, "Timothy!"

They commence what has become the expected back and forth. She asks how he's been. He says great. She asks to see the cannon stuffed inside his white-washed jeans. He lifts his shirt as proof. She claps ecstatically and goes on about having witnessed the prophecy. That the glass she stays perched in front of is a window where she deciphers the future in order to save the present.

Cynthia explains how she's seen his brutal murder.

Chuck insists he has the tools and knowledge necessary to thwart Death's plan.

She warns him of miniature golf.

He gulps whilst leaning over her to pull the slightly cracked window shut. What fool left it ajar this time? He knows whenever they make their brief appearances, the nurses spend half the time huffin' and puffin'. Thus why it constantly reeks of nicotine.

As Chuck tugs on the handle, his grip pops loose.

"Don't," Cynthia lisps, reaching out, "the nice man promised he'd visit again."

"I'm the nice man, Nana."

"No," the words are getting caught in her swollen throat, "the fellow who climbed the ladder." She lowers herself to a whisper. "He delivered a smoothie. It was grape." That would explain her purplish lips, but not the cold sweat which breaks and races down her forehead. "My favorite." She blinks those pale, spotted lids, but the streams rush into her fading eyes. It stings, this he can tell.

"Want me to carry you out, Nana?"

"Where in the Heavens are we going?"

Chuck consults his floppy wrist: 22:09 to get them there.

"Enieolf."

"What's that, Dear?"

"Enie…olf."

She digs a permanently bent finger inside her ear to clear the blockage. "Come again?"

Does he really have to put her through this? Chuck scans the room, can't imagine how anybody could be listening in on their conversation. But there's the lingering fear that if he doesn't tell her where they're going, the killer will make good on his promise and blow Mia to bits.

Chuck fires it off quickly: "We're going miniature golfing."

Her eyes flare open.

"Nothing bad's gonna happen, Nana, I swear."

She trembles.

"Nana?" Is she lost inside that prison formally known as a brain again?

And then out it comes, the most ferocious shriek Chuck's ever heard escape her lips. It's like she's possessed by a banshee. This had to be how she sounded on the day Timmy was erased from existence. Chuck can't deal with such an alarming noise, especially with t-minus 19:43 and counting, so he muzzles her regardless of how searing her skin feels and proceeds to lift his shirt to highlight the cannon once again.

"Hey!" Michelle S. rushes in. She unknowingly or uncaringly dawns a chocolate pudding mustache. "What do you think you're doing?"

"You fucking kidding me?" Chuck doesn't finish this frazzled statement, but it's in reference to the fact that whenever he's needed a nurse in the past, like when Cynthia fell down and went boom, nobody ever came, not when he yelled up and down the hallway, not when he rang the front desk, not even when he yanked the fire alarm.

"I'll testify against you in court."

Chuck lets his shirt drop. "Listen here, Chunk-a-lunk." He's always wanted to call her that. "I don't see any food lying around here, so why don't you go harass someone else?" That'll be the day he explains himself to the likes of a thief. Even if it means clarifying how the day in question was a fluke. He'd take it back if he could.

49

*A year earlier, Chuck had been sulking in the visitor's chair next to Cynthia's bed, tossing his cannon from hand to hand. He couldn't look at her even though she had been deemed nonresponsive. Lying in that plastic-wrapped bed, she appeared coffin-ready. Before the seizure knocked her out, she whispered through a tiny hole in her mouth, "Help." Chuck had pressed the tip of his cannon firmly into her breastplate and whispered back, "I love you." But Michelle S. rushed in shouting, "What's going on here?" with the neighboring patient's mashed potatoes oozing down her chin.*

*Chuck had been caught gun-handed, a moment away from ending his Nana's pain and suffering.*

At present, Michelle S. waddles all agitated-walrus-like over to Chuck and *achooooooooos* right in his face. Bits of undigested food vault inside his mouth, and even though he spits them out just as fast, the taste of spoiled Spam lingers, perhaps forever.

Chuck unleashes Cynthia's shriek to crank back his loosely balled fist, but it hangs there for quite some time.

"Guess what?" Michelle S. grins from dimple to dimple. "I have the flu."

He cranks back further.

"You're not going to hit me. Not with that pathetic thing anyway."

Sure enough, Chuck's fingers, which are supposed to be balled into a tight fist, look like five droopy ding-a-lings.

"And turn her off already—my double ear infections can't take any more."

"Nana, *NANA!*" Still she shrieks. "Would you like to...*WOULD YOU LIKE TO SEE A COOL TRICK?*"

She finally ceases, or maybe she runs out of gas, who knows? Chuck doesn't care as he scoops Nana into his arms and twirls, roundhouse-kicking Michelle S. in the face with Cynthia's bony troll feet.

But Michelle S. is too stubborn for unconsciousness. She wobbles to her feet, at which point Nana rasps, "Again."

"The nerve!" Michelle S. blurts, feeling over the five raised scars running the length of her plump cheek.

"Should've trimmed her nails, Bitch." Chuck performs the trick again, and that does the...*gimmick?*

Cynthia's a corpse in his arms, so Chuck shakes her eyes open. "You missed it, Nana." She hacks a ball of phlegm up her throat, and it gets stuck halfway, making her choke. Chuck plants his kisser over her hard, waxy lips and sucks the same way he would if he were siphoning gas through a tube from a stranger's vehicle. Not like he's done this before. Okay, *once*. But that was when he was a little shit and had decided to drain every vehicle in the city. He was quick to abandon this dream after sucking down a gulp of gasoline from the first car.

It's more of the same at present as Chuck squirms and twitches as the ball of phlegm tumbles violently down *his* throat, the fleshy tentacles tickling his esophagus. He swallows back vomit as Nana pries open her stiff lids and ekes out a rigid smile.

Only 11:12 to go!

Are you enjoying the book? Great! An epic fight scene between Chuck and roughly nineteen clowns once filled this gap. It's since been omitted. Be sure to purchase it as DLC (Downloadable Content), that is if you enjoy action. The industry says you don't. Prove them wrong. Make me rich.

Oh, and hi there! I'm The Narrator.

Let me clear one thing up. *Why's this story in present tense? Present tense sucks, WAAAAAAAAAH!*

Look, listen. Listen. I'm a ghost, and I'm watching the action live, and I'm conveying it to my ghost buddies who live on the other side of the world (through a microphone of course), and the live feed is being used for the audiobook which will be scribed into book format, but during this conversion, the scriber won't change the tense. She wants it to remain authentic. So don't be a pussy about present tense, because one day you're going to die, and this will be the very least of your problems.

Besides, there's something awfully suspicious about to happen inside a nearby hospital. You should check it out.

Okay, see ya later!

*Time to switch POV, bitches!*

A hooded figure drifts by Larry the receptionist. Larry leans sideways, putting the sliced-apart, bleeding, wheel-chair-bound customer seated across his desk out of view, and Larry waves. The hooded figure waves. Larry says, "Rough night?" And the hooded figure says, "Sure."

In the bright white hallway, a doctor turns his attention from his babbling assistant toward the hooded figure and says, "Good morning! Or is it good afternoon?"

"Sure."

Further along, another doctor says, "How're things going?"

"Sure."

Even the janitor gets a *sure*, and all the dusty-looking woman said was, "Don't go in there."

In the tight elevator, it stinks like someone passed gas or away.

On the 4th floor, the hooded figure turns right for surgery. This was the same route Chuck had taken a few months ago—maybe five or six or seven. He pushed Mia in a wheelchair as she hissed and clutched at her ribcage. To Chuck's knowledge, Mia had been in the middle of an intense workout session when the trainer accidentally let a barbell freefall onto her stomach after Mia's arms gave out. The trainer had been told to flee the scene before Chuck arrived so Chuck wouldn't kill him. "I'd never," Chuck said. "Not over an accident. But hey, what's this guy's name anyway? And does he live around the area? Like what street's he on? What's his address? I'd just like to tell him in-person no hard feelings." And Mia laughed and winced and said, "We'll never see that idiot again."

The hooded figure pretends to read a bulletin board while a teary-eyed couple passes by, then slips into the surgery preparation room. Inside, a backpack's slammed onto a metal table, unzipped, and a faded blue, dented cooler is pried out. That cooler is left as an eyesore in the rather pristine room lined with walls of neatly organized, unopened medical supplies.

This was the exact same table the bomb planted inside of Mia had been left on.

The hooded figure sneaks out of the room.

Next stop: the surveillance room.

*Sorry, you're probably not bitches. Let's switch POV again, buddies.*

Chuck punches the gas, he also punches the dashboard as the PT cruiser swerves and hops the curb. His Nana rolls off the backseat and thumps against the floor. He twists to assess the damage, although she's been rendered a 2x4, and his frontend punts a pedestrian into next week. Okay, not next week, but definitely the next block. Maybe half a block. The point is, Chuck punches the brake pedal, punches the roof, punches everything in sight, and grinds to a complete stop.

The watch continually flashes 0:00. Scanning the area, looking passed those gravitating toward his vehicle and its mangled grill, he estimates they've arrived incredibly fucking short of their destination.

Chuck gets out, follows the trail of maroon splats and pretzel-shaped bicycle parts to a spandex-clad woman clenching a popped-open knee to her chest. Each time she fidgets in agony, more maroon spits onto the street and nearby pavement.

"Hey," Chuck says, leaning in.

"Ahhhhhhhhh," she moans.

"I wouldn't do that."

"Ahhhhhhhhh."

"Gotta say, you lucked out, you know? Since you weren't wearing a helmet and all."

"A-hem!" A regular old Joe steps forward. In fact, his name is Joe. He points at the cracked helmet clogging the gutter further down the block.

"Thanks, Dick."

"Actually, it's Joe, and you're the lucky one. Not only were you speeding, but you also ran a red light."

The inevitable call comes through on the mystery cell.

"You could've killed this poor woman."

Chuck can't help himself: "Wow, that's super offensive."

"Nice try, Pal, but I always remain politically correct."

"Then howddya know we're dealing with a woman?"

Joe quickly examines the busted leg, notices the shreds of exposed skin, how they *are* awfully hairy. His eyeballs climb the throbbing thigh and examine the crotch area. With so much fidgeting, he can't be sure if the small bulge is genuine or not.

"Listen," Joe says, turning, "if you keep your mouth shut about this, I won't rat you out—" but Chuck has since wandered over to the PT Cruiser. He hovers over the back window with the cell pressed into his flustered cheek. Nana's eyes display the same amount of pain as the biker's, yet her body won't budge. She must lie there straight and take it.

"She's dying, Chuck," the killer says, "and so is your hand."

Surely enough, his fingers have turned as icy blue as Nana's skin. He feels the watch tighten as if a link has been removed. It burrows further into his wrist, vanishing inside bright red skin and hair.

"Did you honestly think you were going golfing today? Really, Chuck? Didn't think I'd come up with a clever twist?"

He's at a loss.

"Don't worry, your precise Mia will live to see another day. But one of these, either your Nana or your right hand, won't. You see, I poisoned her smoothie, and now her trachea's slowly closing.

And that watch you're wearing? It's cutting off your blood supply. If you don't get Nana to the nearest hospital ASAP, she won't make it to your wedding. Hell, they may not even be able to save her. She's old as shit, Chuck, you know it, I know it, everybody knows it. So perhaps this will make your decision all the easier. Because the key to your watch lies back at the nursing home, buried in the trash, taped to the bottom of the smoothie container. There's certainly enough time left to save your hand, and let's face it, you're no lefty. I remember a headline reading, *Hero Cop Uses Left Hand against Criminals to 'Make it Interesting'*. So go ahead, Hotshot, show the world what kind of hero you really are."

Click.

Chuck dives into the car and says to the rearview mirror, his face all blown-up and veiny, "Hold tight, Nana!" Then, after punching it into drive, he punches the brakes and steering wheel and windshield. "MOVE!" he screams at Joe who's since planted himself in front of the grill. The guy goes off like a wacky, waving, inflatable, arm-flailing tube man: "He's trying to flee the scene of a crime! I repeat, he's trying to—"

Chuck reverses it but is quick to break as a robed man topped with a turban brings his hands together in prayer and kneels before the back bumper.

"Don't bring religion into this!"

The turban doesn't budge.

Chuck punches it back into drive, figures if his Nana's life hangs in the balance, nice knowing ya, Joe. But Joe's been sandwiched by two more robed, turban-wielding dudes. They both kneel in front of the grill and pray. More spill out of a nearby temple. As Chuck lays on the itty-bitty-sounding horn and revs the pathetic engine, the kneeling duo let their eyes fall shut and pray harder.

Nana breaks out into a hacking fit, each wave sounding like a hatchet trying to chop through her throat so her lungs can reach oxygen. Chuck stretches into the back and socks her in the gut with his dead squid of a hand, and she spews mucus all over the cloth roof. The yellow goo hangs there like mushy stalactites. A glob drips back into Nana's slightly ajar mouth. Chuck listens for her thin rasp of air before deciding it's time to take action.

Outside, Chuck approaches an ever-expanding wall of kneeling, praying whatchamacallits? "Yo, guys, seriously!" One of them removes their turban, unleashing their long-flowing, black hair.

"Ha, that's clearly a woman!" Joe shouts. "How's it feel, Douche?"

There's no time for this nonsense. To remain politically correct, there's no timer at all.

Chuck digs Nana out of the backseat, which proves interesting given his limp hand, and figures he'll make a getaway on foot, then commandeer a vehicle past the jam, preferably something helpful like a hillbilly truck on steroids.

But the rapidly-reproducing turbans surround him and interlock hands. There must be twenty in all. They tighten, like the watch, and chant in a different language. Even without a beat, they sound terrific. And if Chuck's being totally honest with himself, it's finally nice to see these people portrayed as selfless heroes instead of evil terrorists.

"*These people?*" Joe says, shrugging to the high heavens.

"You heard that?"

"You said it out loud, Genius."

Chuck attempts to limbo his way under a strand of hands, but they lower accordingly. He steps back to hurdle them, but the hands rise to an impossible height.

Nana's body begins to shake violently as her eyes roll away. "I swear I'll do something stupid if you people don't move."

"*You people?*" Joe smiles, then tries to jumpstart the chant, "Ra-cist! Ra-cist! Ra-cist!" but fails miserably.

Chuck attempts to march through the hands, but they slingshot him back. That's when he does the stupid thing. He heaves Nana onto his left shoulder and holds her there as though he's lugging around a canoe, and he stabs several turbans in the face with her ice-cold-looking, but smoldering hot spears for feet, punching out a hole. The rest of the turbans crash in around him, throwing wild punches. Their improperly formed fists ricochet off Chuck's rock-hard body, busting their knuckles.

"Really though," Chuck shouts as he slips free and skips away, "it was a lovely gesture! Perhaps next time you'll get 'em!" He rear-ends a meathead wearing a giant onesie. This meathead's covered in sweat, or rather, *was* until Chuck wiped him clean. "Dude, take a shower."

"Release the elderly woman!"

"No need to shout."

"NOW!"

"You heard 'em," another meathead says. Chuck rotates, finds himself being surrounded all over again, this time by greasy bodybuilders. They reek of cheesy popcorn.

"Let me guess," he pinpoints the gym, "of course."

One of the lugs strikes from behind, but Chuck roundhouse kicks him into his friend's wet arms. They slip and slide all over each other, and after gaining their footing, shout, "Hey!" and, "Yo!" and, "Get over here!" But Chuck sprints through the idle traffic with Nana foaming in his arms and Joe right on his tail, screaming, "RA-CIST! RA-CIST! RA-CIST!"

A herd of bikers answer the call. They fill the street as if they've been spread with a butter knife. There's no way out but through. And there's no getting through, not with them whipping out knives and clubs and brass knuckles.

Nana's as hot as a comet, and as heavy as one, too. A dark red line sneaks out of her waxy nostril and seeps into her porous skin. The bodybuilders and turbans stampede toward Chuck. They're slow and out-of-breath, obviously cardio isn't part of their regimes. But still, they're coming.

With options limited, Chuck rushes toward the temple and Rocky's his way to the tippy top of the concrete stairs. There, he rushes inside and kicks the two massive, ornate doors closed. They don't seal shut, so he lays Nana out across several mats, and before the diverse mob rams their collective way inside, Chuck jams his cannon through the handles.

A girl smothered in garments approaches as Chuck cradles Nana close to his rapidly-beating heart. The skin of his wrist has been sliced open, and it bleeds in unison with Nana's nose. He hurries across the carpet, but the girl pulls alongside and requests for him to take his boots off.

As Chuck kicks out of them, one goes sailing and whacks a man's turban clean off. "How many points was that?"

The girl giggles.

Nana hacks her throat apart some more, this time with red mist accentuating the severity.

Chuck rushes to the front of the temple where he believes an altar of some sort should be but clearly is not, and deposits Nana underneath a low-hanging chandelier which looks like it could be one of Saturn's rings. He beats a mouthful of puss-filled gunk out of her, then glances at the girl and says, "Quick, what god lives here?"

"You mean Allah?"

"He got a last name?"

She shakes her head.

Chuck forms the prayer hands and leans over Nana's body. He asks the chandelier a lot of questions, mostly why? Why, why, why? He utters "fuck" once, but quickly calls taksies backsies.

And then Cynthia speaks to him. Her eyes roll back into place for the occasion. She goes to war with the words but manages to pry them out of her devastated throat. "You…were—"

Chuck plops his dying hand across her stomach and fits both of hers inside. Then he tucks them in, using his decaying fingers as a blanket. And he squeezes the entire mess together with his lefty.

"—the best…thing—"

Tears build in his eyes as the entrance doors beat like a drum.

"—to ever…happen to…me." She somehow manages to twist her lips into something resembling bliss. "Chuck."

She knows it's him!

If she could do it, so can he. Chuck digs deep, squashes the tears, and sputters through clenched teeth, "I love you so much, Nana. You saved me." He jolts an ounce of life into his right hand, and it's enough to eke out a squeeze. "I don't want you to go, you hear me? You're my world. You're my mom. And I'm…I'm—"

"Who are…you?" She has seaweed for hair and daggers for eyes. "Why?"

"Why what, Nana?"

"Are you…killing me?"

Her final tears are blood, and her final breath comes from a gurgle. Chuck falls into her chest. There's a crack, like tree bark splitting, as the watch crushes every bone in his blackened wrist.

# SUNDAY?

A moment ago, Chuck had been squeezing his nana to death. Trying to anyway. He reaches for her and hugs thin air. They've both been transported. Him to the hospital, and her split like a wishbone—the bigger piece shipped to Heaven (or so he'd like to think), the smaller hauled over to the morgue.

Perhaps Nana's having a reunion with her real son, Timothy, and he continues squeezing her tight where Chuck had left off. Tis a nice visual, especially compared to Chuck's right hand which is smothered in a cocoon of hardened, brown bandages. His protruding, blackened fingertips won't move, not yet anyway, but at least the doctor restored order. The feeling will return, Chuck's sure, and certainly there's something to be done about the blackness. Perhaps his dead skin will crack and flake off, and a new layer will grow in its place. Not that he cares about the color. He doesn't. He's not racist. Fuck Joe Schmo. Most of his adolescent friends were black, and they were in gangs, and most tried to convince him to murder rivaling gang members in the name of, so actually, they're not a good representation of black people at all.

Starting over, Chuck's favorite color is black! And for Christ's sake, his girlfriend's black, and her family, which is now his family through association, is also black. Not to mention *Blackish* is one of the only shows on his DVR.

So there. The proof is in the chocolate pudding.

It all happens quickly now. The tearing of wires and tubes from his flesh. The deafening sound of a flat-line. The nurse gliding into the room, who happens to be male. Even though he is not, per se, a stereotype, the words which come out of his mouth are: "Stop! What do you think you're doing?" But Chuck has already stripped himself free of the machines.

Suddenly, more nurses rush in, some male, some female. One's black, one's Asian, one's even Hispanic, such a great mix. For the cherry on top, the doctor on-call turns out to be a Native American. She yells, "How?" and everybody gasps. But then she finishes: "How'd this happen?" at which point everybody sighs.

Disaster averted.

"Mr. Steak," the doc says, motioning at the bed, "please, sit. You've lost a lot of blood."

With the exit clogged, Chuck plops on the bed Indian style. "Oh shit, sorry!" he blurts, catching his pose, shifting into something more politically correct like a straight-up bed straddle. But he worries such a sight appears too sexually suggestive, so he shifts into a smart lean.

"How about you just lie down?"

"You got it, Chief."

All the nurses and murses gasp.

"Christ, I meant boss. *Boss.*"

The doc presses a gloved finger into the groove of his chest and eases him onto his back. Then she gently places a pillow atop his erection.

"Sweet Jesus," Chuck yips, "that's not because of you. Not because I don't find you attractive. You're definitely hot. I mean Native American girls are beautiful, don't get me wrong, but what

I'm saying is I don't know why I have a boner. I just said *boner.*" Chuck makes a sad face.

She maneuvers around the lively pillow to check his vitals and reinsert the IV. "You're doing extremely well, considering."

"Considering what, exactly?"

"Please," she addresses her subordinates, "leave us."

They leave them.

"That's never a good sign, right?" Chuck chuckles.

The door's pressed shut. "Mr. Steak, your hand is black."

"I noticed."

"I mean it's African American."

"Oh." His mouth hangs open. "*Oh* shit. I mean *oh snap.* And not in a bad way—I've always kinda thought of myself as black anyway. I mean look." He points out how high he's "elevated" the pillow. "Sorry, you're blushing. Don't file harassment charges against me."

As the doc explains the intricate details of the complicated emergency hand surgery they performed, how they had no other choice than to amputate, how the new hand was conveniently delivered in a cooler filled with ice, addressed to Chuck, left on the surgery preparation table, how security checked surveillance but found the entire day's footage wiped clean, how *irregardless* of the convenience surrounding this, now Chuck's got pins and needles in there. While explaining all the ins and outs of the lengthy recovery awaiting him, what he should and should not do (including leave the hospital before they determine whether the hand will reject or accept him, and not based upon his "whiteness"—this rejection will boil down to blood), the pillow drops like an elevator. Talk about a real "boner killer".

"Did you hear a word I said?"

"Totem." He did not.

She stares at him hawk-like.

"I meant totally! You gotta believe me."

It's time for her to leave. As she click-clacks out of the room, Ted pokes his head inside, waves and says, "Howdy, Chuck."

Not Ted (A.K.A. Teddy Bear), the guy who's been on the force long enough to have outgrown the title rookie yet still bumbles around like one, so much so that nobody on the force considers him a real officer. He's like a twelve-year-old with a binky—neither the babies nor the middle grade kids accept or understand him.

"Just a courtesy notice, Chuck: I've been standing guard this entire time."

"You want a cookie?"

"Obviously!" Ted trips on his untied shoelaces, stumbles over to the bed, catches himself on the rolling table and plucks an oatmeal raisin cookie out from under a landslide of cold mashed potatoes and shoves the entire thing inside his mouth. The cookie melts on his tongue, that's how soggy it's become. Ted's mouth freezes as his eyes narrow in horror. But not one to be rude, he manages a smile while forcing the lump down. Afterwards, he jumps right back into his thought: "Guess what? I think I'm a natural at guard duty! Yup, some scary-looking black lady tried to sneak by, but I, Ted, the one and only, managed to fend her off."

Chuck shows off his fingertips and says, "I'm part black now."

"Oh fudge."

"And that was probably my fiancée, you fucktard."

"Double fudge sundae. I didn't know you were engaged! Heck, I didn't even know you had a girlfriend, and don't you think for a second that I'm implying anything about your sexuality!"

In Ted's defense, nobody knew Mia existed.

Chuck strips himself of the machines' tentacles and rolls onto his feet. Then he firmly pats Ted's left shoulder, causing the set to tip like the scales of justice. "Where'd they put my gun?"

"Gosh, I sure hate being the bearer of awful news!" Chuck stares at Ted while Ted stares at the ground and chews on his thumb's cuticle like bubblegum. "Lieutenant Anderson might have, out of safety for our city, not saying I agree with him, which

I don't, I obviously know you're ridiculously safe, not to mention quite handsome, but that's beside the point, isn't it? Okay, he might have confiscated it."

"Figur—"

"And he might have fired you."

"Do you know how many times he's threatened that?"

"And he might have ordered me to give this to you." Ted fumbles a folded, pink piece of paper out of his pocket, unfolds it, and fumbles it into Chuck's white hand. There's a lot of legal mumbo-jumbo on the page, but scribbled across it in permanent, capital letters reads: *YOU'RE GODDAMN FIRED*.

"By the way, Anderson's one floor above us if you'd like to check in on him, and have him check in on you, too, I guess. It'd be a double check-in, he, he." Ted taps his foot. "Let's see, you already know about being part black, and now I do, too, so my condolences."

Chuck is two seconds away from ending Ted.

"And I think we both know how much Mondays stink, but hey," Ted lifts Chuck's chin with one sweaty hand while the other drops a cell into his hospital gown's breast pocket, "at least I found your phone and brought it back to you! It was lying next to your…um, you know. And I figured it was yours, because, well, elderly people like your Nana, God rest her soul, don't usually have phones, and if they do, they tend to use those Jitterbug thingy-ma-jiggers. You know, the mobiles with the enormous buttons? Not that there's anything wrong with those. I find them smart and savvy if I'm being completely honest. But anyway, I was trying to do you a solid, so I took the phone in as one of my own. I would've—"

"Ted?" Chuck latches onto his grape-sized Adam's apple.

"Yes, Chuck," Ted rasps.

"Go back to that thing you said about Mondays."

# MONDAY

## Chapter 7
## Dead Memories

Mia enters through the back. She slams the sliding glass door, but he doesn't answer. In the hallway, she makes a racket with her heels and calls out his name, but still he doesn't answer. She's drawn to the front door where a puddle of toothpick-sized splinters, chunks of glass, twisted metal, papier-mâché and a balled-up brochure of exotic flowers has spilled across the hardwood.

She leans across the wall and pokes her head inside the memorabilia room. It reeks of iron. The glass towers have been leveled. Every past achievement smashed and shredded. Chuck lounges on the floor in half of his torn-apart chair which has been rendered legless. His lips are outlined in smears of chocolate, strawberry and vanilla icing, and there's a trail of cupcake crumbs leading all the way from his chin to his buttocks where a colony of ants have begun their ascent. His left hand's bright red and throbbing, his fingers resting inside empty cupcake wrappers. His right hand resembles a bloody tampon. Both arms rest at his sides, bunched-up mounds of debris acting as armrests. He bleeds watery blood all over old newspaper clippings—over old, original photos he's never made copies of—over one-of-a-kind metals and ribbons and pins and even the key to the city.

"I came to see you earlier," Mia says, "but some fool threatened to use his taser on me." She cocks her head, gives Chuck a funny look, but he's lost to a daze. She doesn't mention the two wishes she had to grant for dying children today, thus why she's only now showing her face (which looks lovely by the way, and not because of the painted-on expressions and wig). "I'm so sorry about what happened to Nana."

"You didn't do it."

"Chuck?"

"Uh huh?"

"Is my family in jeopardy—" She stops short of saying *too*.

"Of course not."

"Am *I*?"

"Don't be silly."

"Then what happened the other night?"

"You know how sometimes people confuse people for other people?"

She glares at him.

"That didn't happen here. Some moron followed me to your place, thinking he'd kill me or something. Dumb move though, because I ran him down and took him out with a…trash can. One of those steel ones. It was filled with bricks…from a building which had recently been demolished."

"Funny, I didn't see anything about this on the news."

"Wasn't creative enough I guess." He shrugs. "Goes to show how sick today's society has become."

"Right."

They go quiet, which has become familiar territory as of late.

Scanning the aftermath, Mia's not surprised Chuck pulverized something. She *is* surprised, however, the something was his beloved memorabilia room. And the carnage didn't end with the towers—the overhead light has been pried out of the ceiling and dangles like an eyeball popped from its socket. And the walls have been fisted several dozen times over. The studs stamped with maroon knuckles. The only window in the room had its white blinds yanked from the drywall. It has since been smeared in a coat of blood to blot out the sun. As it hardens, so fades the light.

Mia's V-shaped stilettos act as ships plowing through the spillage. She steers herself into a comfortable position underneath the doorframe and its peeled molding. "Why don't you go back to the hospital and rest?" She doesn't mention the pair of hanging tighty-whities, but if she had, Chuck would've told her he ripped them off fake-wrestling-style and hammered them into the front door to cover the peephole so when anyone tried to peek inside, they wouldn't know it, but they'd be staring deep into his underwear. The message was supposed to be, "Eat my ass." In retrospect, Chuck doesn't think he relayed the message properly. Thankfully Mia hasn't mentioned it. She's also skipped over him being completely naked.

"I'm freaking out, Mia. There's just too much to do, so little time." He drives his fist inside a mound of debris and fishes out a fistful of shredded tulips. "Do you like these?"

She sort-of laughs.

"Didn't think so." He tosses them over his shoulder, and they rain specs of purple.

"Are you planning our wedding, *right now*?"

Chuck nods whilst saying, "Aaban offered to host it. He owns the temple. He's super nice, and so are all the others. Maybe I didn't see it before when I was 100% white. Aaban may be a little too nice, because there was some confusion over what the event was. I think he's under the impression it's a funeral for Nana, so it might get a little awkward Saturday."

"From the way you're talking, it sounds like our wedding's this coming Saturday."

"Correct." He showers her with another clump of flowers. "Surprise."

Mia crouches, tries to sink to Chuck's level, but it's not possible. She'd have to lay flat on the floor, so she stares at him like *really?* "That's in five days."

"I don't have a calculator handy, but the math sounds about right."

"We're not getting married in five days."

"We have to. I made Nana a dying promise."

"That we'd get married in five days?"

"That I'd marry you before the burial so someone could take her place. So I wouldn't be alone. So I'd still be loved."

Mia struggles to find a patch of his skin not covered in sticky blood. She places a peck atop his right ear and says, "I'm going to pretend you're not lying to me and only acting this strange because love makes people do stupid things."

"I promise to never be rational again."

She smiles, he smiles. Everything seems okay. Then she leaves, and he finds himself alone in the crimson-tinted room. Chuck dig's Nana's urn out from under the mound of cupcake wrappers. He picks a few more pieces of stuffing out of the empty chair, then places them piece by piece around the cold brass, forming a blanket to keep his Nana warm. It was only a few, short years ago when they would come together every Friday night, her seated in that once sturdy chair, him in the other, and they'd both lounge while staring at the wall of memories. They'd munch on popcorn as their imaginations turned pictures into movies. One night they'd watch a framed photo of Chuck accepting a golden cheeseburger award (good for a year's supply of free cheeseburgers—bacon was unfortunately an upcharge). Another it'd be a framed headline reading, *Rookie on the Rise Accidentally Drops Public Enemy from Hot Air Balloon.* And then there was Chuck's personal favorite magazine cover, *The Year of Chuck Steak: Not the Meat.*

The room had been built specifically for Nana. Chuck would direct her attention to a particular level on a particular tower, and through the glass they'd both gaze as Chuck narrated the story behind the memorabilia. At the close of each movie, he didn't have to remind Nana how he had taken her advice—how he had practiced day in and day out—how he could, when the time came, thwart the punks. She knew from his towers of success how prepared he was. She'd grin majestically and lend over her frail, spotted hand. Their arms would hang in-between the chairs to form a V. They'd squeeze, and she'd smile brighter, the death pooling inside of her all but flushed. The inevitable end all but forgotten.

In those moments, they were both frozen in time.

And then when Chuck would drive her home, her memory would bounce on top of her head like an open box of rocks. Some rocks would already have skipped out the window along the drive. Days later, the box would be empty again, so Chuck dropped by and picked her up in an Avis rental. Took her out for a night at the Chuck Steak movie theater. Over and over, rinse and repeat. Until, of course, she took a turn for the worse. Something happened, and her box seemed flattened. She couldn't retain much for long. Her window seemed to have been reduced to minutes, almost.

*Worthless.* Chuck chucks the golden cheeseburger across the room and scores inside a hole. It wasn't hard—he did, in fact, have a 50/50 chance since his wall is about 50% wall and 50% holes.

*Fuck that cheeseburger anyway—it hasn't been valid for ages.*

What Chuck's referring to is life. It seems worthless, but maybe a better word is pointless. What's the point? What's Chuck's endgame here? What's he ultimately want to get out of his life?

To never end, of course, but there's no such wizardry to make it so.

The philosophical bullshit mutates into a headache, so he thinks about something else—about Mia—about how they began opposed to how they might very well end...

*Buddies, there will be a sweet backstory DLC released in the near future, probably, maybe.*

The mystery cell goes ballistic. Chuck reaches inside the wall and fishes it out of a layer of drywall dust. "What now?"

"You look…I mean you sound lonely," the killer says, laughing.

Chuck analyzes the room.

"It's not like I'm inside your walls. Or outside your window. Or across the street. Or down the block. Or watching Mia as she struts to her car. How could I be everywhere at once, Chuck?"

Still analyzing.

"I think you need help, *too*, Pal—wink, wink!"

# Chapter 8
# Signage

Bernard apologized.

*OH HELL, PAST TENSE ALERT! But only because when I was watching the action live, one of my ghost buddies distracted me with a funny joke, so I had to go back and summarize this part, thus why it's past tense, because, as a friendly reminder, this story is 100% raw and authentic!*

To repeat, Bernard apologized.

Chuck asked why, since *he* was the one barging into Avis in the middle of the night, well past closing time.

"Because," Bernard said, "of what happened to Cynthia. It was god-awful. Dreadful. Unwarranted. Disgust—"

"Enough already," Chuck said. "Were you the one who killed her?"

"Heaven's no!" Bernard tensed, his face reddening, his sweaty hands gripping the keyboard. He must have pressed one of the buttons too long, because his computer went, "EEERRRRRNT!" and he said, "Damn you!" He made it a point to look directly at Chuck and say, "Not you, this lousy computer." He cleared his throat. "And I was working all day during that mess. Sorry, it wasn't

72

a mess. It was sad. Truth be told, I'm always working, you know this. Don't you?"

"Bernard, I'm just pulling your fucking chain. Relax."

Bernard's body went limp as he sucked in a big one. Then he presented a set of clunky car keys resting in his palm, and as the two engaged in their ceremonial midair arm-wrestling match, Bernard said, "Chuck Steak, you son-of-a-bitch—here's your purple Mazda."

The purple Mazda coasts into a concrete parking lot with grass sprouting from the cracks.

Every spot's taken, so Chuck pulls into a field and parks a few feet from the vaulted chain-link fence with the curved top. Beyond the gate lies an airstrip. A plane strolls by as Chuck steps out. He follows it a hundred feet or so to 4592 East 5th Avenue, which looks like an upside-down, square, abandoned box with two white doors scribbled on in crayon.

A plane takes off a few strips over, its twin jets erupting, shaking the earth below. After it slices through the cloud-filled tropopause, Chuck twists the aching knob and tries to ease the door open, but the hunk of metal cries out in orgasmic squeals. There, he meets a sea of dilapidated faces slapped atop disheveled bodies all huddled together in the middle of the open space, each using their picketing signs as crutches.

This place could've been a hangar for personal jets once. It's since been commandeered. The bald, soot-covered, thirty-something-year-old woman in gray overalls, who had probably been preaching about an important matter, stands idly on her crate podium while staring and listening intently to the climax of Chuck's door-knob-romp. Everybody, in fact, is turned and staring. All sixty-some of them. All women.

*SWEEEEEEEEEEEEEEEEEEEEEEEEEAAAAAAAA AAAAAAAAAAAAAK!*

And he's done.

"Can we help you?" Ms. Baldy says.

"Yeah, what the hell?" shouts a face lost inside the beating mob.

"Ahem." Chuck steps into the pit, and several women hiss at his nerve. "I happened to be in the neighborhood." He glances around. There's really nothing to look at besides angry women and rafters shrouded in thick spider webs. "Figured I'd explore unknown territory. So here I am. What's this all about?"

"What's this all *about?*" Ms. Baldy laughs at the ceiling—at the plane rumbling overhead. "What's *this* all about?"

Jesus Christ, yes, that's what he asked.

"Betsy, Dear," she takes aim with her blackened finger, "show 'em what this here's all about."

"Okay," Betsy says, fumbling with her sign, knocking it into others. She's a sweet, elderly lady sporting belly-high jeans, a tucked-in, decade-old, practically sheer OSU t-shirt which shows her massively sagging bosoms flopping out her hot pink bra, she's also wearing bottle cap glasses and is topped with a permed bush of white hair. Pretty innocent. But then she squeezes the wooden handle like it's a neck in need of wringing and thrusts her sign into the air. It's a huge, white rectangle with letters written in blood-red marker—maybe even blood, who knows? The sign reads:

*Asian Lives…*
*Native Lives…*
*Black Lives…*
*Latino Lives…*
*Queer lives…*
*Trans Lives…*
*Women's Lives…*

*Children's Lives…*
*MATTER!!!!!!!!*

*Oh shit,* Chuck thinks, worried about what he's stepped into, *I'm not on that list.*

"Hooks!"

"Yeah, Tune-up?"

Great, Hooks has talon piercings outlining her lips, a big bull ring knocker tugging her nose toward the ground, and devil horns screwed into her temples. From the chin down, one can't decipher what is and isn't a tattoo, but her entire body is certainly covered in *something.*

"Show this bozo here what we're all about!"

Hooks pumps her sign with unrivaled emotion. Black background with neon green lettering:

*MORE THAN MEETS YOUR EYES*

Tune-up nods proudly and shouts all drill-instructor-like, "What inspired you to create your sign, Hooks?"

"I didn't always look like this. You might think it's gross, and stupid, and that's how it started out—after I got my first tat, I think it was a dolphin," she sighs, "how dumb—every girl's first tat is either a dolphin or a flower. My second tat was a flower." She shakes her head, but her sign never once wavers. "I got a couple piercings, too. Not much, you know? I had these things in moderation. But then people started judging me. Anything they saw on my body not on theirs, they'd find a way to ridicule me over. You try to let those insults slide, but then you learn you're getting turned down for jobs by looking a certain way. By having a little metal ball in your cheek instead of a mole, because a mole's excusable even though it's ugly and potentially cancerous, but a metal ball? Get out of my office already, Loser. Aaannnd I'm ranting."

"Ranting's good," Tune-up reminds her.

"After years of feeling people's eyes constantly smothering me, I figured I'd do something to tell them the only thing abnormal was the way they stared at me, and judged me, and chastised me. So I started getting tattoos of those who wronged me. I'd go into a parlor and give the artist a mug-shot description of every single one of them. Sometimes it was a guy who forced himself upon me because he saw all the tats and figured I'd be an easy lay. Sometimes it was a store owner who called the cops 'cause I was apparently a thief and had to have been stealing something. I mean, why did someone like me need to be shopping for fine jewelry anyway?"

"Pigs!", "Jackoffs!", "Scumbags!" a few women shout.

"Same deal with the piercings," Hooks says, "I want everyone to look at this body, and I want them to see the faces of those who've turned me into this monster." Upon further inspection, her limbs do appear as though they're glass jars filled with severed heads.

Everyone claps. Chuck even joins in with a slow-clap of his own. Then when it quiets down, he says, "Wow, okay...well...you ladies sure are interesting and everything, but I'm actually here to speak to someone named Rosa Costello."

As if Moses suddenly appears, the sea parts, leaving behind a single woman standing in the center. And not any ordinary woman. This one's at least four inches taller than the rest. This one's got her hair tied into a harsh topknot—so harsh, her hairline seems ready to tear. This one's got calves the size of cantaloupes piercing her jeans. What could be a plate of medieval armor fitted snug under her plaid, rolled-up-to-the-elbows shirt. And delts. *Delts!* She's got big, silver hoops for earrings and sunset orange lipstick. And she's also wearing Keds.

This is Rosa.

She struts forward, dragging her sign haphazardly across the cement like a shovel used to dig a hole for the bodies she had just mass-murdered with her bare fists.

Rosa chest-bumps Chuck. He plants his boots to maintain balance and remain upright. The two come face to face. He's got at least three inches of height on her, but they're tied at roughly 7%

body fat, which is an advantage for Rosa. Here's why: men require 3% of their body mass for essential body fat whereas women require 12%. There's essential body fat in nerve tissues, bone marrow and organs. For athletic men, body fats range from 5-10%, meaning Chuck is in superior shape, both on a muscular and lean level. For athletic women, the range is 8-12%, meaning Rosa is insane.

The rivaling strangers breathe into each other's mouths. She smells fun, like a bowl filled with coconuts, Malay apples, raspberries and sandalwood. He reeks of death and decay, like his Q-tip had been plugging the hospital's sewage system, backing up all the toilets, but Rosa doesn't seem to mind.

They breathe harder, slapping each other with hot and hotter air. Chuck's not sure what this is—a breathe-off? An Oxygen transplant?

But then a sign strikes down between them. It's as tall and wide as Rosa. Chuck takes a step back to read the text. Once done, he mumbles, "Fuck."

This is what the bright white sign featuring police-blue lettering and outlined in caution tape reads:

*TO PROTECT AND SERVE, RIGHT?*

There's a blown-up picture of a sidewalk. Drawn across two of the slabs is a white chalk outline. It's obvious where the blood had been wiped away due to the blotchy, pink smears. At the tip of the outline's outreached hand is a numbered marker for evidence. Inside the chalk, around the heart area, a bystander (could have been a loved one) scribbled in red chalk, *Mateo, just 6*.

Below this picture:

*WHY DON'T YOU TRY TO PROTECT AND SERVE ME, PIG-FUCKS?*

The sign slides away, bringing them face to face again.

No wonder the killer handpicked Rosa—she seems to be under the assumption police shot Mateo dead. Mateo's connection to her remains uncertain. Perhaps he was a friend, a cousin, a nephew, or worst-case-scenario, a son. Regardless, she appears to be in a state of constant rage judging by the punishment she's put her body through. The woman's molded herself into the ultimate fighting machine, and it's logical to assume the intent was to use it against police.

"Why're you looking for me, little man?" Rosa says, the only hint of her former self shining through in her honeyed voice.

Chuck skips the part where he looks down further and mentions the three-inch difference in height with a devilish grin. "I came to offer you a job."

Finally, a smile cracks her penetrating stare. "You don't think I know who you are?"

"Figured you might."

"Then you got a lot of nerve."

"Thanks?"

"Because you see this?" She highlights her statuesque body with Vanna White hands. "This is for you."

"Shucks," he can't resist any longer, "I *just* got engaged. Sorry, Doll."

Perhaps *Doll* was taking it a bit too far, especially when the doll in question slugs him square in the gut. He takes a hunched-over moment to collect his breath, after which he pries himself straight—the pain evident through a hiss he's quick to suck in.

"What?" Rosa says, tapping her chest with fingernails painted like toucans, before throwing her arms wide. "Huh? What?"

"What are you talking about? What, *what?*"

"Chuck Steak's always looking for a good fight." One of her toucans flicks him in the chin. "So what's the problem?"

"Lady…" Her freshly plucked, black, commas for eyebrows drop as low as a car with chopped springs, and her eyelids squeeze out haterade. "…*Rosa*. I don't want to fight you."

"Because I'm a chick?"

A disembodied woman pumps her sign into view. It reads: *Resistance is Fertile!*

"You afraid of losing to a lousy woman?"

"As if!"

"A minority then, is that it?" She flicks his chin again.

Another sign pops into view, this one reading:

*Remember, dumbasses, ALL of us descended from IMMIGRANTS!*

"God, no!" Chuck blurts. "My fiancée's African American."

"Oh, I see." Rosa's bubbly with laughter. "Since this guy knows a black girl, he automatically knows all about her people and their struggles."

"Come on, you're putting words in my—"

She throws a jab, trying to put her entire fist inside his mouth, but it's not a good fit. Instead her knuckles collide with his pearly white walls of teeth.

Chuck staggers back cradling his crunched lips. Through a quilt of finger slits, he muffles, "Seriously, enough!"

Another sign:

*TAKE IT,*

*LIKE A WOMAN!*

"Awww," Rosa struts toward him, "can't the big baby handle a little love tap?"

"That sounded sexual."

Another sign:

*Get your mind*

*out of the gutter*

*PIG/PERVERT*

"Holy Hell," Chuck says, "do you ladies have a sign for everything?"

Last one:

*YES!*

Rosa jabs him again, this time in the cheek, not the butt. "You've got a little something-something right there."

He doesn't look, because it's physically impossible.

"Made ya look!"

Chuck tries to get out, "No I—" but she bitchslaps the rest into oblivion.

Another backward stagger. Another, "Enough!"

Rosa performs a full split, dropping her crotch to the concrete. Her jeans bend with every contour of her muscular thighs. It's as if they've been down this road many times before—worn to unimaginable lengths of flexibility. For this very reason, the jeans aren't surprised when Rosa cocks her fist and prepares a devastating blow to Chuck's manhood.

"Don't do it!" Chuck shields himself, but even he knows his sausage-like fingers and the fingerless glove of Duct tape he had concocted and self-applied at home aren't enough to soften the blow. He'll feel it, and he'll probably, against his own will, cry. There will be sixty-some witnesses, and he'll never live the moment down for as long as he lives. In fact, it very well could follow his name around for the rest of eternity.

"Then hit me." Rosa pumps her chest.

Chuck performs his own split, dropping so his bulge joins her crotch on the floor.

"Clever boy," she says, grinning. She strains to cock her fist back another tick.

He doesn't know where to station his barricade of hands. "Please." They waver. "Listen to what I have to say."

"Make it fast—no idea how long I can hold this." She's already got veins sprouting up from her neck, into her throat, pushing beads of blood through them.

"Okay, if you joined the force, imagine what you could accomplish. You wouldn't have to stand outside whatever buildings you're planning on protesting. By the look of it," Chuck peruses the signs, "that would seem to be all of the buildings."

She grunts.

"Sorry, I couldn't help myself."

The oxygen in her face wears thin.

"Listen—you could make an actual difference on the inside, Rosa." A brief montage of all the ways this could backfire flash through his thoughts. For one, he's not even an officer anymore, so how's this even going to work? "Or are you just another social justice warrior who somehow loses their voice once given the opportunity to take action?"

Too many women gasp.

Rosa grinds her top teeth into her bottom lip and lisps through the gaps, "Why me? You even give a shit? Or your department look at their staff and figure they lacked women and minorities?" She's losing steam. "So a big ass light bulb went on inside your head, and you said, 'Shucks, let's just hire ourselves that there Hispanic chick'?"

*Wow, does she really think I talk like that?*

"We'd never!" Even though when he thinks about it, the department *is* running awfully low on minorities, and there's a high probability the building contains more blowup dolls than actual women.

"Better hurry," Rosa warns. She's broken a fuckin' sweat.

"Here's the truth! I've been scouting you for months. My boss has been riding my nuts about getting a partner, and I didn't think anyone was good enough, so I kept putting it off. Until you came along. A big, Hispanic woman from the…*a* neighborhood." He almost said *ghetto*. "I knew I had to have you…ask you to, you know? Join me. Because, well, I can't keep fighting the city by myself. Do you see my hand?"

She sees his hand.

"The bandaged hand?"

The bandaged hand.

"See how it's clearly not mine?"

She sees how it's clearly not his.

"I need help, Rosa, and seriously, all this gender bullshit aside, you're the most badass person in this city—well, besides me." He throws out a Bernard-ready handshake and awaits her reply. Shake or face-fist, which will it be. "I *need* you."

"If I get to choose the cases."

"How about 10% of them. That's fair."

"Fair's 50/50, mother fucker."

"Fine, 50/50 it is!"

"Deal."

Chuck's hand bobs. "Now shake on it."

She blasts him in the face.

# Chapter 9
## Hairy Ball-sack

Chuck awakens on a blistered crate. Having noticed, the gaggle crashes in around him. He says, "What—"

"—day is it?" one of them says back, and the rest snort.

"—'s so goddamn funny?"

Hooks snaps open her compact mirror and slides it in front of Chuck's nose. He examines his face in the tiny circle. The gaggle tries to hide behind the golf-ball-sized reflection. When it drops out of view, most of the women can be seen clutching their mouths shut, or their friends' mouths shut, holding back the laughter.

"Really?" There are juvenile phrases and comic doodles etched into every square inch of his face.

The gaggle giggles.

"Is it permanent?" He already knows the answer before popping a thumb into his mouth and dragging the slimy tip across his forehead.

Tune-up steps forward, the skin under her ashen cheeks bright red, and says through some tears, "We thought it hilarious at first, but when you didn't wake after like 10-15 minutes, we got a bit freaked out."

The gaggle bobs their heads.

"But don't worry, Pal," she pats him on the back, "you were in the best of hands. Hooks here is a sleep doctor. She takes care of passed-out dipshits for a living."

"They refer to me as an anesthesiologist at work," Hooks says, "amongst other things."

"Hold up," Chuck says.

"Surprised by my profession?"

"Hell no. Anybody can be whatever they want. Now tell me, how long was I out?"

"For pity's sake," a thick woman who goes by Info Hub says, digging out her phone, "do I have to do everything around here?" She's literally done nothing so far. "It's 11:11. Make a wish."

Chuck's already on his feet, shaking his jelly-like legs back into action. That much time couldn't have passed, so he demands a recount.

Info Hub loathes backtracking. Loathes it every single time her boss tells her to go back and check all the memos and reports and presentations she's been labeled the overseer of, even though it wasn't in her initial job description—in essence, she didn't sign up for that shit. Info Hub's work fury is triggered, and she calls Chuck what she calls her female boss: "Poozer."

"Whoa," Chuck says, "I've never heard that one before, but it sounds bad."

Info Hub has already reclaimed her phone. She plans to do what she always does—recheck the work, then throw it in her boss's face with extremely sassy passive-aggressiveness. But when Info Hub brings the actual time to life, she shrugs and says, "My bad, I told you the incorrect time."

Chuck sighs. He knew it had to be off.

"Forgot my phone's all screwy. It's really 11:18."

"What?!?" Midnight has snuck within striking distance. "NO!" The gaggle look at him like, *yes, Bitch, you can't refute the facts.* "Where's Rosa?" He stands atop the crate, searching for the high-rise amongst the duplexes. "Rosa!"

"Rosa left, Pal." Tune-up laughs, but not at his misfortune— at the giant, hairy ball-sack scribbled down the length of his neck.

"11:20," Info Hub announces.

For tonight's mission, Rosa must agree to become Chuck's partner in crime, and then Chuck must obtain an official, in-person verbal okay from Anderson, all before midnight.

"11:21!"

Chuck doesn't know where to turn, so he spins in circles. Tune-up jams him to a stop with a stiff-arm. "When I said *left*, I meant *stepped outside*."

Chuck's there in a jiff. Sure enough, Rosa's parked on a stack of pallets, her folded arms pulling the heels of her Keds into her buttocks. She watches the next plane peel its tires from the tarmac and crawl into the sky. With her gaze locked onto the tail end's red, blinking light, Rosa delves into some completely uncalled for babbling. "I remember the first time my father ever brought me here. I was six."

*Jesus Christ,* Chuck thinks, the current time blinking rapidly inside his mind like a strobe light, *don't start at six!*

"I was blown away, you know?"

"Most definitely."

She doesn't catch his sarcasm, or perhaps she doesn't care. By all appearances, this woman doesn't have a single fuck to give. "I watched a few planes go up and disappear. It seemed like magic. When Dad finally kicked old Beatrice back to life, I begged him for a few more minutes. Kids, right? Always asking for more and more. Never enough."

"Fucking kids."

"I think I was eleven the next time Dad parked us a ways down the road."

Too many years left.

"I watched the same amount of planes, but when he kicked old Beatrice into gear, I didn't put up a fuss. I had seen enough." She stretches and yawns, and it appears she's acting. "I watched those planes take off and vanish, and you know what I felt? Not-a-thing." She untucks and hops to her feet. The two come face to face yet again. Her heavy, hot breath ignites his face and forces itself down his throat, choking him as she says, "It's what happens to everyone. People," her Ps feel like hot-air-balloon explosions, "people become content. And when people become content, other people, innocent people, die." She has to be fucking with him. "If

I were to take this job, I'd want to give it my all every single day for the rest of my career. The public deserves as much."

"I agree, wholeheartedly. 1,000%. Couldn't have said it better myself. Tell you what—let's do something special for you, because *you're* special. *You're* different. *Unique.* And not just because of your skin color. Because of what's on the inside. How's about we swing by my lieutenant's…ummm…room…and get you sworn in before midnight?"

She frowns. "Are you already mocking me?"

"Jesus, no! Or whoever you believe in, no. It's just…just…just…"

She clears her throat.

"…just…don't you wanna start as early as possible?" Before she can answer, "That way we can set out first thing and beat some crime's ass."

"Is this the type of shit I'm gonna have to put up with?"

"I think so."

She sighs, massively. "Let me go grab my keys, and a Prozac."

"Wait!" he blurts. "I'll drive."

She turns and grins. "Nice try."

This can't be happening.

"Look." He dangles the Mazda's keys. "We'll take mine since, you know, they're in my goddamn hand."

"Oh, is this your personal vehicle?"

"You bet!"

She flicks the chunky tags. They read loud and proud, *AVIS.*

"Well, the vehicle's not mine per se—"

"How many cars have my taxes paid for?"

"Seven?" If she had said "vehicles", the answer would have been thirteen.

"*I'm* driving." She drags her feet on the way inside the building, at which point Info Hub cups her hands and yells, "F.Y.I., it's 11:32, *Poozer!*"

The candy apple Camaro pulls out, slowly. Rosa must think it's Sunday, but it's really Monday, and in a handful of minutes, it'll be Tuesday.

Chuck gallops into the hospital room with three minutes to go. Rosa trots in twenty-four seconds later—she elected for the stairs over the elevator, figuring she'd treat her calves to a cardio-based midnight snack.

The curtain's yanked closed, and Anderson apologizes for the stench, explaining how his roomie had passed a few hours earlier. Everybody is solemn.

But then Anderson convulses, buckling in bed. The multicolored wires he's hooked to swing wildly. They make him look like a puppet nobody can possibly lift. He strains to say, "Chuck, goddamn you." Is that foam forming at the sides of his mouth, seeping into the grays of his beard? "Seconds after you escape the hospital against everybody's wishes, a citizen tries to arrest you?"

"I threw him into a sheet of glass which didn't break, because this is real life, Sir," Chuck says, his mind replaying the entire ordeal...

*A citizen had exited the hospital. He carried his belongings in a man purse, but who cares? He was taking the concrete stairs three at a time and noticed a hand gripping the railing. It was Chuck's hand. He had unraveled the bandages while exiting the room, while bouncing between the walls of the hallway, and while landing in the elevator. He had left the dozens of feet of thin, bloody cotton lying there, stretched across the hospital's innards like an extracted tapeworm.*

*The meds meant to kick Chuck's ass were doing a fine job. But he stumbled out of the hospital anyway. He made it to the handicap ramp but wasn't ready for the grade, so he took a nasty tumble and had been trying to pull himself to his bare feet as the man purse man blew by.*

*Chuck sloshed some words around in his numbed mouth, which the man purse man duly noted, stopped, but upon realization that the hand was black, the man purse man jumped in place with two white hands shielding his purse and yowled, "EWWWWWWWWW!"*

*And then Chuck's other hand, the white hand, clamped onto the railing. He pulled his very white, so-pale-it-could've-been-transparent face into view. The man purse man let out an enormous sigh of relief and immediately hopped the railing, putting on display his athleticism in case a female happened to be looking their way, and burrowed his mass into Chuck's armpit to hoist him up in case the female wished to see his kind and gentle side, how he had went out of his way to aid a total stranger in need.*

*Chuck had mumbled, "Tank you, odor der peas."* Odor der *meant* over there, *which was in reference to a mighty, rectangular, glass sign which protruded the curb, which Chuck then shoved the man purse man face-first into. The man purse man went splat, and Chuck gave him a black middle finger and said, "Fuck in race ist."*

*The man purse man, unaffected by the collision, sprung to his loafers, said, "I knew I should've stuck to my beliefs! You're evil, and you're under arrest! A citizen's arrest!"*

*And then Chuck shoved him face-first into the glass again. And again. And again, until the sign was so smudged with spit and slobber that the next few vehicles to funnel into the hospital parking lot dead-stopped at the sign, shrugged, and screamed, "WHERE THE HELL AM I SUPPOSED TO GO?"*

1:23 remain.

"You were right, Sir," Chuck says, forming an impressive pair of prayer hands since he's had a lot of forced practice, "I needed a break, Sir. Desperately, Sir."

Anderson may have very well soiled himself with the way his face twitches, hard, and there's a pop of hot and sour air.

"Sir, you need me sane, and I need you healthy," all facts, "and we both need Rosa, Sir. Sir?"

Anderson tries to shift but rattles like a Jell-O mold instead. "Who the Hell's Rosa?"

Rosa doesn't take too kindly to this bitter tone and readies a medium-powered punch. She attempts to preface this with an ill-mannered comment regarding the lieutenant being a lard ass, but Chuck catches her words and shoves them back down her throat. She chomps his white palm (would she have used such violence against the other?).

Chuck thrashes and yelps. Rosa laughs. With 53 seconds to go, Chuck says, "Why would you do that?"

"I've always wanted to bite the hand that—"

"Feeds?"

"—suppresses."

"Probably gave me rabbis."

She steps into him. "You must be itchin' for me to lay you out again. It'd be convenient this time around with an empty bed nearby and all. I could even notify the staff of a huge pussy alert."

With 32 seconds remaining, Anderson chrispers (a combination of a cry and whisper), "I like this gal. She doesn't put up with your shit."

Rosa beams, and despite the fact that an orthodontist would probably fit her with braces due to her lower left-hand side canine tooth bullied to the backrow by the incisor and premolar, and the second premolar on her upper, left-hand side having been punched out some odd years ago, leaving the surrounding teeth to lean into the gap, and the fact that one of her front central incisor's has had 1/8 of its bottom chipped off, something about her smile is…*charming*.

*Must be the orange lipstick,* Chuck rationalizes, *even so, get to a dentist already.*

With 19 seconds to go, Chuck shuffles his hands. "So, Boss, you wanted me to get a partner, and here we are."

"Five goddamn years ago!" Anderson foams. His beard's so frothy, and wet, it looks like boiling, vegetable spaghetti.

Rosa glares at Chuck while Chuck stares at Anderson while Anderson envisions a heaping bowl of brown maple ice cream topped with caramelized bacon as Chuck clears his throat with 15 seconds left and plealls (a pleading yell), "Sir, please," *with caramelized bacon on top,* "I just need one more chance! I promise I won't blow stuff up *or* leave corpses lying around. Hell, I swear I won't even kill anybody anymore, not even bad guys."

"Hot damn, I never thought I'd live to see the day when Chuck Steak pleaded for his job back." Anderson chuckles, causing yellow bubbles to form and pop. He chokes on the concoction for six precious seconds, and then says slow and slurred, "You know," cough, cough, "wha—" cough, cough, cough, cough, cough, "wha—" cough, cough, cough, cough, cough, cough, is he dead?, cough, cough, "what?"

# Hairy Ball-sack

Oh what's it even matter? The clock's struck midnight.

"I'll hire Rosa," Anderson says, "for *your* position." This makes him happy, but not as happy as he knows he'll be when he finds out the answer to this question: "And Chuck, what's the goddamn truth behind those testicles on your neck? And those nipples on your cheeks? Are they...are they lactating?"

"Screw you," Chuck says, having wanted to say it ever since the firing. He digs the cell out of his back pocket...

*Wait a minute,* he realizes, *I've had this on me the entire time!*

In retrospect, there was no need to ask Hooks for the time other than to give her character something worthwhile to do. How sexist.

Anyway, it looks like Chuck is removing an ass tumor, that's how big the phone is. He flips it open in anticipation of the "game over" call, and despite it not containing neither a make nor model number (according to the red sticker plastered to the back, it was made in Zimbabwe), the proper, universal time is revealed in Calibri: *11:59pm*

"JUST KIDDING," Chuck blurts. "Twas my final joke, Sir, I swear! Now what were you saying?"

Anderson burns two seconds clearing his throat. "I said—" cough, cough, "said—" cough, cough, cough, "you want—"

*Want what?*

"You want—"

*COME ON!*

"—back in?"

That's literally what he just asked for, but Chuck can't nod any faster.

"Then," cough, cough, cough, "this Rosa lady takes—" cough, cough, "takes—"

*Takes what, the cake?*

"Takes the—"

*THE CAKE? IS IT THE CAKE?*

"—your position," cough, cough, "and you—" cough cough, cough, cough, cough, cough, cough, "you become *her*—"

*I'M NOT GETTING A SEX CHANGE! TOO FAR!*

"—*her* partner."

"My *rookie*," Rosa snarks.

"Real funny, Sir."

"This isn't," cough, cough, "a goddamn joke."

"I'm not doing the rookie thing again. I'm Chuck Fucking Steak." Yes, he legally changed his middle name to "Fucking". Mia still, to this very day, pretends he didn't.

"Oh, so you're too good to be my rookie," Rosa says, "but yet you were fine with me being yours? You saying you're better than me?"

*Do I have to?* "Never."

"You implying women need to take whatever scraps men leave behind? You think we can't be leaders?"

Chuck huffs and puffs. "You know what?"

She huffs and puffs right back. "Don't even—"

"You're the boss." He turns to his actual boss and says, "There, happy? We good here?"

Cough, cough.

*FOR THE LOVE OF GOD!*

Cough, cough.

A slurred "Yar" is all Anderson can muster, but that means yes in pirate slang and occurs seconds before universal midnight.

Even though Chuck should feel thrilled with having defied the odds yet again, this all seems like one small step for Chuck, and one, giant leap for the killer.

# TUESDAY

## Chapter 11
## Peaches and Fucking Cream

There's a neatly folded, plastic-wrapped uniform tucked away in Chuck's bedroom closet. Underneath this is a lockbox containing his first standard issue firearm. Of course he doesn't remember the combination, so he clobbers the lid with a fist and expects it to bounce open. It doesn't. Not until Rosa stomps on it with the heel of her Ked.

"Merry Christmas." Chuck hands the uniform over. "Never worn." Then the gun. "Never fired."

"You know," she says, already tearing into the plastic, "some people don't celebrate Christmas and take offense to those types of comments."

"A lot of stuff used to offend me back in the day." He caresses his chin, wishes he was wearing a pair of smart-looking glasses while staring smugly at the ceiling. "Then I turned five."

Rosa already kicked her jeans into the far corner, missing the hamper by a good foot. Her smooth and shiny, latte, curvaceous legs seem to stretch on for miles and miles.

"Up here," she says, taking aim with the gun. "I'm not a man toy."

He shakes his head *of course not.*

"Get out."

Rosa's in there for all of three minutes putting the puzzle together, after which she steps out a legitimate police officer. She dawns the uniform Chuck had always been yelled at for never wearing. It's black and has still retained some sense of sleek newness. Even though her chest's mostly muscle, Rosa can't fasten the top three buttons, so the white T-shirt highlights her neckline. This brings into view the thin, silver chain running like a V down her collar bones. At the end, there's a shiny cat's-eye-shaped pendant, and inside, if one could fend off the dragon and pry that sucker open, they'd probably find a treasured picture of Mateo, just 6.

"Well?" she says, posing. "Thoughts?"

"It's snug." Indeed. Even though the fabric stretches to an extent, the seams appear as though they could pop free at a moment's notice. Perhaps due to this uniform having been tailored for a younger Chuck who had yet to reach his peak physical form. "It was made many years ago when I was little and weak."

"Then it probably still fits, huh?"

He kneels and presses his thumb into the tip of her right, black, high gloss tactical shoe, revealing a huge chunk of unused space. "Seems like you've got a ways to go. You know, to fill these in and all."

Rosa leads herself out, down the hall, down the stairs, across the living room, through another hallway, and at the front door, instead of addressing the detonated bomb which seems to have gone off in the memorabilia room, she nods at the underwear nailed into the front door, covering the peephole, and says, "Someone give you an atomic wedgie?"

"Ha—ha—ha—"

"For this?" She flicks the ivory book he had grabbed from his nightstand and tried to conceal under the bulk of his arm. "Don't tell me you're planning a wedding."

"I'm—"

"Hate to break the news to ya, but lit cigars make for terrible centerpieces."

"I'd—"

She grabs his knob, the door kind, and twists. "And you can't engrave the invitations onto bullets and shoot people."

"I'll—"

She opens the door. "And don't even think about giving the flower girl grenades."

"Let me—"

"Look over there!" Rosa peers into the distance.

"I'm over and under that joke."

"Your loss."

"Yeah, how so?"

"Because some guy's taking your picture."

Sure enough, there's a Lincoln parked next to a fire hydrant further up the street. The shadowy driver yanks an obscenely large camera back inside and squeals into traffic.

"You sure it was a guy?"

"I assume all peeping Toms are guys, thus the name."

"So sexist."

They hop inside the Camaro, rocking the shimmering hunk of metal back and forth like a see-saw, and head off toward their first case. Rosa had insisted they christen their new relationship with hers, because "ladies first".

"Still sexist," Chuck had said.

"Or would you rather file unemployment?"

Through an earlier text message, the killer had said, *Treat her with respect, Chuck. People need to know, without a shadow of a doubt, you're no chauvinistic pig. Especially if we expect to capture the female demographic. Now, look at her (not like that), and listen to her words (even if you don't agree with them), and aid her in her journey. Because no matter how small or pointless her endeavors seem, equality makes them just as, if not more important than yours.*

In other words, Chuck was to become *her* bitch.

During the commute, Chuck does something unbefitting his character. He sets the planner atop his rocks for thighs, flips open past Mia's smudge-riddled dreams, extracts the red pen he hooked onto the back flap, pops the cap into his mouth and nibbles on the end in-between jotting stuff down. This is called keeping track. At a later stage, it'll be called organization. It's all very new to Chuck who dives in with no direction whatsoever.

This is what he writes:

*Dear diary,*

*I hate snugglin*

He giggles while crossing that out.

*OK seriously*

*shit to get done:*

    *1.~~book church~~ DONE (hahahahah I rule)*

    *2.fix ~~Orf Orrphu~~ Mia's dad and bro*

    *3.*

He slips Rosa a calculating eye—she's fixated on the road and only has one hand on the wheel.

    *3. keep R around til Sat then have fired (and deported???)*

    *4. did the killer just take my pic?*

    *5. what significance does this POS half-used planner hold?*

    *6. get Mia to say I do*

    *7. are 4 and 5 connected?*

    *8. this is a mess this blows*

"You should paint a portrait of your man-gina," Rosa says, grinning, "and hang it above your hot pink, tufted headboard."

Chuck slams the planner shut and shifts upright, cheeks tight (all of them). "You know, I could reprimand you for not using two hands."

She uses her second to mimic the jerkoff motion.

The Camaro scrapes against the curb leading into a vast parking lot lined with rows of gleaming cars. It doesn't occur to Chuck where they're actually headed until they judder to a halt. It all happens fast. Rosa hops out of the car before the engine dies and stomps toward AVIS. Chuck hustles to catch up. He snags her hand as it flirts with her newly appointed firearm.

"Why're we here?" Chuck says, flushed. "And why're you getting ready to shoot someone?"

She sighs. "If you must know, there's a notorious drug dealer running this establishment."

"Bernard?"

She shrugs. "On the street he goes by Beardy."

"Now you're definitely messing with me."

"Beardy's responsible for most, if not all of the crime on the East Side."

Chuck snorts.

"This man's a drug trafficker, Chuck." She pricks his chest with her fingernail toucan. "A sex trafficker." Another prick. "And an arms and exotic animals trafficker." Now he's the prick.

Chuck peeks through the glass to ensure his Bro-nard isn't overhearing any of this. The big lug's probably busy up to his eyeballs in the back, per usual. And when he comes barreling toward the counter, he's always disheveled and out-of-breathe, so it's not like he'd notice anyway.

Hold on. *Disheveled and out-of-breathe.* This had never once seemed odd to Chuck, but now he can't help but wonder why? Why would Bernard, a man in superior shape, a man who lifts the frontends of cars (although electric and foreign), always be stuck in such a state? What's he so busy doing back there?

Rosa tugs her hand free and muscles her way through the door to the sound of DING, DONG!

Behind the vacant counter lies the tight hallway which leads to two rooms. Bernard steps out of one, careful to seal the door behind him shut, then barrels toward his computer's dead monitor. He appears disheveled and out-of-breathe, and to boot, doesn't look to see who's entered. He shakes his mouse to bring the monitor back to life and says, finally acknowledging the patron, "What can I do for—"

The air rushes out of him like an enema blowing all the way through his digestive track.

Rosa unpins her badge, Chuck's old one, and slaps it against the tacky oak. She turns it after noticing how the engraved name and number (both of which aren't hers) appear upside-down. Now it's proper. Now it clearly states: *CHUCK F. STEAK.* "Why hello there, Beardy."

Bernard gulps, unleashing three beads of sweat which paint glossy lines down his lobster-baked face.

"What's in the trunks today? Drugs? Guns? Knives? Corpses? Maybe a little bit of everything?"

"I...I don't—"

"You don't what, Beardy?"

Beardy, no, *Bernard*, pounds his mouse, and his monitor finally awakens, painting his face green—he looks like a swamp. "Stop calling me Beardy."

*Disheveled and out-of-breathe.*

"What were you doing back there anyway?" She points at the *EMPLOYEES ONLY* sign.

"Paper...paperwork."

"Which is it? Paper or paperwork?"

"Both, I guess? I don't know."

"For your 'patrons'?" She finger-quotes patrons, but he doesn't get it. "Gangs and syndicates?"

"What?" Bernard wraps his paws around his neck and squeezes veins into his face and hacks through his dry throat.

"We know you're not really choking."

"Okay, listen," the charade drops like a swatted, dead fly, "I'm not associated with those types anymore—haven't been for ages."

"So you willingly admit to past involvement," she claps her hands and rubs them violently—excitedly, "which means it's not a stretch by any means to assume you've relapsed."

"The...I...Miss..."

Rosa stabs her spade-shaped badge, pointy-side-first, into the warped wood. It remains upright after releasing her grasp, a tombstone of sorts. The words *SPECIAL POLICE OFFICER* peer into Bernard's dilated eyes, straight into his tattered and torn soul. The word *SPECIAL* appears to have been haphazardly carved into the golden metal by hand.

"It's Ms., Mother Fucker," Rosa says, leaning in.

"Sorry," Bernard shakes, beads of sweat springing off his head every which way, "Ms. Mother Fucker."

"No!" She palm-smashes the badge further into the wood. "It's Ms., comma, Mother Fucker."

"I don't really understand."

Chuck steps in. "She's referring to her title, like Miss, Ms., and Mrs. She also called you a mother fucker."

"They all sound the same," Bernard whines.

"I know, Man, English is tough. Here, why don't you take a second to Google it?" Chuck slings an arm around the large of Rosa's back. "And we'll just step outside to have a quick word."

Rosa points two fingers at her eyeballs, then directs them at Bernard.

Once outside, she plants herself in front of the tinted glass, right below the orange V in AVIS.

"Are you psychotic?" Chuck says directly below the S. "That's my best friend in there."

"Then what's his favorite color?" She bobs a thumb over her shoulder but smudges the glass.

"That's a dumb question."

"How so?" She smudges again.

"Because I don't know the answer." If his planner were present, he'd jot down, *8. what's Bernard's favorite color? 9. throw the answer in Rosa's face.* "Listen, you can't just barge into someone's place of business and accuse them of an assload of crimes."

"Isn't that how you've," smudge, smudge, "built your legacy?" Smudge, smudge. Jesus, doesn't she know Bernard's gonna have to Windex that shit later?

"Fine, go, and when you botch the only case of your career, I'll—"

Too late.

DING, DONG!

Rosa hurdles the counter with her gun drawn and knocks the monitor over flat on its face. "Come out!" She plants herself in front of the *EMPLOYEES ONLY* door. Nobody answers her within the allotted half second, so she cocks her knee to her chest and...

While repositioning the monitor atop the counter, because Chuck might not know Bernard's favorite color, but he knows how neat and tidy and obsessive the red-bearded-one can be when it comes to his work station setup, Chuck says, "Rosa, don't you even—"

...she boots the door in, popping the metal frame loose and sinking the handle into the dry wall. She's not in there long. In fact, it appears she only broke into and entered the room to create more runway, because she gallops across the hallway with a low shoulder and batter rams through the second flimsy piece of wood. It must be made of Styrofoam with how easy she's making it look.

"Why didn't you peek out the back first?" Chuck says, bobbing his head at the wide-open, emergency exit blinking at the end of the hallway.

"Why'd you let him escape?"

"The more likely scenario is he had to take a leak."

A vehicle peels out of the parking lot and cuts into the thick of traffic which honks wildly.

Just to make certain, Chuck peeks out the emergency exit to scan the desolate wooded area. "I'm sure there's another logical explanation. He could've swung over to the bar next door so you wouldn't arrest him for urinating in public."

"You're too close to this one."

"And you're a walking cliché."

A creative name-calling battle ensues for a good amount of time. When the good amount turns into the bad amount, the partners get to rummaging through the abandoned AVIS office.

Rosa selects option *EMPLOYEES ONLY*. It's an interesting choice. The room could fit four dumpsters inside but doubles as half gym (a power rack/bench and a two-tier rack loaded with mismatched dumbbells), half storage (secured filing cabinets lining the far wall). Rosa punches each one open. The drawers are packed tight with stuffed folders. Each is filled with personal information.

"What're those?" Chuck asks from inside the split frame mid-chew. He's already cleared the other room. It contains a fridge and water cooler and microwave and a sad table with one chair. He snuck a tilapia from the top shelf, figuring Bernard's missed out all these years on the joys of sharing a communal fridge and leaving food unprotected, so he'll give him a dose of reality.

Rosa flips a folder open. "Did you know your boyfriend does taxes?"

"You mean," Chuck swallows a lump, "I could've been getting a discount this entire time?"

She flings the folder over her shoulder. Papers go everywhere.

"Hey now," Chuck sucks the orange residue from his fingers, "you should," more sucking, "put those back where," even more, "you got them. Maybe file 'em under *I rushed to judgment.*"

Rosa shoves him out of the way and tears a cabinet from the lobby wall and beats it against the edge of Bernard's counter until keys rain down upon the floor. Then she grabs two fistfuls and shakes them in front of Chuck's face.

Outside they go, and there's really no time for this. Clicking the lock buttons to make the corresponding vehicles beep, then doing this several times over in a seemingly endless stretch of smoldering blacktop filled with not only AVIS vehicles, but those belonging to the employees and customers of the rest of the strip center's businesses. It becomes an annoying game of hot and cold which only one person wants to play.

Chuck had been banking on a freed-up afternoon where he'd swing by Chet's apartment, say something like, "About the other night—sorry for ratting you out. I kind of got caught up in the moment." He'd throw a touchy-feely arm around Chet's neck and say, "You know all-too-well how that happens. Remember?" When Chet remembered, he'd probably ask if this was Chuck's revenge, and Chuck would say, "I made a mistake, Chet. I never meant to hurt you." They'd probably share a hug, maybe even a tear. And then Chuck would inspect the pitch-black room, the curtains most likely shut to set the perfect, depressing tone, and he'd say, "For your own wellbeing, I need to get you out of here and drunk." He'd chauffer Chet over to Lucky's on 4th and pump a few drinks into him. Then Chuck would excuse himself, warn Chet it could take upwards of ten minutes before he returned— the liquor would already be loosening his stressed mind, prompting him to flick his wrist and say, "Take your time, Man, no worries, ha, ha, we've got all the time in the world." Before Chet would finish this sentence, Chuck would already have vanished. He'd sprint five doors down the block to Orpheus' State job located inside the Rhodes tower, and he'd catch the disgruntled father off-guard in the lobby during lunch. Orpheus enjoys eating his lunch standing in corners. Since he sits most of the day, this is his only chance to exercise and also judge everybody who passes by. Orpheus likes to make educated guesses based on appearances and demeanor about who's eventually going to get spiked into Hell or hail-Maryed into Heaven. Sometimes when Orpheus can't derive a logical conclusion, he'll swallow, and with his lunch still in hand, lain out across a crumpled tray of tinfoil, he'll approach these mysterious beings and ask them personal questions like, "Hey there, doing anything in particular this evening?"

Yes, this explains why sometimes a total stranger will approach another and ask them odd questions which throw the victim all out-of-sorts, prompting them to respond with something equally as puzzling like, "Thanks."

Orpheus has received many of these replies. He determines those to be the purgatory souls. Before they can flee his presence, he calls out to them, "Hey, sorry."

"Thanks?"

"Sorry you're going to spend eternity in limbo. I can help you find your way." He slips them what first appears to be a run-of-the-mill business card, but really, it's a tiny portrait of his church along with the sacred address. "There, I helped you find your way. It's up to you to walk the path."

Orpheus has had sixteen incident reports filed against him over the years for similar stunts. But he continues the great fight in the name of his lord and savior, Jesus Christ. And God, too. And don't forget the Holy Ghost.

Anyway, Chuck would approach Orpheus. Orpheus would swallow and say, "Hell." Chuck would apologize. Orpheus would cram his tiny church into his pocket and say, "There's no salvation for you." Chuck would beg for Orpheus to join him at Lucky's for unlimited virgin Bloody Marys—it'd be Chuck's treat. Orpheus would say, "Sure, Dumbass, I'll take your money," and off they'd go.

Chuck would set Orpheus at a table located across the way from tipsy Chet. He'd place an order before excusing himself. Then he'd mosey on over to Chet who'd be all shits and giggles while saying, "That was sure fast," and Chuck would laugh, because it would have already been like thirty minutes.

"I need to make a call," Chuck would say, ordering them another round—both of which would eventually drain down Chet's throat.

Switch.

Chuck would excuse himself after ordering drinks with Orpheus and intercept the waitress to switch the virgins to sluts.

Switch.

Rinse and repeat until the father and son were nice and blitzed. Then and only then would Chuck take Chet's hand and say, "There's someone I'd like you to meet."

Boom, a little bit of creativity and liquor saves the day.

But Chuck's stuck rooting through the backseat of a Tundra. Annoyed, he calls out from underneath the passenger's seat, "No little kids in here! How about you?"

"Found your backbone!" Rosa hollers from inside the trunk of a Civic. She even pumps a tire iron into the sky.

"Least we know you'd never be able to break it!"

No retort.

Chuck slams the Tundra's hitch shut and selects a fresh pair of keys with his middle finger. He beeps the vehicle for a long while, each passing second grating on his nerves. A Prius is next. Fits the depressing mood exceptionally well, because nothing's more depressing than a top speed of slow.

To the trunk.

Despite being a 2008 model, the felt lining looks brand-spanking new save for a loose, long, curled, white piece of string. The previous renter must have opened the trunk to retrieve their luggage, noticed the fray on their shirt, figured they'd take hold and tear with haste and all would be right with the world again, but instead of splitting, the string grew thrice over. Chuck chuckles at the thought of the person pulling so hard that their sleeve fell clean off.

This is what his mind has been reduced to. The insides of the vehicles are set to broil, and there's a limit to how many times one mortal can dunk their head inside without losing one's sanity.

Chuck undunks his head from the trunk and redunks it into the glove box. Nope. Into the center console. Nothing. He shifts, because the seat's terribly uncomfortable. He gets back to dunking. Into the ashtray. Under the seats. Through the remaining hidden and not-so-hidden compartments, and there's literally nothing to see here.

But when Chuck slides out the car, he feels over the lump which had been digging into his rear.

*Could it be?*

He kneels to fondle. It's soft. He presses firmly into the center, treating this as a breast examination, and finds a hard mass.

"What is it?" Rosa *would* appear directly behind him at this exact moment. It had been at least twenty-some-odd minutes since they last saw each other. But now she lingers over him like a bad hangover.

"Gee, I don't know, it's only been one second since I found it. Probably just a hardened spill."

"Sure it is." She winks, then muscles her way into his place, then goes at the side of the seat with the hands of a molester. Her fingers run along the bottom where the fabric hangs loosely, as if it had been methodically undone. "Hmmm...seems awfully suspicious." Her grin widens as she reaches up the seat's polyester skirt. Her hand caresses the junk and squeezes. "It's big."

"You've got a bad case of 'the Dad jokes'."

She yanks free a bag of cocaine, or Baby Powder (which Chuck could certainly use right about now), but probably cocaine.

"And I've also got 'I'm Right Syndrome'," Rosa says, and Chuck has to admit, twas a fine comeback.

*Jesus, Bernard, what have you done?*

# Chapter 12
# The Devil's Gay

Their initial greeting felt odd. Chuck extended his white hand, bobbed it there, and lured Chet's hesitant, shaky, nimble fingers into his sweaty palm. As Chuck performed a finger vice on Chet's dead fish, he realized a second hand was needed and came down softly with the new addition, eased up on the old, and transitioned seamlessly into a hand hug, which seemed to have won Chet's heart over.

"We could be real brothers now," Chet had mumbled, kind of, sort of smiling, fixated on the pavement.

"We'd probably have to devise a Cirque du Soleil handshake to make it official."

Fast forward through the multiple rounds of liquor and beer. Nobody could quite remember which came first to remain in the clear, not even the waitress despite her outspoken love of getting "fudged up". Chuck excused himself, stating a number two was in order.

Twelve minutes later, Chuck appears. He extends his black hand, and Chet takes hold, performing a hand crusher. Chuck follows this with a hand crusher of his own. They both crank back, then fire pound cakes which connect at the knuckles and turn into exploding fingers and absurd, slurred blasts. Then Chuck wraps Chet's demolished fingers up with his cupped hands formed into something of a cocoon. He rolls Chet's fingers together like a dough maker, and when he pops a hand lid off, Chet's hand has been rebuilt. Afterwards, Chet rebuilds Chuck's hand, and this happens four times, since there are four hands in need of repair. After all this, the hands pat each other on the backs, or knuckles, gently massaging them to sleep, and then two hands get tucked in, and a few seconds later, the other two hands which are still wide awake slap the shit out of the asleep hands and yell, "PARTY TIME, PARTY TIME!"

"Holy cow," Chet blurts, "this is the best handshake ever!"

"I know, right?" Chuck whips out the controller shake, in which he assumes control of where they go, thus the name. "There's somebody," Chuck says, "I'd like you to meet."

For Chet, this transition is abrupt. One second he's standing. The next he's dropped into a seat at Orpheus' unbalanced table. For the past ten minutes, Orpheus has been obsessing over the lean, which he's only made worse by shoving napkins and coasters and even a spoon underneath the wrong leg. The lean has since become unbearable. Orpheus is practically in tears when he acknowledges Chuck and says, "Why can't I fix it?"

"Hey now," Chuck says, "get your shit together. We have a guest for God's sake."

For God's sake, of course. Orpheus quickly drops below the table and retrieves a handful of dirtied napkins which he buries his face inside and unleashes an avalanche of mucus into. He's wanted to exorcize this congestion ever since it started to build immediately following his son's dreadful revelation. But real men don't cry, and they certainly don't question their maker.

"Who do we's have here?" Drunk Orpheus rises to the occasion, above the tabletop, and he and Drunk Chet make eye-contact for the first time since their shouting match back in Chuck's condo's formal dining room—the one which ended with Orpheus hurling his chair at the wall and yelling, "FAG!"

"Oh," Orpheus says, burping up some slutty Mary. "Oh Jesus." His eyes swim over to Chuck. "You rotten bastard. You think me fool?"

Chuck snaps his fingers, so Orpheus follows them to a second version of Chuck. The real version. "I overstepped my boundaries the other night, guys."

"And girls," Orpheus says. He doesn't find it funny. He says it as though he's stating a well-known fact.

"Goddamn it!" Drunk Chet blurts, pounding the table, making it wobble violently, not only alerting all patrons that this table's got a good show to put on, but also highlighting another problem in Orpheus' life which he's not been able to fix. "I've done things your way my entire life."

"Wednesday a know?" Orpheus swallows some barf. "I means, when's did ya know, huh? Hubbub? Whaaaa age?"

"Nine."

Orpheus laughs and whispers, *"Nine."*

"Shut it you old, bitter man!"

Chet appears magically flushed of his drunkenness, while Orpheus not so much.

"Watch yo—"

"I don't care...any...more! I'm done trying to impress you. You made me pretend to be somebody I wasn't. I'm soft, and kind, and I love another man, his name's—" Noticing his father's massive eye-roll, Chet says, "—you don't deserve to know. Not because it's a secret—I'm done hiding those. It's been causing me so much unnecessary stress. And why? To impress my father? Because all I've ever wanted was for you to admire me the way I thought I admired you?" He shakes his head, dripping tears. *"Fudge* you, evil man." The waitress taught him that. She nods and smirks in the distance, because she's eavesdropping. "You act like a Godsend, but you're nothing." His voice rises, and all the patrons secretly cheer, because they're finally able to hear what's going on. "You're a sham! You're a coward!" Chuck leans in, parts his lips, readies a *whoa, whoa, whoa,* because this sure took a turn for the worse, but Chet's on fire, and he wants to bring the entire world down. "All you'll ever be is a buuuuuuuuullllllllllllllllly!" he screams, just like in that song.

Orpheus lowers his voice to a whisper, because this sure is embarrassing. Both the reference to that gay band *and* his gay son. "Would you love ta know why ya got ta repent?"

Such a condescending bastard. Chet can't help but snicker out a nonresponse.

Orpheus leans into his son and places a hand, sunny-side-up, on the table. "I shudda...shudda-a-nah, ca...ca...called ya a fag. I, I...hate meself for sayin' that. Real lies this. Understand this."

He's got Chet's attention, as well as Chuck's, because this—*this* is progress.

"But nuttin' changes defacts. If you do-do-do-do-do-do-not stop this homosexist behave your, and-and-and ask, pray fo God's fogivenessessess, I won't, won't be able ta help you."

"Fudge you, and fudge God."

"Don't, Chet, don't say it. Fudge? Dun use gay slurs gainst God." Orpheus' glistening eyes bulge. "Pa...peas, Budders."

"Dad, I don't even believe in God. Not your God, anyway. Why would I?"

Orpheus almost smacks his son like he almost smacked Henriette at dinner, thinking maybe, just maybe, it might knock some sense into him. "YOU are DOOMED, Chet. You even understand may? You rememba anything I taught you? Ever? Because this serious." To Orpheus, nobody outside of him and Chet exist. With the table acting as a confessional, he realizes this is the only chance he's ever going to get to save his son's life. "I'va luved you morer than you coulda ever...eva known, *know*, Son."

Chet looks away, sniffling, but can't stop the flow. "Yeah, okay."

"Damn me! I dun ever-e-thing ta raise ya proper. All effort I put into church, it been for hour family. We lead good lives in a evol world. I have dun bestest ta ensure nun yous ever mess up. Maybe sometime I too tough," Drunk Orpheus sounds awfully similar to a caveman, "or it seem like I ova...ova-re-ack......" an uneducated caveman, "or ack shell-fish," he means *selfish*, "but yew knowers what, Chet? I sacrifice so-sooo much. I dedicate my wife," he means *life*, "ta follow-king an tiring to understand ever Bible rule no matta how silly or cupid they seem. Why, you ass?" He means *ask*. "Goud question. Why? *Why*?" Okay, everybody (meaning the entire patio) gets it. "Cause I tiring to get hour entire fam-i-ly inta Heaven. Why again? So we an Jesus live together for paternity. But! Butt, butts! This gayness you there've sprung on may, if you dun lies, you tell me sooner, I coulda talk so much sense into that tiny Brian, *brain* a yours."

"I WAS BORN GAY!!!!!!!!"

"Dis here's a choice. You choose to bed a woman, which the right way, or you choose bad way—yuck way—which the man way, then you go direct to Hell. What then? What happen when Mom, me, Sis be in Heaven, and if we loooook down, there, loooook, it Chet, he in Hell! What then, when you trapped for paternity? And there no-thang-no-bod-dee can do-do ta save you? You think anya us can live lives like dat, knowin' yer ski-rewed? Fagive my language, Father." He kisses a finger and points it at God.

Chet laughs through the snot. "You really are this far gone, aren't you?"

Orpheus doesn't hesitate to nod. "It be da honest-ta-God truth." He must have answered a different question inside his blurry head.

"Get over it already! Get over God! We're alone in the darkness, and if you can't see that, I wish I could be there on the day you die, when you close your eyes and never see again."

"Who even are you?" Orpheus says, leaning in to stare deeper into his son's eyes. "Where my whittle boy gone? What devil possess him, her, both?"

And it happens, as swift as lightning. SMACK! Chuck's distracted by the way Chet kicks out of his chair and sprints away wildly. It's only when Chuck attempts to explain to Orpheus how this has been yet another misunderstanding when he discovers Chet's bright red handprint tattooed across the side of Orpheus' stunned face.

# Chapter 13
## Kill with Kindness

Chuck raps on the glass, startling Rosa awake. Her uniform has since become a sponge, absorbing an amount of sweat which has surely left her severely dehydrated. Her once ironed shirt is covered in mostly hard, wet wrinkles. To add tackiness to untidiness, hundreds if not thousands of random, frizzy hairs have escaped her topknot. They sway ungracefully with the faintest of movements in the air, like the way everybody imagines Einstein's doo did.

It takes Rosa the average amount of time to locate the unlock button, which is 14 seconds.

"Don't you know," Chuck says, plopping into the fiery passenger seat, "you're supposed to crack the window if there's a dog in the car."

"Hot air helps me sleep." As she shifts her seat upright, the accordion of fabric covering her belly makes a squishy noise as puddles of sweat run down her sides. "Sometimes I think I'll like it in Hell."

"Don't have a comment for that one."

"Good, because I'm too groggy to come up with one for you."

It takes a second for it to register, but then Chuck smiles.

Then Rosa smiles.

Then a businesswoman outside smiles because her Bison Frise finally took a dump on the sidewalk.

"You hungry?" Rosa says, turning the key.

"Starving."

The businesswoman struts away from the steaming pile of shit as the partners pull out.

They approach a diner on foot. It's three-fourths the way into a city block. It's modeled after a World War II airplane with aluminum plating for walls and fat squares for windows with rounded edges. The sign bolted into the second story's maze of red bricks reads *MAC'S LANDING* in big, red, Coca-Cola lettering.

Chuck stops short to snatch a penny from the pavement, but with a latex glove suctioned to his right hand which was given to him by the restaurant's hostess the third time he reentered, after of course she said, "Why don't you cover that up?", no telling if it was meant as a racist remark or because several of Chuck's stitches had popped open thanks to those slightly exaggerated handshakes with Chet and began bleeding down his forearm, penny-picking turns into quite the production. He picks and peels, but the coin only slides and hops. He kicks it, but that results in him chasing it several stores yonder. Eventually, he decides to drag the coin by thumb over the edge of the curb, into his cupped hand.

Somewhat pleased, somewhat annoyed, he hustles over to Rosa and says, "I've got this." He turns to the Indian woman with the dark face outlined in sun-bleached, ratty hair and presents the tarnished drop of copper. "Here ya go," he says, waiting for her gracious, fingerless-mitten-wearing hand to pounce from her side. But it remains there, limp. "FOR YOU," Chuck practically screams. It's odd, really, for he's never seen a homeless Indian person before.

The lady bats the penny out of her face, and it bounces back home where it belongs.

"Wow," Chuck says, "I know pennies aren't what they used to be, but beggars can't be choosers."

Rosa shakes her head, steps around Chuck and says, "This here the joint?"

The Indian lady nods. "Owner's Mac Henry. See him over there?" She points through a window at a man sporting a stark-white jumpsuit. His back's turned to them as he swims through a stainless steel grill's eruption of steam. There must be a hundred pieces of meat packed onto that bitch. Chuck can taste the greasy goodness. For all he knows, this could be the one spot in the entire world where the oxygen contains calories, because each gulp contains a hint of oil.

"That's your guy," the Indian lady says, and this doesn't feel right, so Chuck says, "Excuse me, but I didn't catch your name," so she says, "Vishnu."

"That's your guy," Vishnu says.

"Ready to head in?" Rosa pats Chuck on the back, but he's got a bad feeling eating isn't on their agenda. She nudges him inside. There's a cowbell attached to the inner handle. The metallic clank prompts the entire diner to turn. Most nod and tilt their trucker hats, while some shout, "MORE COWBELL!" Everybody laughs, because it's the joke which keeps on giving. Then they turn back to their white plates filled with avalanches of yellow food.

"Howdy," a prune-skinned woman says as she chomps a line across her dripping wet corn on the cob. After she swallows, she smiles, revealing deflated corn kernels stuffed between each of her false teeth.

A gentleman at the very next booth lowers his newspaper to nose-level and says, "How's it going?"

Chuck tips his head and says, "Thanks."

"Have a seat," the man says, no idea telling how old, because he's simply a set of brown eyes hovering between a newspaper and straw hat.

"I'm people," Chuck says, turning completely around, "I mean I'm here with people." He looks for those people, for Rosa and Vishnu, but they're outside, their two heads pressed together behind one of the windows. They shoo Chuck toward the counter.

"I don't see anybody," the eyes say, rolling all around.

"Thanks," Chuck says as he drifts over to the counter and straddles a cherry red stool. The place mat *is* the menu. It's littered with portraits of Mac's bestsellers. With a burger oozing BBQ sauce and caramelized onions, with crispy, golden brown fries smothered in chunks of gravy, cheese lava and bits of shiny bacon, and with logs of buttered garlic bread floating in a bowl of steaming marinara.

Mac finally turns and plucks a pad from his breast pocket and an uncapped pen from the spindle. This is the moment of truth, but Chuck can't decide—can't envision himself settling. His stomach growls, at which Mac bobs his bicced-bald head and says out the peppered handlebar mustache outlining his weathered lips, "Poor guy, you're starving, aren't ya?"

Chuck whimpers.

Mac stuffs his order-taking tools back into his pocket and slides a bent coaster into place. "How's about I fix you a real man's dinner?"

Chuck drools.

"Something with balls."

Chuck winces, and Mac turns back to the grill grinning, and a woman wearing an old, faded XXXL band T-shirt and no bra so her balloon breasts rest on her beer belly as it rests on her lap, slaps the vacant stool between them and says, "Pretty sure he means steak. Here." She slides her plate over. "Take a bite."

Chuck stabs a cube of succulent steak with her slimy fork and pops it inside his mouth.

"Did you just cream your pants?" the woman says, "and by the way, the name's Donna."

As Chuck chokes getting the steak down, Donna stands erect, ready to suck face, to suck the piece of steak out of Steak's throat, as do most of the patrons, but the scare's over in a jiff, so everybody eases back into shoving their pie holes.

"Wash it down with this." Donna slides her mug over with 20% Coors remaining. It doesn't tip. This must not be her first rodeo.

Someone once mentioned to Chuck in passing, "The last 10% of any drink if scientifically proven to be backwash."

With a 50/50 chance, Chuck pounds 50% of the 20% leaving behind a frothing 10%.

"Polish it off," Donna says, smacking the counter.

*What the hell,* Chuck thinks since he's ridiculously parched.

"Next round's on me, Mac!" An absurdly tall woman in knee-high cowboy boots, her torso a white, blotchy stem sprouting from a pair of unbuttoned, low-rise, frayed jean shorts, her boobs, or lack of, hidden inside a black velvet vest drenched in cat hair, half-hugs Chuck and plants a kiss atop his head. To Chuck, she says, "Sure looks like you need one, Mister. Rough day?"

"Rough week."

To Donna, she says, "This seat taken, Ma'am?"

"Not at all, Dear."

"The name's Dolly." Dolly crams her legs under the counter and extends a full head above Chuck while seated.

"Hey, Dolly, Dear, would you mind passing my plate back this way. That's if, oh what's your name, Muscles?"

"Chuck."

"That's if Chuck's finished."

"You finished, Chuck?" Dolly says.

"Yeah, thanks, Dolly." As Dolly slides the plate to Donna, Donna leans into the counter, her boobs and belly eating into the white wood, and says, "How was everything?"

"Oh, excellent. Thanks."

"Don't thank me, thank Mac."

"And don't thank me," Mac says, sliding a beer into his hands, "thank Dolly."

"And don't thank me," Dolly says, "thank the scratch-off I just cashed in."

"Amen!" a surprising amount of people chant.

This is odd. But in a good way. Like this is what having a real family feels like. Not only a mom. And not only a Nana. And not only a girlfriend. But all those things together, at the same time, plus more.

The fellow seated on Chuck's immediate right nudges him in the ball of his shoulder, slides *his* plate over and says, "You ain't leaving here 'til you try the scrapple, 'cause you look like you ain't ever had yourself some." Chuck takes hold of the greasy fork and cuts around a black-as-night hair from the man's bushy neck, although it does look like it could have also come from down under.

*Damn it,* Chuck thinks, chewing while also trying to spit out yet another hair.

For what appears to be no reason, people start cheering wildly, and moments later, Chuck finds himself chugging beer, racing the entire counter. Dolly slams her mug first, and Donna says with one gulp to go, "You shark, you!" and Dolly says, wiping away a mustache of bubbles with her tattooed wrist, "It's my first of the day."

"But errr won't be yer last," a greasy mechanic with a decently-washed mullet shouts near the counter's end. He snaps his grimy fingers and shouts, "How's bout another go fur ma friends, Mac?"

Ten cold breskis coming right up!

"Take one more bite," the scrapple fellow says.

"No, that's quite—"

"I *insist.*" The scrapple fellow airplanes a clump inside Chuck's mouth, and another hair tickles the roof of his mouth.

"Don't you go getting full on me now," Mac says, having replenished every beer.

Chuck swallows, and the hair scrapes through his esophagus. "I'm hungrier than ever, Mac." Lines of glossy drool rush down his square chin. "My body's ready."

Mac disappears inside the wall of rising steam. As he shuffles meats around, he says out of the back of his head, "Lovely weather we're having."

"Sure is."

"Supposed to remain in the mid-80s with nuttin' but clear skies."

"Hope so."

"Got any big plans for the weekend? Going anywhere fancy? Doing anything fun?"

"Well, actually," he lubes his throat with another swig, "I'm getting married on Saturday."

Mac drops his spatula. Donna spits a mouthful of beer. Dolly's eyes grow to the size of planets. The scrapple guy slides his plate over and says, "Have the rest." The man concealed by the newspaper folds the newspaper and sets it down—his hairless face is comprised of melted bars of skin, looks to have been from an accident. An elderly man plants a sandpapery kiss against his wife's spotted forehead. A five-year-old boy says, "GROSS," and his mother shakes her head and says, "Not gross—it's beautiful," and everybody in the entire joint agrees, because they rise to their boots and applaud and whistle and hoot and holler. "Oh," the mother says, noticing the elderly couple, "you meant them." She brings her voice to a whisper. "Yeah, they're gross."

Something of a line forms. It's not straight, and customers constantly rotate positions. They don't seem to mind though. They only care to shake Chuck's hand and wish him the best life has to offer. But the sixth guy in line doesn't playfully smack Chuck's rear or fist him lightly in the chest. No, the sixth guy in line pardons himself as he cuts through Dolly and Chuck with a fat guitar case, pardons himself again as he uses the case to bulldoze plates and glasses out of the way on the counter, and then he flips the lid open and hoists an acoustic guitar into the air. People oooh and ahhh.

Dolly slides off the stool and says, "Here, Mister, have a seat."

"Johnny," Johnny says, "just plain, ole Johnny." He slides a piece of barley into the side of his mouth and nibbles on the end. "Nuttin' fancy, nuttin' fake. Just me, Johnny from the block." He sits. He hoists the guitar onto his lap. He fondles the frets. "I hear ya got a big day coming up."

Chuck blushes and nods.

"I don't do hugs, sorry, but I do songs. How's about one?"

Everybody wants.

"Hold on," Johnny says, tuning his strings, "what does *Chuck* want?"

It has since become a noiseless vacuum.

"Um," Chuck really, really, *really* dislikes country music, "I guess—"

"He guesses what?" someone says.

"I guess I want one."

Cheers.

When it dies down, Johnny leans forward into position and says, "Everything you're about to hear, well, it'll be off the top of my head."

"AN ORIGINAL?" someone shouts.

"An original," Johnny says.

That someone faints. A waitress fetches them an ice-cold glass of water. The fainter regains consciousness the moment the strings are strummed. Nobody knows if the strumming had anything to do with it.

"Tate-ter, tate-ter, tat-ter," Johnny spits, "tate-ter, tate-ter, tate-ter." His tongue does gymnastics. "Tuning my voice," he says, noticing Chuck noticing him noticing the pitch.

The song begins.

"IIIIIIIIIIIIIIIIIIIIIIIIIIIII," Johnny sings, his voice thick like molasses, "walked into the diner for some food...and I met this here dude...he said his name was Chuck...and he sure looked like he could fuck."

Chuck chokes on drool. The women clap and laugh. The men pump their fists into the air and cat-call.

"Chuck was a certified ten…he satisfied both women and men…"

"Um—" Chuck begins, but an audience member clangs a butter knife against an empty tea glass. They have no rhythm, and perhaps this is why Chuck loses his train of thought.

"…dogs liked him, too, and never left behind poo…he was even a hit at the local and national zoo…back to the ladies, he could have any…speaking of ladies, Chuck had many…he did not discriminate, big, small, short, tall…they were like Pokémon, he just had to collect them all…"

Chuck verifies the math, and sure enough, he's only ever slept with two women (at separate times) and zero men. But before he can fact-check the shit out of Johnny, a chorus has amassed within the crowd, and together they howl in nails-on-chalkboard harmony, "HE JUST HAD TO COLLECT THEM ALLLLLLLLL!"

"And then Chuck met this gal…"

"HE MET THIS GAL!"

"…her name was Val…"

"VAL!"

"…she said if you want to get with me…"

"ME!"

"…win the battle royale…"

"ROYALE!"

"…so Chuck fought…"

"HE FOUGHT!"

"…and he won…"

"HE WON!"

"…and Val was like 'come get some'…"

"COME GET SOME!"

"…but Chuck was like 'nay'…"

"NAY!"

"…and not like a horse…"

"GOTCH YA!"

"…more like a British dork…"

"DORK!"

"Chuck said he wanted to wait…"

"WAIT!"

"…for marriage…"

"MARRIAGE!"

"…and a horsy carriage…"

"CARRIAGE!"

"…to whisk them far, far away…"

"AWAY!"

"…NOW           EVERYBODY           SCREAM NEIGHHHHHHHHHHHHHHHHH!"

"NEIGHHHHHHHHHHHHHHHHHH!"

And the crowd goes wild. And Johnny rests his guitar on his turkey-leg thighs. And Mac's moved onto plating the food. And Dolly gushes, explaining how magnificent that was, and how she'll never, ever forget, and Chuck says, "I probably will, but the first part was accurate—you did, ummm, great."

Johnny bobs his head as if to say, "Don't even mention it."

Chuck offers his hand, because he doesn't do hugs either. Johnny takes hold and yanks, and the latex glove slides right off due to being lubed by blood and sweat. Johnny immediately falls off the stool, his eyes narrow, and his chin tucks into his neck.

The look's contagious, because one by one, the entire diner does "The Johnny".

The grill sizzles, and eyes burn red. Chuck spins around slowly and finds Mac standing there with a ginormous, porcelain tray laid out across his mitts. There's a foundation of mashed potatoes with chunks of blackened steak sprinkled about. And there are fried, crisp onion rings piled on top with succulent shrimp tossed into their centers. And then there are fences of fries pierced into the mashed potatoes, sectioning off the onion rings like they're homes, and don't forget the rivers of white gravy running through and over and under it all.

"Holy—" Chuck's mouth hangs open. "—holy shit." His stomach knots, squealing in agony, as he stretches forward to grasp the mother of meals. "You—" He swallows. "—you shouldn't have." He over-stretches, the burn in his chest proving exquisite. As his fingers float underneath the tray, it begins to float away. *That's odd,* Chuck thinks, and he stretches more, the counter's hard edge slicing his pelvis into two, but Chuck needs this food more than he's ever needed anything in life.

"All right," Chuck says, "I see what you're doing." He smirks. "Very funny."

Nobody else finds this funny, especially Mac. The tray continues to drift away.

"Wait, where's it going?"

Further now.

"Mac?" As far away as the sun. "Are you there, Mac? It's me, Chuck." He waves. Mac doesn't blink, but he does pause the tray above a bulky trash can half-filled with slimy waste. And it finally clicks. And Chuck leans forward, stretches again and says, "No, Mac! No!"

Mac shakes his head in disapproval, but of what?

"I'll pay double what it costs! Triple?"

No reply. No emotion. The tray tilts, and a glob of loaded potatoes splats inside the can.

"Dude—" More splats. "—dude, don't!" But the dude does. He tilts further, and half the tray separates and slides into the barrel and goes splat, splat, splat, splat, splat, splat!

Chuck's fast, and he sets out to prove it by swiping for the tray, but Mac lets it drop a fraction of a second before Chuck can get a grip, and the entire meal splats facedown into the mound of grease-covered gunk.

"We don't serve your kind here!" someone shouts, and Chuck doesn't need to wait for Mac's nod of approval to know it's true.

He can feel it in the air, a storm brewing, only hatred building instead of H2O.

"Uh huh," someone else shouts, "you sir suck!"

"Where'in tarnations your master at?"

"You pick dat der cotton wit dat hand? HAHAHAHA!"

"HAHAHAHAHAHAHAHA!

"LOL!"

"HAH, HAH, HAH, HAH!"

"MUAHAHAHAHAHAHAHAHAHAHAHAHA!"

Chuck feels bent over and spanked, and the trek toward the exit (while short) cuts deep. Five feet shy of the door, Chuck stops at the furthest table. The man of the table glances at Chuck and shrugs, then swallows his mushy biscuit. The man takes another bite, and as butter glazes his teeth, he mumbles through the crumbs, "An I elp you?"

Chuck forklifts his black hand under the white plate and raises it with the same condescending tone Mac did.

"I still eat that!" the man barks with crumbs spilling everywhere, even onto his wife and kids.

Chuck tilts the plate and dumps what looks like triple cheeseburger hamburger helper atop the man's head, and it oozes like boogers down his stunned face, repeatedly scalding and scolding him.

"WHAT THE HELL!" The man shoots out of the booth and gets on his tippy-toes to tower over Chuck. He's unafraid and very pissed. "WE'RE NOT RACIST! WE JUST COME HERE FOR THE FOOD!"

A burnt, triangle-shaped hash brown cuts between the two and explodes against the greasy wall. An angry customer stands and pumps his middle finger. "Then get outta Dodge, ya fuckin' non-racist!"

Suddenly, more and more customers take sides and lob handfuls of food across the room. By the time Chuck steps outside and the door dings shut, the racists and non-racists have engaged in a full-fledged war.

"How'd it go?" Rosa says, hustling over. "Tell us all about it."

"How about I tell you about something else entirely?"

Vishnu stretches onto her tippy toes and peers giddily through a square window at the wrestling match which has since broken out. "I think one guy just broke his arm!" she yelps, the glass fogging momentarily. Yup, definitely broken. Snapped right in half. The guy's dangling it midair, and nobody seems to give a rat's ass. What a bunch of inconsiderate pricks."

"Okay, Vishnu," Rosa says, "keep us updated."

"Sure will!"

"Go ahead, Chuck, tell your story."

"Once there was this guy," Chuck says, and Vishnu says, "There go some shirts, and those women were NOT wearing bras," and Chuck says, "I don't remember his exact name, because I'm terrible with them," and Vishnu says, "For the record, they SHOULD HAVE been wearing them," and Chuck says, "but I remember his face from TV, or maybe the paper, but I don't read the paper, so maybe the Internet, I don't know," and Vishnu says, "OH GOD, is that a real, live pig?" and Chuck says, "Let's call him Pete," and Vishnu says, "GUYS, the pig is on the loose! I repeat, THE PIG IS ON THE LOOSE," and Chuck says, "I failed Pete."

Chuck recounts the tale:

*Six years ago, Chuck came—*

"NOW THERE'S A CHICKEN, NO, TWO CHICKENS! THREE!"

"Do you mind?" Chuck shouts. "I'm trying to tell a story."

"Oh, sorry. I didn't know. Now I'm the prick. Go ahead, go about your business. I'll shut my yapper."

Six years ago, Chuck came—

Vishnu bursts out laughing. "Oh," the laughter escapes her, "I'll quit that out, too."

*Six years ago, Chuck came to a crossroads when he encountered The Bitches, a female-only gang led by a porcelain gal terminally ill with breast cancer. When Chuck blazed onto the scene riding a Moped (don't ask), he had two options—catch the big bad who had stumbled off on her own, four days removed from the expiration date doctors had placed on her decaying body, or hunt down her small but extremely volatile army of nineteen members who had sped off in an armored bus.*

*Chuck chose the former, nabbing the leader in under an hour, but by then, the rest of the gang had already made a pit stop at a local elementary school which had been hosting an evening play. Pete had stepped out during the brief intermission for a few quick puffs. He held a grin the entire time, because his son, Pete II, was killing it as Romeo. He didn't need to brag, because the other smokers waved their orange tips around and said, "Talented kid you've got, Pete."*

*"Way better than mine," another said.*

*"I didn't even see Carl," another said.*

*"That's because he's part of the fence. I told him to blink once in a while to let people know he exists, but you know how stupid kids are these days."*

*Pete hadn't caught much after that—he was too excited about the surprise trip he had planned to spring on his unsuspecting wife and kid a few days later. At the looks they'd give him when he mentioned how they'd be flying to New York City to catch Phantom of the Opera.*

*Pete had pinched pennies for months. His wife took notice near the end. She accused him of being unfaithful. As to not ruin the surprise, the best defense he could offer was his word. But his wife demanded proof. Where had all their money gone? Yet Pete remained diligent even after numerous threats of divorce.*

*The armored bus pulled alongside the curb in a hurry, and the dads gave it their full attention. They ran their fingers along the steel slabs barricading the windows. Along the tires wrapped in barbed wire. Along the grill painted to resemble a cartoonish mouth with fat links for lips and cone-shaped drills for teeth.*

*One dad said, "Hot damn, nice ride."*

*He wouldn't say that seconds later when The Bitches flooded out of the hatches and took hostages. Within a jiff, the bus had sped off.*

*Pete was one of the five who couldn't manage to get away fast enough. He had inched closer to examine the paint job. Sure enough, what he thought might have been flesh-colored storm clouds were a sea of cut-off breasts raining blood. Still, he had time to get away but tripped on the curb.*

*As the bus raced down the freeway, The Bitches hacked off each of their victim's genitals, placed the jewels in a massive, blue barrel which read A Dick for a Breast in dripping, white paint down the side. Then they tossed the men one by one out the side hatch, over the concrete barrier, and into oncoming traffic. Pete caused a nine-car pileup, and his wife had to cancel the trip to fund his funeral.*

"I don't know," Chuck says, shaking his head, "don't know why I make certain decisions. I wanna help, wanna make a difference, that's why I became a cop, and I do what I do because the bad guys' leader is always supposed to die, especially first, you cut off the head, but sometimes when I look back, I realize maybe this rule doesn't apply to every situation, but I know I don't have the tools to deal with such BS, so I continue to do what I know how to, maybe out of fear I'm only good at one thing, and those sorts of people," he bobs a thumb at Mac's Landing, "if they're not committing violent crimes, I can't kill them, so what's the point? I can't even comprehend how people hate a black hand, let alone why minorities can't eat there. And that's putting a lot of things into perspective. When I was leaving the hospital, I tripped and fell like an asshole, but this even bigger asshole wouldn't help me when he saw my blackness. Then there was this officer who almost tazed me when he found out. Point is, I'm starting to connect all the dots, and I'm seeing things I should've seen all along, and I wonder how many racist remarks I've turned a blind eye to, and I wonder how long it's been going on (all my life?), and have I never noticed we have a cultural problem, or am *I* the problem?, in which case I don't even know because my head is about to explode, but my arm hurts ways worse because the narcotics wore off long ago. Honestly, I think I need a higher dosage, but I know they won't up the prescription because they think I've lost my mind, which I very well could have, plus it doesn't help that I ran away."

Rosa, not one for hugs either, extends her callused hand, and whilst beaming, her teeth (crooked ones included) shimmer, and she says, "Hi, I'm Rosa."

Chuck hesitantly shakes, swaying back into a dodgy lean.

"We haven't been properly introduced yet."

"We haven't?"

"You think you're above stereotyping, but sometimes it creeps up on you."

"You mean me?"

"I was referencing myself."

"Oh, good." Chuck nods, grins, smiles, beams, winks, sniffs, bobs his brows, smiles some more, grins some more, laughs, laughs harder, chuckles, giggles, farts, and smiles again, this time extravagantly.

"Even though you're an ass," Rosa says, clamping her grip around his already throbbing, black hand, "I think you might be one of the good guys."

Chuck unravels the cord which keeps getting tangled around the stump of his neck by spinning counterclockwise, but that's the wrong direction, and the cord chokes him blue, so he twirls clockwise and goes too far, so here we are again, choking, to which Mia says through the speaker, raising her voice above the wind's monstrous swooshing, "Hello?"

"Sorry," Chuck says, "and hi." He had just rung her, so these are the first words he's spoken. Who opens with sorry, anyway? And who even owns a landline anymore, anyway?

Anyway, Chuck double fists two diverse spatulas and says, "Hi."

"You already said that." She can tell when he's not paying attention, which is odd since *he* called *her*.

"Sorry."

"Said that, too." Her ear tries to sort through the mess of sounds. The clanking. The dinging. The crashing. The gushing of water. "Is something on fire?" He had once rung her from inside a burning building to see if she wanted to maybe, sorta watch the newest *Terminator* which had finally arrived on Netflix, even though he proceeded this with, "I know it's gonna be bad, but—" and then he paused, and she heard the fire's tendrils lashing out at him, to which he said, "—sorry, gotta *jet*." And before he severed the call, he giggled. She'd later learn this was in reference to a fighter jet which had crashed into the building Chuck had been trapped inside as they conversed about the latest *Terminator*.

"Apologies," Chuck says since he already used "sorry" twice, "you're hearing the kitchen's vent—it's on high. I refuse to apologize for the steaks and eggs and sausages and chicken and pork though," he's going down the grill, "and all this other awesome goodness I'm cookin'."

"Look, if you're calling to explain about that nonsense you pulled between my dad and Chet earlier, save it—I already know the full story, and I'm not happy."

"I'm trying to change, Babe, seriously." He grabs a plate from the top of a stack suspended above the grill, but it slips from his greasy grip and smashes against the floor. He swipes another plate, this time faster, and whips it across the room like a Frisbee so it smashes clear through a window. "For you, but more importantly, for myself." He takes a third plate and swipes it repeatedly between his ass cheeks. Then he tosses it over yonder, and it smashes against something hard. The fourth plate is the charm, and with it sturdily in-hand, Chuck packs the meats aboard like he's Noah, and this plate is his ark. "I want to become a better man, the best man, for…you know…when we start our family, which I'm kinda hoping is…now."

She's speechless, maybe because the entire stack of plates gets bulldozed off the side of the shelf and explodes against the floor, all because Chuck went into rage mode after accidentally fish-flopping the juiciest piece of steak onto the ground and the 5 or even 10 second rule can't possibly apply because it bounced underneath the stove which looks like it hasn't been cleaned nor dusted since its installation back in 1912.

Realistically, Mia's speechless due to the abruptness. For what's felt like forever, Chuck's avoided the topic of marriage and danced around the possibility of children, so excuse her if his drastic rise in interest seems like another publicity stunt.

Mia had always dreamed of children, no less than four. By the time Chuck started entertaining the idea, she didn't even know if he'd be capable of caring for one, let alone several. After their first in-depth conversation, Mia wandered home and cried herself to sleep, because his unreadiness terrified her, especially after several years of already having been together, so she sunk into a soggy slumber wondering if they were truly meant to be.

"Hey," Chuck says, nonchalantly tossing around pots and pans, "now you're the one who's not paying attention."

"Sorry. Hi." They both snort. "You're acting unusual—not yourself."

"Am, too."

"Just tell me what's going on already."

"Who knows? Maybe I'm having a third of a life crisis, no biggie." Sounds like he's hanging out with a bull in a China shop. "Say, you're…*different*. Have you ever been judged for the color of your skin?"

"Of course I have, *and* for being a woman."

"Why haven't you ever told me?"

She laughs. He doesn't. "I don't know, maybe because of your temper."

He hurls another plate at an overheard light, causing it to explode with sparks. "So?"

"When we first met, if I had told you some punk called me the N word for forgetting part of his order, you would've damn-neared killed him."

"Did that really happen?"

"Maybe."

"You wouldn't happen to remember his name, would you?"

"See?!"

"I just wanna check if he's on Headbook. See what he looks like."

"Why—"

"Sorry, and I wanna find out where he lives, and I wanna go knock on the marble door of his gazillion-dollar house, and I wanna grab him by the popped collar of his salmon-colored polo and lift him into the air while his collection of servants watch, and I wanna say right to his face after not having brushed my teeth for at least a week, 'Why don't you call me the N word, mother fucker?' He'd probably gulp and be like, 'But you're white,' and I guess you have a point, because I'd have to snap his head off." He leaps into the air and bashes the shelf off the wall with his black hand balled into a hammer. Every plate in the joint rains ceramic chaos down upon the tiled floor.

"I'm going to assume you're trying to be romantic," Mia sighs, "but honestly, why are you asking me this all the sudden?" She means after all these years.

"Sorry, what? I was plotting out what happens after he pisses his capris."

She sighs louder.

"Okay, okay. I was only messin' around, but not about changing. And not really about that guy."

"You think he's the only one?"

Chuck gulps.

She shares the tip of the iceberg, recounting several times in her life when she's been made to feel less than human.

"Oh fuck," is all Chuck can muster.

Cling, clang, bang, BOOM, rattle, cattle, caw, chew, what in the hell is even going on over there?

"None of this ever occurred to me," captain obvious strikes, "seems people see what they wanna see, and for that," splat, crack, gurgle, "I'm so sorry—I should've asked, it's my job to ask, to make sure you're safe and sound, and I fucked up. I've only seen what I've wanted to." It's called tunnel vision, and it's placed their futures in jeopardy yet again. "We should talk more."

She nods, he can't see it.

"Go on dates more."

Another nod.

"Hold hands more, cuddle more, kiss more."

"Chuck?"

"Yes, Mia?"

"Are you…"

"Gay? Hell no, not that there's anything wrong with it. I love your brother, but in a brotherly way, even though I've never had one. Rest assured—"

"…happy?"

"Of course! Why do you think I've been wanting to get married ASAP?"

They go back and forth for a bit, the exchange like old times, rather cringe-worthy and filled with lovey-dovey stuff, so moving on.

"I love you," he wails above the mechanical chug, chug, chug attempting to drown him out.

"And I love you," she wails above the burp, burp, burp attempting to eat her words.

"We can make—"

"What?" It's getting too loud.

"We can make this—"

"WHAT?"

"WE CAN MAKE THIS WORK!"

"OH!"

"I JUST KNOW WE CAN!"

"I KNOW! I WANT TO, BUT—"

"NO BUTTS, HAHA, BUT FOR REAL, THINGS ARE GOING TO BE DIFFERENT!"

"I HOPE!"

It sounds like Chuck's leaning against a great redwood tree which splits straight down the center.

"I HAVE TO RUN, SORRY!"

"BE SAFE!"

If this were the movies, he'd hang up immediately.

"OKAY!"

"GOOD!"

"OKAY, I'M GOING FOR REAL!"

"GO!"

"HANGING UP!"

"DO IT!"

"IN ROUTE!"

"LESS TALK, MORE HANGING UP!"

"I LOVE YOU!"

"I LOVE YOU, TOO!"

"I LOVE YOU MORE!"

"I DOUBT THAT!"

"YOU DO?"

"I THOUGHT YOU HAD TO LEAVE?"

Whatever's making the cracking tree sound snaps and nearly crushes Chuck's legs, but he hops onto the grill in the nick of time, but the still-red-hot slab of tarnished metal smelts through his rubber soles.

"SHIT, NOW I'VE REALLY GOT TO GO!"

"ALL RIGHT!"

"SINCERELY!"

"WHAT?"

"I MEAN BEST WISHES! I MEAN SALUTATIONS! I MEAN GOODBYE!"

"WHATEVER YOU SAY, WEIRDO!"

Chuck peels each boot from the surface, thin strings of rubber stretching and snapping off, creating long hair for his soles.

Chuck slams the phone against the wall-mounted housing unit, and then his hairy mops for boots carry him across the counter, making the briefest of stops to allow Chuck to bend over and fetch the giant plate overflowing with meats and gravy. Then he boots a window out of the frame, clears a few loose shards of glass with his heel, then fits himself through, into an alleyway, then he waits a moment to admire the tsunami of wet cement crawling toward him. It flows over the toppled counter and sizzles as it splashes across the grill. The concrete mixer Chuck commandeered in the name of justice is parked directly out front in two handicap spots, it's rear-end aimed at Mac's Landing. The feed-in device, a big, metal shoot, has been pierced through one of the storefront's square windows and spews a chunky, gray river inside, flooding the joint.

133

As Chuck wanders off, he tosses a chunk of steak inside his mouth, and whilst mid-chew, remarks, "Mac's sure gonna have a *hard* time cleaning that mess up."

# WEDNESDAY

## Chapter 15
## The Wedding Planner

The Camaro roars as Chuck guns it, because Rosa had ordered him to do so.

But, "Keep your eyes on the road," she warns, yet such a task proves difficult since Chuck doesn't entirely trust her. There must be a catch if she's urging him to throttle her "baby".

A little further down the road, Rosa says, "I know what you did."

Here it comes, get ready.

"Get your hand on the wheel," she slugs him in the arm, which shields the bulk of his head. "I'm referring to last night. At Mac's."

"How'd you—"

"This may come as a surprise, but I'm literate." She's right. "Besides, it was all over social media."

"I don't chirp, or Headbook, so I wouldn't know."

"Too bad—you can find everything and anything you want about a person, especially YOU, online."

"Been stalking me much?"

"Never." She's all smiley. "But if I *had* stalked you, I'd probably want to ask why you always drive the lamest vehicles possible? A

Prius, an Aztek, one of those boxy cars? I mean seriously, what's wrong with your taste?"

"That's just reality, Rosa. The people I typically commandeer vehicles from are either poor or middle-class. This one time I ordered some rich guy out of his Mercedes, and he wouldn't budge, so I went to put my fist through the window and broke my wrist. The bastard tapped the glass, and as he rolled away, mouthed 'bulletproof.'"

"You happen to remember his name?"

"Holy shit."

"Holy shit what?" She promptly looks around.

"I just realized something."

"What?"

"You're me."

"Ha-ha, no."

"Except you don't have any balls."

"Figuratively, I've got bigger ones than you."

This back and forth gets worse, much, much worse, so...

The Camaro eats through the street, widening its potholes and annoying the pedestrians who happen to be out using their legs.

They zip into the parking lot five minutes early. The entrance remains locked with the "We're Closed" sign still wobbling back and forth from Chuck having rapped on the glass. Nobody answers, not even with three minutes until open time.

"Question," Rosa says, pacing the creaky porch, "what's the deal with this wedding? Who's it for?"

Chuck thumbs himself.

"Seriously?"

He grins.

Her brows rise moderately. "Congratulations." No exclamation point needed, it was that dry. She must have noticed her blatant lack of enthusiasm, because she forces out a stale, wrinkled grin. "I'm happy for you."

*Lies.*

A plump face layered from cheek to cheek in foundation appears above the closed sign and bats its eyelashes at the mismatched duo—or what appears to be an officer escorting some hobo. The woman's heavy sigh fills the glass, and when it dissipates, the sign reads, *Yes, We're Open*, and the face is missing.

As the partners enter, the face remains absent for quite some time. They drift amongst the racks, Chuck smearing tiaras and shoes and bags and candelabras and long, tulip-shaped wine glasses with his grubby, big fingers, Rosa constantly batting them away, each time repeating, "What's wrong with you?"

"It's my A.D.D."

"You don't have A.D.D."

"Like hell I don't."

"Like hell you do."

"The F I don't."

"The F you do."

"May I help you?" The face, the blown-up blonde hair, the fat ears weighed down by golden anchors, suddenly appears between them. The body's lost behind a rack. The woman must be seven-feet tall. She's a high-maintenance giraffe. "And please, no profanities."

"Yeah, Chuck," Rosa elbows him, "watch the language."

"Um," he gets high on his tippy-toes to have a looksee, but what he's doing is obvious—he could never be as tall as this giraffe, and this makes him feel small, lesser even, as he mumbles, "I'm looking for a ―."

"What's that?" The woman tilts her head, an anchor almost decapitating him. "Speak up."

"Yeah, Chuck," another Rosa elbow, "speak up, would ya?" She's *not* helping.

"I'm," he clears his throat, "looking for a dress."

Okay, too far.

137

"Right." She must have meant "right this way" since she struts that-a-way.

"Right," Rosa quips and elbows Chuck forward. He has to hustle to keep pace.

The woman's planted herself near the start of an aisle. She motions at the crammed-together row of wrinkled dresses. "I think you'll find these in your price range."

Chuck leans sideways and can judge this entire book by its cover. "Actually—"

The woman's black bars for eyebrows flinch.

"—why don't you go ahead and show me your most expensive dress."

The brows nearly leap off her forehead. "Excuse me?"

"Yeah, excuse me, Chuck."

"You heard me," Chuck says, stepping onto a stool to rise a half-inch above the woman. He peers down at her. "Well, what're you waiting for?"

As she scoffs off, Rosa calls out from behind, "Hey, pssst!"

"Huh?"

"You're rich all the sudden?"

"I might have withdrawn my pension."

The woman outlines an elegant ivory dress fitted snug around a mannequin without a head or arms. The woman's crimson talons for fingernails follow the seam line comprised of…are those actual diamonds?

Chuck gulps.

"If you haven't already taken notice," the woman crouches low, "the waist to hem is comprised of silver Duchess Satin." She runs her claws down the length. "Heavenly, isn't it?"

GULP.

The woman comes to tower over Chuck, casting both a shadow and a shadow of a doubt. "Shall we take measurements?"

"Um—" Huge gulp. "—I'll take it in an extra large."

"HA-HA, oh, sorry, did I just laugh out loud?" She winks. "Why doesn't your fiancée simply try it on? Our fitting rooms are wider than you think."

"Whoa, hold on there," Chuck blurts, stepping away from Rosa who appears flushed, "we're not together, not to mention she's practically a dude."

"We certainly cater to 'dude' weddings."

"Look, Lady, my fiancée's at home, so I'll take an extra large and be on my way."

Rosa catches herself on a rack. She's lost her caramel tint and has since become another run-of-the-mill Caucasian. She also, but not limited to, slumps over herself and mildly hyperventilates.

"Fine," the woman says, "I'll find you an 'extra large'." She goes to fetch it, but Chuck calls out, "And by the way, just curious, but what's the, you know?"

"I have no idea."

"The tag."

"The what, Sir?"

"The thingy."

"No idea what you're saying."

"The price!"

She winks, again. "This particular dress runs roughly one thousand."

"Only one?"

"Yes, one is a lot."

"So in the entire store, this is your finest dress?"

Rosa stumbles into the equation, mumbles, "You brought us to a knockoff store, Chuck, what the fuck did you expect?" and then stumbles past the equation, dripping beads of sweat across the laminate wood flooring.

"I'll take it." Chuck looks around, notices Rosa stumbling toward the entrance. She's left a wet trail to follow. "Hell, maybe I should buy the entire store."

The woman's brows disappear inside her straight-cut bangs. "Why I think that's a wonderful idea!"

"You do?"

She winks. "If you're as rich as you think you are, why hold back?"

Because his $35,417 pension could probably only net him half the store. "Actually, on second thought—"

"Don't second-guess yourself, Chuck," she says, elbowing him lightly but sharply in the side of the head.

"Well will you look at that," he says, pointing, "my partner...she's...got her period or something."

As he takes chase, the lady winks and says, "O-K," and even forms both her hands into the universal symbol for okay.

Outside, Chuck catches Rosa in the middle of the lot, hunched over and retching at the blacktop. Nothing comes out but stinky air. "I'm fine," she says, waving him off. "Go back inside, I'll get over this."

"Can't, now I have to know what's wrong."

She sighs at the rising sun, but seriously, if you don't want someone to know something, don't hint at it.

"There used to be this boy," Rosa says, "his name was Mateo. He lived three doors down and had this thing for me. In case you forgot, he was only six."

Chuck's fully immersed despite the blatant lack of setting.

"I had a soft spot for him." Funny, because she looks like she's never had a soft spot. Not even on her head as a baby. "Local cops gave him shit because he was a mix—Dad was black, Mom was white. They wanted him to pick a race, because he couldn't be both—not in their town."

Chuck sits Indian style to show support. He wishes there was a black style, and maybe there is, and maybe one day he'll learn about that, too, but at the moment, he's still a student learner, so this'll have to do.

"Mateo wanted to be black, plain and simple, but he wasn't a fool. The cops were white, so he knew they wanted him to be, too. He didn't come right out and ask me for my two cents, but I offered them anyway—told him to stay true to himself. I thought since he looked up to me, I'd offer some wisdom, but as you know, he was just six."

Such has been made abundantly clear.

"My little buddy was prepared to charge head-first into war, but I couldn't let him go it alone. I knew he loved me, had told me many times over. And not young, dumb love, Mateo called us soulmates. I figured what the hell and asked him to marry me."

"Whaaaaaaaaaat?"

"You heard me—I wanted to make a big deal about it, give him all the confidence in the world. I started planning this stupid, fake wedding. Everything from flowers and dresses to a DJ for the after dark party. That's when I got into bodybuilding. I wanted to be Mateo's muscle. That way he'd have no problem showing those cops his true color.

"But on the big day, Mateo was a no show. I thought he might have gotten cold feet, or maybe he was watching cartoons or something. What did I know? He was only six.

"He wasn't home when I checked, and none of his friends had seen him. I searched tirelessly for hours, and most of the community joined along. Not a single cop offered help, not even when we tried to open a missing child's case. They said he'd eventually show up, our kind always did.

"Police didn't surface until the worst possible moment—when I had already crashed at home, passed out on my couch. Five of them beat on my front door around two in the morning. Three of them aimed their guns at me after I answered, rationalizing the fists I rubbed into my eyes were weapons. I knew what came next—they screamed at me to get the fuck in their cruiser, or else. Naturally, I told them to go fuck themselves, and before I knew it, I was being tag-teamed to the ground. I beat a few of their asses before they managed to cuff me. I thought they'd unload their magazines into my back, exactly how it happens every day on the news, but they had prepared a surprise and were hell-bent on ensuring I received it.

"They paraded me over to the morgue, four cruisers in total. Then they shoved me through these red-bricked hallways, then into a tiny death room. I knew before they peeled the tarp away that the small lump of mass below was Mateo's body. I knew they had murdered him long before they dug in with their spiteful questions. Like, 'Do you know anybody who would've wanted to do this?' They couldn't hide their smiles while flicking Mateo's head. It had been amateurishly hacked from his body.

"I spun around to bash their noses in with my forehead, but they already had their tazers drawn and proceeded to light me up. I woke behind bars for what they called five accounts of 'assaulting an officer' and one of 'defecating on a corpse'."

*We're supposed to be better than this,* Chuck thinks. *No, we've got to be fucking better than this.*

"I spent two years in a cage, but don't you think I wasted a single second. That's where I got huge. That's where I turned my body into a blunt weapon.

"The point I'm trying to make, Chuck, is even after everything I've been through, I'm still out there trying to make a real difference. I failed Mateo, but somehow, some way, I have to see justice brought back into this shitty world. The urge burns within my soul, a pain so deep, sometimes I feel like I could scratch and claw my skin and bones apart. Why do you think I fight on behalf of others who haven't quite found their voices yet? Because their voices matter no matter how small. I don't want to see them end up like Mateo, or like all the other murdered minorities you never hear about on the news because they weren't important enough."

Chuck stands, faces her, forms his arms into a pair of tongs, goes in around her steep shoulders, tightens his grip, but as everybody very well knows, tongs suck, so Chuck's hands get all touchy-feely trying to maintain any semblance of grip, to which, after several seconds of this, Rosa says, "Really, have you never given a hug?" She drives her hands through his pits, interlocks them behind his back and reverse-Heimlich's his breath away. He transforms his tongs into vice-grips and squeezes her shoulders, not to pop her head like a pimple, but it comes off as such. The pressure forces a few tears out of Rosa as she nestles her head into the divot of Chuck's neck, and in return, he nestles his cheek atop her skull, and the two hug it out with that dolled-up face looming on the other side of a nearby window.

# Chapter 16
# The Obligatory Montage

Chuck and Rosa meet in front of the Camaro's mouth with raised right arms bent into meaty Ls. Then they throw open their hands, then they throw them together, then they lock dukes and take turns pumping each other's like the inflation bulbs of blood pressure cuffs, the cuffs in this instance being their biceps.

The Camaro hauls ass.

The partners stand idly on a typical sidewalk as a disgruntled Japanese woman with a droopy sign reading *Fired for not holding door...and being Asian* blows her loaded story all over them.

"They promoted me to executive," the woman says, a building which looks like the next great, baffling piece of modern art looming over her shoulder, "and that's when it started."

"What started, Miki?" Rosa says.

"Racism," Miki says.

If a passerby were to study the continents of clouds rolling by in the sky, they'd see a leather whip snap, a mysterious, genderless face in agony, a boatload of shackled slaves, and a sea of pumping fists.

A man in a nifty suit takes a seat behind his pristine desk. He directs Rosa and Chuck's attention to his plethora of elegant, one-of-a-kind, hand-built miniature buildings positioned strategically around his most revered office.

"I received the promotion over Mr. Winchester," Miki had said.

Mr. Winchester caresses a bottle of Scotch while Rosa caresses a banana-shaped high-rise and Chuck caresses a peach-shaped townhall.

Mr. Winchester throws his hands out, dropping the bottle of Scotch.

"In retaliation," Miki had kept saying, "he became buddy-buddy with my white bosses, and he told them Asian jokes, and he turned the big wigs against me, and he eventually became so irate that he said they only promoted me because they required more diversity in the workplace."

The bottle of Scotch smashes against the ebony flooring and gives Mr. Winchester a golden shower.

"Then one day," Miki had still been saying, "Mr. Winchester was entering the building, and I did not wait to hold the door for him because of how disrespectful he had been toward me. He informed my bosses about the incident and coaxed them into believing my behavior was uncalled for. Not even two days later, my bosses called me into a conference room and explained how the firm wasn't generating enough money, so they had to make cuts. Then they let me go. I was the only one."

"NOOOOOOOOO!" Mr. Winchester shrieks like a bitch.

"HELL YESSSSSSSSS!" Rosa and Chuck shout as they hurl the models at the floor.

A massive, something-to-behold high-five ensues.

The clouds outside whisk by, casting flickers of shadows and bursts of light, and within some, there're images, one of a bald eagle soaring, one of copper keys being tossed at a slave's bare feet, one of the American flag being hoisted to full mast.

The Camaro roars, and bugs attack the windshield like specs of light during warp speed, and Chuck looks left, and Rosa looks right, and they nod slightly.

They parallel park and get out and high-five again, and several pedestrians can't quite tell if this was a result of successfully parallel parking, which is hard, or not, but whatever.

Someone holds the door open for Rosa. That someone is white.

A voice booms, "NOW WE'RE GETTING SOMEWHERE."

Hold your fucking horses.

An upbeat man, perhaps too upbeat, leans over his counter and motions at a busy stand of exotic flowers.

Chuck points.

Everybody laughs, because Mia's diary dreamt of Lily of the Valley, not Cherry Blossom.

Even Chuck has to laugh and say, "Very funny, Guys."

They gang-nudge each other, all four of them, including a customer who had been previously perusing the daisies. So much for that, and so much for this.

The Camaro does donuts in an empty parking lot.

People cheer. These people happen to be located across the street. They're picketing KFC. One's dressed in a chicken suit.

The American flag in the clouds rises higher, and there're three children jumping rope, all different colors, and singing tunes, all different genres.

*YOUR RACE TIME IS: ???* reads the next sign.

A hostess asks Chuck, "How many?"

And Chuck gives her the peace sign.

And the hostess takes them right away.

Dayita stood outside the restaurant with her sign slung over her salwarkameez and said, "Me and my husband had come here to eat on many occasions."

A server approaches the partners' tiny table. The partners ask to be relocated to something much bigger. They're sat at a gigantic round table meant for eight. They high-five. The server, of sorority type, scoffs.

"The hostess always asks us how many," Dayita had said. "We always say two. And they always say, 'Okay, it'll be about a half hour.'"

The clouds above the restaurant brew.

"My name's Tessica, and I'll be your server today," Tessica says, biting on her pen's cap. "What can I start you off with to drink?" She rolls her eyes, because she's already writing down, WATER x 2.

"Actually," Chuck says, slamming the menu down flat, "we're ready to order." Before Tessica can spit out more of her script, Chuck stabs at a picture and says, "I'll take that." Before Tessica can correct him, say, "That's not how we order, Sir. We say the name, and then we say please," Chuck stabs at another picture and says, "and that," and another, "and that," and another, "and that…"

Up in the clouds, lightning strikes Hell-fire, and a million souls reach from inside the swirling flames, their melted skin raining down upon the masses.

In the restaurant parking lot, a couple exit their vehicle and upon passing Rosa's Camaro, the man remarks, "Beautiful," and his wife says, "Gee, thanks," and he shakes his head, because she just doesn't get it.

Dayita sneezed politely into her elbow, turning it swampy, then continued to say, "While we were waiting patiently for our table, we noticed white couples were seated almost immediately, even if their parties were much larger, say eight. Black couples came in second with a ten-minute wait, usually. Asians were last, because they don't think Asians tip well. The only reason we're third is because they don't really understand us."

A parade of servers march the food over to Chuck and Rosa's table. Those who are present for lunch follow the action and ready their hands because they believe this to be a birthday celebration.

Before Tessica can start setting the table, Chuck and Rosa leap to their boots and Keds and uppercut each overloaded tray. All nine servers panic and freeze and watch in horror as explosions of food erupt above them.

In the clouds, a gavel strikes an anvil and a chorus of robed children sing hymns.

Inside the restaurant, people had prepared to do it, so they applaud anyway.

While the Camaro does more donuts, Chuck hangs out the passenger-side window and lets the wind take his arms and hollers, "WEEEEEEEEEEEEEEEEEEEEEEE!"

Everything happens faster now.

A DJ in a dank room performs a backward flip while neon lights slice his body into atomic plaid patterns.

He's told to bring it down a notch.

He scratches out a slow song.

Rosa and Chuck believe that'll do. Chuck hands over a check. On the memo line, it reads, *Be there Saturday, 12:00pm.*

The Camaro fishtails around a corner.

Chuck smears white paint over a black woman's face, even her lips. She appears albino-ish whilst smiling.

She performs the smile on a property manager.

The property manager says they have several apartments available. He points at a printed-out map.

She points at her face in-between wipes.

He squints.

She wipes harder.

He taps his watch.

She wipes frantically and says, "Is this actual paint, Chuck?"

"Oops," Chuck says, then to the property manager, "This woman's trying to show you that she's black."

"And that you're racist," the woman says, "because just yesterday, you told me you wouldn't have any availability for at least a few weeks, if not months."

The property manager smirks. "So sue me."

A lawyer enters, one from Rosa's posse at the abandoned aircraft hangar, serves a stack of papers over the counter and says with a more sinister smirk, "Wish granted."

The Camaro flies over a hill and lands in a heap of sparks.

The DJ appears in the sky now, skipping on his turntables to the beat of a happy song, perhaps even that song called "Happy Song".

Rosa stares at what a disheveled man has to offer and says, "Got anything longer?"

Chuck laughs and says, "No, longer."

"Even longer!"

"Even more longer!"

"Even more longer than that!"

# "THE LONGEST YOU'VE GOT!"

And the disheveled man says, "We're not talking about limousines anymore, are we?"

One more high-five for the road.

Mia's making a difference in her office.

There's a light knock at the door.

"Yeah?" she says, nose-deep in a folder. Her desk's cluttered. Her title, *Director*, buried. She hears heavy footsteps and looks forward. "Chuck." All the air deflates out of her as she drops the folder and pushes backward in the rolling chair. She stands, hips bent to the right, knuckles resting on her love handles. The love handles are concealed by a cream-colored, silk blouse. Tis lovely. The dirty look she gives him, not so much.

"Mia." He nods. Seems appropriate, no? She said, "Chuck", he said, "Mia." They've now acknowledged each other as if they're bitter yet formal enemies.

"What do you think you're doing here?"

He doesn't like this game, mainly because he always manages to lose. He'll state his purpose, which is to make sure she still wants Orpheus to give her away, which of course she'll say, "Of course," and of course he'll have to say, "Yeah, of course indeed—just checking," then he'll have to figure that mess out later, and then it's onto figuring out who's going to be in their wedding parties and how they're getting fitted, if rice *and* bubbles are really necessary after the ceremony, and honestly, the main reason he stopped by was to smooch her on the lips because he's missed her dearly.

Chuck leans halfway across the desk, figuring he'll nail the smooch first.

"Close the door."

He closes it eagerly along with the blinds then turns with a quarter-of-a-stiffy to find a sliced-open shipping envelope staring him in the face. It's addressed to Mia with no return address. She slides a handful of grainy-ass pictures out and grimaces at the top-most.

"What?" Chuck says, craning his neck. "What is it?"

She flips the picture over. It's from yesterday morning and shows Chuck stripped down to shorts, his elbows raised high above his head, resting on the frame of his doorway entrance, and there's a too-muscular-for-words woman waiting impatiently on his unwelcome mat. She's in civilian clothing—frayed, jean shorty shorts and a sunset orange beater.

"That's Rosa," Chuck says, "my new partner."

"Oh please," Mia says. "The mere mention of a partner makes you physically ill."

"Look, listen—I fought this partner bullshit all the way, but—"

Mia ignites the next photo. It shoots sparks in his face. It's the same scene, only Rosa appears to be going in for a one-armed hug.

"She slugged me," Chuck says, knowing all-too-well where this mess is headed, "for saying something cocky, but only because *she* said something bitchy first, and I wasn't in the—"

Another picture's lit. The fuse is awfully short. This one shows Rosa exiting the premises, only she's sporting Chuck's never-before-touched police uniform. The picture explodes.

"Roleplaying?" Mia says.

"Only with you!" She's gonna need more to go on, so he starts stretching. According to the garbage which flies out of his mouth, Rosa's an exchange woman from, um, Mexico. The department had to ship someone down there in exchange. That's right, this was an exchange police officer program. Bruce Matthews drew the shortest straw, so away he went. He could be dead by now, because as Rosa continues to blab on and on about, it's no joke across the border. The department hasn't received a single letter from Bruce, so they're constantly praying for his well-being and safe return. But that won't happen until Chuck shows Rosa the ropes. He wishes he could boot her ass back down there, and not in a racist way or anything. Everybody knows he loves Tacos, especially from the Bell.

Mia collects her purse from the floor. "I'm not playing this game anymore." While strutting by, she slaps the envelope against his chest.

He takes hold. "There's more?"

No response as Mia click-clacks to the door, but she dead-stops in front of the window.

Chuck tips the envelope and fishes the object out of a corner. It's her engagement ring. The sight sinks his heart. He turns to find her there, a gargoyle peering out at Rosa who's pretending to read a pamphlet in the lounge.

"Who's that?" Mia's nostrils flare and fog the glass.

"My partner. You know, from the pictures? Rosa? Jeez, and I thought I was bad with names."

"You are—" Mia swoops into his personal space, "—because her real name's Alejandra."

"Ha, ha, okay."

"Really, Chuck? She was my personal trainer." Chuck blankly stares. "You two formally introduced yourselves to each other." He shrugs. "I cooked us dinner, but she had to run at the last minute. You two held like a twenty-minute conversation on my couch. Seriously, nothing?"

Come to think of it, Rosa does seem familiar.

"Ooooooooooh," Chuck lets out. "She probably wasn't wearing makeup, was she?"

"You don't even seem concerned about her name change."

"Mia," it's probably not the best time to chuckle, "have you ever heard of a nickname?" Or phrase a question that way. "Why're you getting so uptight?" Or that way.

"And why're you being so defensive of *her*?"

Before Chuck can drum up an answer, Mia takes off. She sweeps through the cubicles, her draft capsizing one of Dolly's dust-covered, plastic flower pots in H-223, and doesn't cease until she rams into Rosa's chest, knocking the hot tamale back two annoying steps.

"Oops," Mia says, "didn't see you there."

"Lady, I'm kind of hard to...*Mia*?" Rosa's caramel cheeks flush with red. "You're looking good, no *great*!" Lies. "It's been awhile, hasn't it? Have you been keeping up with your routine?" Rosa reaches out with an opened, gentle hand, but Mia snaps back and cocks a fist.

"I see what's going on now—you're the one pulling the strings here, not Chuck."

"Come again?"

Mia launches her fist. Rosa thrusts her palm forward. The sound of meat smacking meat overtakes the office. All coworkers cease typing and lean across their cubicles to listen intently.

"Did you put Chuck up to that stunt with my family?" Mia spits, digging her heels into the carpet and driving her bulging battering-ram of an arm forward.

Rosa turns, her palm now closed into a tight, sweaty fist, her arm being driven into her ribs, her feet slipping on the carpet, and says to Chuck, "Is everybody you know on drugs?"

"I saw instructions," Mia snaps, "written on Chuck's napkin! I saw him checking a timer!" She whips her fist back and fires a left hook which Rosa blocks with a forearm. "I know my Chuck, he wouldn't willingly out my brother!" Her wild right misses. "And he sure as hell wouldn't invite my parents over for dinner!" She stumbles while throwing a left and catches herself on Diana's cubicle. Mia says, "Sorry, Diana." Diana jolts upright, pretends to type and says, "No worries, Mia!"

Turning around, Mia says, "That was you outside my basement window, wasn't it?" and with the grace of an elephant, she uppercuts Rosa in the chin, knocking the behemoth through Terry's cubed wall. Terry immediately oversteps Rosa's fidgeting body and announces, "I'm taking an early lunch, thanks, bye!"

Mia plops atop Rosa's hip, clutches her topknot and yanks her swollen face into view. Rosa has tears bleeding down her face. No way to tell if they're from the uppercut or something else entirely. But the tears do something to Mia—they cause her to drop another balled fist—cause her to slide off Rosa, crawl to her heels, look around, perhaps question her existence, then she eases herself into Terry's rolling chair. Then she pulls on the side lever and lowers herself a few inches, which is really going to throw Terry off—that and the demolished wall. Then she leans back as far as the chair will extend, points at Rosa and says, "Could you take the trash out, Chuck?"

# Chapter 18
## WTF?

Rosa parks abruptly and puts her flashers on.

Chuck stops counting telephone poles.

"Just so you know, I'm not upset or anything. And Rosa's my nickname."

"That's what I tried to tell her!"

"She has a right to be pissed. You might be too after what I'm about to tell you. But I want to be one-hundred-percent honest with you. You deserve as much."

"There's always gotta be a twist."

"Maybe if you paid attention, there wouldn't be. You truly don't remember me at all, do you?"

He studies her face like he's studying for a test he'll soon fail.

"It was obvious you weren't paying any attention to me that night. I figured you were fantasizing about some bad guy you had just nabbed. Mia even noticed and made a comment to that extent."

"She knows me better than Wikipedia."

"For the record, you told me Mia was your friend, not girlfriend."

"I had to keep her a secret."

"I would've done the same…*if* she would've allowed it."

"Is this the twist?"

Rosa laughs at her inflamed face in the rearview mirror. "No, this—*this* is just silly."

"I'll kill you if you don't tell me." He laughs, then quickly wipes his face serious.

"I'm bi, Chuck, okay? Are you happy? Congrats on your outing streak."

"I'm so, so sorry."

155

"Don't be, it's not a goddamn disease, and I'm just busting your little balls. The truth is, I had a thing for Mia. I didn't know she was in a relationship, and then things got weird during our workouts, and we had a stupid falling out which got blown way out of proportion, ending with weights being thrown around, one of which happened to clip her."

"You're the dude who broke her ribs?"

"Thanks, I still feel like a giant asshole for how it all went down. And now she's under the impression I'm trying to ruin her family and frame you for it, I guess so she'll choose me over you in the end?"

Chuck yanks on his collar.

"I promise you," Rosa says, "I'm over her. I've been over her. It was a silly crush, nothing more."

"Oh yeah. Definitely." This is not the response Rosa was hoping for.

"Besides, you sought me out. I've never asked for any of the bullshit which keeps coming my way. But I woman up and deal with it."

"True dat."

Rosa sighs. "Are things gonna be weird between us now?"

"No."

"If it matters, I'd rather be with you than her."

"What?"

"Obviously I wouldn't touch you, you're fuckin' gross, but if it's any indication as to where my feelings lie with her, I want you to know."

"You're saying even though you really dislike men, you'd rather date me than her?"

"If you were like the last two people in the world, yeah, no doubt. That's what I'm trying to say."

"Oh, duh, I get it now. No offense, but if it were you and Anderson left, I'd, um, I guess I'd fuck myself."

"Shit, I didn't even think of that. I'm changing my answer. I'm going to fuck myself, too."

"Good call."

"Thanks!"

# Chapter 19
## Few Chunks Remain

An itty-bitty Mexican lady stands on the heel of a shiny tower. Her ginormous sign reads:

*REAL VILLAINS WEAR SUITS*

Chuck and Rosa sandwich the woman. They admire the paperboard's heft. Chuck explains that if she continues to pump it around in the air all day, she's going to get "jacked". And Rosa explains, "No, Kathy, not like carjacked."

"Oh, good," Kathy says, giggling.

"Wanna tell us what you're protesting, Dear?"

"Certainly, Ma'am," Kathy says, bowing her bean of a head. "We brought here with many promises. Our lives in Mexico bad, very bad. I sex slave. My daughters sex slave. My son sex slave. My husband sex slave."

"So everybody," Chuck says. Rosa chops him in the throat. He gasps for air.

Kathy isn't deterred. "Sometimes, they make me sex slave with donkey. We leave there when men come and promise better life. We come here. We work miles that-a-way." She points. "We work in building with no windows. In a forest no one know. It secret. We work all day, all night. They make us fight each other for food. Sometimes they like to select person and punch until unconscious. They say if we do not follow orders, they give us back to cartels. Cartels still angry at us for running. They will do worse things than I can imagine. We can't go back. It is not even an answer. We have questioned mass suicide. But I try this, at least." She thumps the hollow pole against the sidewalk. "Maybe someone listen, maybe someone care."

"We care," Rosa says, lifting Chuck's bent head, "right, Partner?"

"I *have* been itching to knock an old, white guy's head off."

Kathy giggles, and her cheeks jiggle. "You cannot touch the men in suits. You will pay dearly."

"Lady, do you know who I am?"

"No, Sir. I live sheltered life."

"Duh, of course. Well don't worry, Kathy, we'll figure out how to handle this, isn't that why we're here, Rosa?"

Rosa's mouth hangs open as she stares down the length of her stretched arm, at the brown goo dripping from her spread fingers. "Did I just get shit on by a bird?"

"Ha, ha!" Kathy cradles her stomach while giggling feverously. "You get shit on by man. *The* man."

The partners peer into the sky and spot the shadowy, marble-sized heads perched over the side of the roof.

"They my masters. They make game out of spitting on me. I do not know how many points I am worth."

"You're worth two-hundred, Kathy, and don't you ever forget it." Chuck pats her on top of the head before leading Rosa around back. There's a tight alley between buildings made even tighter by a handful of dumpsters.

At the slab of steel with a keycard reader, Rosa says, "Now what?"

"I think I still have the key." Chuck pulls his knee to his chest, then nails the knob at a slight angle so it snaps off and hangs by its mechanical intestines. The door then drifts opens by itself. "Yup, still got it."

During the thirty-four-floor adrenaline-filled hike to the tippy top, Chuck shouts up through the void in the center of the stairwell (because Rosa's increased her lead to one-and-a-half floors), "How do you...you wanna...wanna handle...this one?"

"I'd like to think we're on the same page by now." Jesus, she doesn't miss a beat.

There's no need to kick the door leading to the roof in since it's been propped open by a rustic brick. The sun's blinding. Even with hands for visors, the partners only recognize the men as dancing shadows.

"Don't do this!" Rosa shouts, her voice getting swept up by the wicked wind which makes the tower sway ever-so-gently.

One of the suits spouts off complete gibberish.

The duo marches toward the edge of the building, Rosa shouting the entire time, "Your life is meaningful! You don't have to do this! Step away from the ledge!"

*Ah!* Chuck gets it—scare tactics—so he tries to force the issue, ram it down these gentlemen's throats. "Yeah," he shouts, "it looks to us, two police officers, me being Chuck Steak, that each of you...are contemplating...suicide!" He takes a moment to recoup his breath. "It doesn't look, whatsoever, that you're doing anything else, especially not spitting on a poor...a poor...defenseless...woman! We are here to try and talk you guys out of this! If we can't...cannot...you will definitely...definitely jump, all of you...and it will look exactly like suicides, because it would be...would be our words, two police officers, against a bunch of dead guys! Get it?"

They only caught bits and pieces due to the wind.

Finally, one of them surfaces from the shadows. He fits the stereotype flawlessly—has slicked-back, jet-black hair with sideburns speckled in silver. Wears glasses seemingly chiseled from marble. Has himself a regal chin and even sports a pocket square in the breast pocket of his gun-metal blazer. "What's this all about?" he says, thrusting his body forward, daring anybody to touch the golden Adam's apple in his million-dollar throat.

Rosa clutches it, a gala, and drags the snob over to the toothy, brick edge. She drives his head down to force his gaze upon Kathy who looks like a piece of bubblegum stuck to the pavement.

Since Rosa's filled the role of muscle, Chuck butts through the gaggle of dumbfounded suits to rise as the mouth of reason.

"I'm gonna get straight to the point, Pal." Chuck readjusts the man's gaze so they come to stare deep into each other's eyes. "You're gonna stop manipulating illegal immigrants."

"I don't know what you're talking about!"

"Guy." Chuck massages his temples while pacing. "Everybody already knows where this is headed. We're gonna go back and forth, me accusing you of the obvious, you denying everything under the sun, literally."

"Nice one."

"Thanks, Rosa." Chuck flicks the man in the forehead. "Why don't we just skip ahead to the fun part? Toss him over the side, Rosa." Chuck snorts out a laugh while attempting to guess how many seconds until the scumbag confesses. But Rosa has already flung him from the roof. By the time Chuck rushes over to the ledge, the sidewalk's already covered in chunky meat pie.

"You threw him?!"

"You told me to!"

"It was a goddamn bluff, Rosa!"

Silence for the longest time.

"Okay, it's okay." Chuck overdoses on deep breathes. "He was bad. He deserved it."

"I'm not thinking straight—there's too much adrenaline running through me."

"I've killed a shitload of bad guys, what's one more?" Only, this one doesn't feel right. "I mean he was real bad, wasn't he?" Chuck turns to face the pile of suits, each trying to burrow under the other. He repeats the question.

They shake their heads.

"What do you mean, no?"

"Sir—"

"What do you mean, Sir?"

"Mr. Steak?"

"Why are you being so polite?"

161

"We're just a couple of grunts." This man sounds like he's on the verge of sobbing. "I know we're not allowed to hang out up here, but—"

"Hold the F up—what do you mean 'grunts'?"

"We're noobs." Sensing he still hasn't made his point, the man says, "The lowest guys on the totem pole?"

"But you're wearing suits. You're middle-aged men. By looks alone, you're rich big wigs."

The man chuckles nervously. "They always tell us to dress for the job we want, not the job we have."

"FUCK!" Chuck circles the roof, yanking at his hair.

Rosa mentions a, "Rookie mistake," and Chuck blurts, "Understatement of the year."

"I'm gonna go back to prison for the rest of my life, aren't I?"

"Goddamn it, I need a second to think!" Chuck's still sorting through his landslide of thoughts when the sirens kick in. "Never mind, we have to run."

"But they'll talk." She's referring to the pile of grunts. Her body leans over the edge. "Should I jump?"

"Rosa!" Chuck yanks her back. "You're not killing yourself, at least—"

*Don't say it!* one of the 'grunts' secretly thinks.

"—not on my watch."

The 'grunt' cringes.

Rosa peers at the shivering witnesses. "Are we gonna throw them off instead?"

"*No*, we're certainly not! Listen, you're confused, both sexually and emotionally, which is fine, but not really, but it'll have to do, even though this sucks."

"You're babbling."

"Please don't kill us," one of the grunts says as Chuck crouches before them.

"Guys—*guys!*—look, listen! What'd you see happen here today?"

"Nothing, I swear!"

"ERNNNNNNNNT! You tried to talk some sense into that guy, but then he leapt to his death."

"His name was Jared. He was my friend."

"Didn't all of you try to talk Jared out of suicide?" Chuck digs into his boot and withdraws a tiny pistol. He cocks it, because that's the only way to ensure people know it's not a joke.

They nod.

"Did he listen?"

They shake their heads.

"Good. Well, not good. This is fucking terrible, but it was an honest-to-God mistake. Nobody else needs to get hurt over this. But if someone *were* to rat us out, my buddies, which means the entire police force, would almost definitely murder that person's entire family. Does everybody understand?"

They understand, so Chuck and Rosa barrel down the stairs as fast as their reckless feet will take them. Out on the street, traffic has come to a screeching halt, and a small crowd has amassed around the blood splatter, which measures roughly thirty-seven feet in diameter.

The partners hunt down Kathy who's still loitering lackadaisically with her limp sign. Upon spotting them, Kathy shrugs and says, "What happen?"

"What do you mean 'what happened?'" Chuck yells, then tones it way down when part of the crowd looks their way. "None of those guys were bad, Kathy."

"Ah." She throws a finger up while glancing across the street. "I see now. I mix buildings."

"You mixed…never mind. I'm not going to choke you, Kathy. It wouldn't be nice. But I will be taking this." He yanks the sign from her. "Thanks, Kathy. You've been a ton of fucking help."

Chuck bullies his way through a wall of spectators straddling the edge of splatter and tip-toes into the mess. The pedestrians act as caution tape. "Come on," he tells Rosa, waving her in. She accidentally steps on Jared's dress shoe—there's still a foot inside.

"What're we doing? We're gonna get caught."

"Don't you think that's what I'm trying to prevent?" He shoves the monolith sign into her hands. "You need to cover me."

"That won't be shady or anything."

"Attention, people!" Chuck steps in front of a raised cell phone and slips it the black bird. "This is a pretty horrific scene, so we're gonna try and keep the body concealed until medics arrive. How about showing some respect and not snapping any pictures, especially selfies, because they're annoying?"

As the sirens whip around a corner and fill the street with shrieking wails, Rosa angles the sign, creating a makeshift beach umbrella for Chuck as he crouches low to the ground, his knees avoiding pink chunks, and rummages through the meat pie.

The sign wobbles too far to the right, revealing Chuck's busy hands. "We've got a firetruck and ambulance headed our way," Rosa says.

"I have ears." Chuck yanks the sign back into place. "Now keep it steady for Christ's sake."

"What are you even looking for?"

"A finger."

"By your left foot."

"I thought I already looked there." He peels it from the cement. After a moment of careful examination, he identifies it as a pinky and tosses it over his shoulder. "Nope, need a pointer."

"Over there."

"Where's over there?"

"Your 10 o'clock."

"Do I look like someone who's good with time?"

She spits, and he follows the wad.

"More like it." He yanks the sign an inch lower so the edges kiss the ground, then sneaks his pistol out of his waistline and hooks Jared's severed finger around the trigger. Then he places the gun handle-deep in a pothole brimming with maroon blood. Then he stands and slaps the sign out of his face. Then he pats himself off and sighs.

Rosa leans in and whispers, "Did you just plant a gun on him?"

"I'm leaving no doubt."

"He leapt to his death—how's that even make sense?"

"You're right, now that I'm part black, people may question this."

The firetruck cuts off a BMW. What a role reversal, because the BMW has probably always been the cutter. It will never be known, but the question remains—has the BMW's driver learned anything from wearing the other shoe?

Chuck turns to leave but bumps into a firefighter.

"What's the rush?" Three other firefighters have this one's back. They're armed with axes and shovels.

"None whatsoever."

A pair of medics has since joined the firemen's posse. They stare at the mess with their kits dangling at their sides.

"Sooo," Chuck taps his sticky boot, "looks like you guys got this." He goes to sidestep around them, but a cuff clicks around his black wrist, and a booming voice blurts, "You're under arrest!" Chuck feels the pointy tactical shoe as it grinds into his back, forcing him onto his knees.

"He's resisting!" the voice shouts, faking a struggle.

The firemen strangle their axes and shovels and raise them in anticipation.

"I'm innocent!" Chuck whines as the shoe kicks his face to the bloody ground.

"He's threatening me!" The arresting officer pretends to wrestle with Chuck's other hand, and before he can unlatch his firearm, he lets the hand drop and immediately hops off. He dashes alongside Chuck, and even though there's Jared smeared everywhere skewing the identity of this perp, the officer recognizes his error and is quick to help Chuck back onto his feet. He even goes as far as wiping away some of the blood with his used handkerchief before unlocking the cuffs.

"Sorry about that," the officer says, flushed with embarrassment, "I thought you were—"

"A murderer?"

"—black."

"You're fucking joking, right?" Chuck uses the belly of his shirt to squeegee the gunk off. He knows this guy—his name's Angel, and he's been blessed with the blonde hair of one.

"Chuck, hot damn, I didn't even recognize you!"

"What were you saying about being black?"

Angel twists and yells at his partner who's aiming a shotgun over the passenger-side door, "Yo, it's Steak!"

"Chuck Steak?" the partner shouts back, his voice tiny.

"Yeah, the one and only!"

The partner says something to his radio before waving frantically and shouting, "Hey, boss's going nutso! Wants to have a long-ass chat!"

The firemen bat their axes and shovels against their palms while accompanying Chuck over to the squad car.

"Gee, thanks," Chuck says, swiping the radio, "ya pricks."

The pricks don't budge as Anderson goes off the rails: "Chuck, what the hell? Why aren't you *here*, at the hospital? Why're you with another corpse? What have you done? Have you lost your mind? Why'd you pull Rosa into this nonsense? Ahhhhhhhhh!" A nurse hurries into the room, spews a bunch of mumbo-jumbo about breathing the calm in and pushing the stress out. Anderson throws an elbow. The nurse cries for help. "You see this bullshit, Chuck? You know you're ruining my life, don't you?"

Chuck stretches the radio three feet from his ear.

"Are you going to answer me or what?"

"Which question, Sir? You asked fifty."

"You no-good, rotten, stupid, careless, son-of-a-bastard-prick!"

"Look, Rosa's helping plan my wedding. We were running errands when the guy jumped and smacked the pavement. Trust me, I didn't want to get involved, mainly because I don't do custodial work, but Rosa convinced me it'd be immoral if we didn't cover the body. She has a good heart, Sir, no offense to yours."

"My heart's fine! I told you I have a weight-gain disorder! And everything out of your mouth is either offensive or a lie! I'm calm, get your lousy hands off of me!" Anderson fends off a gang of nurses. "Chuck, get to the station *NOW* and make a statement, and not *I'M THE BEST* like you wrote last time, and then get situated in my office, because you and I, we're gonna have a long, goddamn, serious talk! You hear me, men? Make sure Chuck actually gets there and stays put, or else when I'm done sticking this radio up these nurses' asses, I'm going to stick it up yours!"

So unsanitary.

The radio blares static. Angel shrugs and whispers, "Um, I didn't catch that last part." His partner's quick to nod in agreement.

Chuck turns and bumps into the firefighter yet again. The firefighter says, "I did." He pats the axe. "One way or another," not to be left out, his buddies pat theirs, too, "you're turning yourself in."

"And who are you again?"

"That's the problem, Bud—unlike you, we actually save people on a regular basis, and nobody knows squat about us." He taps the blade's edge against Chuck's pectoral. It sounds like metal dinging metal, but only because the engagement ring's attached to a chain underneath Chuck's shirt. Still, everybody seems impressed, except for the firefighters' ringleader.

"You're funny." Chuck bats the axe away, but it repels into its original, taunting position. It taps again. "Dude, really?" He bats again, but the axe comes back for thirds.

"You know how many of your messes we've had to clean up?"

Chuck shrugs.

"Exactly, nobody does."

"We get it, you're butt hurt."

"Nut uh, you don't get it. Let me take you back eight months ago."

"Please don't."

"We were responding to a code 3 over on 5th ave. By the time we got there, the abandoned storefront was already fully engulfed."

The memory's still fresh in Chuck's mind, so he tunes the firefighter out, because his point of view threatens to spoil what evolved into quite a splendid action sequence.

*A former Air Force pilot who coined herself "The Flamer" had pieced together a suit of armor comprised of Tungsten and Kevlar, making her immune to physical attacks. She also concocted a jetpack to mimic the Harrier Jet she used over the course of an illustrious career filled with precision strikes and massive kills, therefore rendering her nearly uncatchable.*

Nearly.

*Chuck had borrowed a struggling band's roadies and put them to better use by having them setup a stereo system capable of emitting his voice miles in each direction. They parked their gear in front of the abandoned store on 5th. The entire block, for that matter, had long-since been abandoned.*

*Chuck Steak performed not too long after. He opened with, "That'd Be the Day," which was extended in the chorus with, "I'd lose to a girl. The very thought would make me hurl." Other hits included, "She Needs to be in the Kitchen, Bitchin'," and, "Chick Looks Like a Dick (Literally and Figuratively)", but it was during the breakdown of, "She Thought She was Flying a Jet, but a Man was Behind the Controls, He was a Vet," that The Flamer swooped in through gray clouds. She didn't come to exchange words—instead, she let her flamethrower do the talking. As she torched the musical equipment, smelting it into black liquid, and ignited the building, Chuck hopped on his commandeered Harley and fishtailed through the street.*

*And so the chase went, The Flamer lobbing fireballs with Chuck narrowly skidding out of their trajectories. Until, of course, they soared foolishly into an unfinished tunnel still being constructed below the Scioto River. The dirt road contained a complex maze of orange cones. It seemed The Flamer would finally best the mighty Chuck Steak. But she couldn't have foreseen the bomb Chuck had tossed into the river pre-battle. A bomb wrapped in plastic and tied to a boulder.*

*When the bomb was triggered, the ensuing eruption brought down an avalanche of concrete chunks which punched The Flamer's thought-to-be indestructible suit flat, causing her body to spew out the cracks.*

*And that was, well, that.*

"We had to work it from both sides."

The firefighter's still babbling on.

"Is there a point to this story?" Chuck says.

"The *point* is, while we were battling the fire on 5th, another broke out on Lancaster. This one had a family living upstairs. A kid hadn't made it out, so we closed shop and zipped on over there. By the time we got close, three more fires had already erupted— the furthest away was about four blocks. The fire down the block had a mother and her infant daughter trapped in the basement. Another two blocks over held an elderly couple and their hen house hostage.

"Our chief, he cut us loose—said to save whoever we could, however possible. Which left me in the worst of situations, deciding who to save and who to let die."

The next morning, the newspaper ran the old folks' picture along with the nine-year-old boy's on the front page. They were microchip-sized and pushed to the bottom corner of the page by an enlarged photo of the tunnel's entrance vomiting river water. Chuck stood front and center in the picture leaning against the burnt Harley.

"You think I wanted innocent people to die?" Chuck takes hold of the axe's pole and drives the tip methodically into his own boulder-esque boob, drawing blood which dribbles down his shirt. "If that were the case, I would've went home and watched Netflix. But I was the first to act. I always am. And if it weren't for me, the body count in this city would be much fucking higher."

"You ever think you're the one creating all these whackjobs in the first place? That's why more and more keep stepping up to the plate. They dream of being the big bad who finally topples the mighty Chuck Steak. You're nothing but a prize to them."

"I literally don't have time for this."

"Hold on, where you think you're going? You heard the boss man—to the station with you."

Chuck yanks the axe from the firefighter's grasp and tosses it into traffic. The firefighter slugs Chuck clean across the chops. Chuck spins, wipes his busted lip and lisps, "I'd walk away while you still have legs."

The firefighter strips off his coat and pries his shirt over his head. His six-pack's lubed in sweat, and his chest's covered in third-degree burns. "These are the scars of a real hero." He buzzes around Chuck and shoves at random. "I don't need no stinkin' axe."

"You sure could use some deodorant though." Another shove knocks Chuck off-balance. "Okay, that was annoying."

"Now you know how I feel every time you get away with murder." Shove. "Time to pay the piper." Shove. "I fight in the name of all your victims." Shove.

"Go to your happy place, Chuck, and eat tacos."

As a tiny patch of hair behind Chuck's ear gets pinched, he feels the snap of sanity and fires a shot that lays the firefighter flat out. The back of the firefighter's unprotected head cracks the sidewalk, and moments after his body goes limp, his limbs contorted into pretzels, a pool rapidly spreads around his skull, granting him a blood halo.

The firefighters pour in around their fallen comrade. One of them pounds his chest. Another knots a shirt around his fractured skull. And the one without a purpose yells, "MURDERER!"

# Chapter 20
## Forgive Me, Father

It takes four rings for Henriette to answer. She bows her head monk-like, then disappears. Chuck doesn't hear a word through the glass storm door—perhaps she uses sign language to notify Orpheus. Chuck wonders what her symbol for him is. An automatic handgun followed by an explosion? Two middle fingers formed into a cross?

Orpheus makes him wait for a commercial break before floating over. "Can I help you?"

"You can stop rolling your eyes and look at me."

Orpheus gives him that. "I repeat for the hard of hearing: can I help you?"

"I'm here to, what's your word for it? 'Atone'! I'm here to 'atone' for shit. Er, stuff." Not even a blink? "I get it, you despise me. But I'm not as bad as you make me out to be."

"No, you're far, far worse."

"Oh really?" Chuck slaps his black palm against the glass and smears his prints around in a hypnotic circle. "Then whaddya think about this?"

Orpheus leans in and squints. "It sure is interesting, Chuck, but I fail to see how such a development helps your case."

"I'm one of you now."

"Ha, ha, seriously? You could never be one of us."

"Just like Chet, huh?"

"I think we're done here." Orpheus steps back and reaches for the galvanized steel door.

"You're a hateful man, which is such a shame, because if you only opened your goddamn eyes, you'd see how much love you're missing out on."

"I don't hate you, Chuck, and I certainly don't hate Chet either. I don't possess an ounce of hatred within my being. It's not what the good Lord taught me. I've been created to love everybody, even mortal sinners like you." He grins slyly while easing the door shut.

Chuck jams it with his boot. "I'm not finished."

"You don't matter."

"All lives do. A sign taught me that."

Orpheus cackles.

"I want to confess."

"Best of luck finding someone who cares." Orpheus throws his body weight forward but gets nowhere.

"I want a real confession—one where I have to do like twenty Hail Marys or something."

"Maybe in another life."

"Isn't it your duty to listen to everybody's sins?"

"Nice try, but we're not at church."

"So your biblical laws don't apply in the real world?"

"I'm not debating this—"

"Hey, God!" Chuck shouts at the pinkish sky and lavender clouds, "one of your beloved disciples refuses to do your bidding! Maybe a good smiting is in order!"

"This is your bright idea? Insult the very man you desperately need a favor from?"

"Don't flatter yourself. I don't need you, your blessing or your respect. If I really wanted to, I'd take the low road and marry Mia. She'd invite you, of course, but if you refused to show, we'd go on without you. You'd push yourself away, Orpheus, and I'd win. But do you think that's why I'm here? To best you? To steal your daughter? If so, *you're* the fool. I'm trying to open *your* eyes—to make sure you don't miss out on the biggest day of your daughter's life. I'm trying to make amends."

Silence is golden.

"Fine," Chuck starts off, "you couldn't handle what I have to tell you anyway."

Not even a minute later, the two find themselves locked inside Orpheus' Lexus with the fish decal on the rear bumper. The car remains parked in the driveway at a steep enough angle requiring the emergency brake. Orpheus sits prim and proper in the driver's seat, staring at his garage door as Chuck leans forward and speaks into his ear, "I once—"

"Back up."

"Oh, sure." Chuck crashes into the seat, rocking the Lexus. "I once punched a nun in the face."

Orpheus snorts, because of course Chuck did.

"She was standing guard outside the orphanage as it burned to the ground. I was the only kid to make it out alive, and they couldn't have that, so she doused me with a tube of holy kerosene, then lit a match and flicked it at my head. She burst out laughing as I roasted. I guess she expected me to stop, drop and die, but I laid that penguin out with a 9-year-old fist. I managed to run off before the real bad guys came back."

"Wow."

"I know."

"Can't even tell the truth like a man."

"The truth is, I had to forfeit being a kid in order to become one."

"Whatever you say, Chuck."

"Go ahead, Google it sometime. A twenty-some-year-old orphanage fire with multiple fatalities and only one survivor."

"I'll get right on it."

"I became a thief afterward—"

"Now *that* I believe."

"—to stay alive. I'm not proud of my past, but I wouldn't change it, either. It opened my eyes to the horrors of the world, and instead of running away, I decided to take a stand. I fight the battles nobody else will. I get my hands dirty. And yes, sometimes I don't handle every situation properly, but at least I'm out there trying. Who else is going to? You?" Chuck laughs. "You hide inside a building chastising people like me, yet I'm the reason you have such freedom."

"Jesus Christ gave his life for *my* freedom, Chuck, not you." He taps his wrist—the universal sign for "Are we done here yet?"

"I could go on and on."

"The obvious is obvious."

"I never knew my father. Only had my mother growing up. She *was* my father, and I had to watch as an armed gunman blew her brains out. Point is, you don't know how lucky you and Chet are. At least you're both still alive. You have a chance to fix this. Who cares if you can't change him? He is who he is just the same way you are who you are. If you truly believe he's going to Hell, then why not spend as much time with him as humanly possible? Or why not go to Hell with him? If I ever had a kid and thought he was headed there, I'd do everything in my power to ensure I was right by his side, and I'd fuck any demon in the ass who thought of messing with 'em. I'd even go toe to toe with Satan."

Orpheus angles the rearview mirror so his bright, white eyes fill the rectangle. "You know what? You're right."

"I am?"

Orpheus nods, but then the red and blue lights slice across the glass. They hammer a brilliant light show against the garage door. And then an officer taps the tip of his taser against Chuck's window and mumbles, "Chuck Steak?"

"Speaking."

"Hey, it's Ted. Remember me?"

"*Seriously?* How the F can I help you, Ted?"

"I'm doing good."

"I didn't ask."

"Oops, sorry. Well, this is going to be awkward."

"Isn't it already? You kind of ruined the moment."

"Chuck Steak, you're under arrest!"

"There you go again, not making a lick of sense."

"Sorry, but I need you to exit the vehicle immediately and place your hands on the roof, firmly, but you know the drill by now, don't you?"

"Breathe, Chuck, breathe."

Orpheus hits unlock, allowing Ted to pop the door ajar. "Anderson gave me strict orders to bring you in peacefully." Ted laughs at this. "I said you'd never. Anderson agreed. I smiled, because we've never agreed on anything before. I think I'm finally making progress with my career!"

"He sent you of all people?"

"I was just as surprised. I still am. Can't you tell? I'm shaking."

"I'm going to try really, really hard not to punch your smiley face off, Ted. Now would you mind telling me what in the F is going on?"

Ted plucks a crumbled post-it-note from his breast pocket. "You're wanted for questioning regarding a suicidal jumper."

"Okay, and?"

"You're also wanted for assaulting a firefighter and rending him comatose."

"For the record, he struck first."

"Gee, I'm sorry to hear. Perhaps we can get that one removed. Or reversed. Which would be better? Or legally correct?"

"Finish already, Ted."

"Sure! Definitely. I understand. Where was I?" He scans the haphazardly written list. "Bingo! Found it! Sorry, I probably shouldn't be so excited. Last one, I promise."

"Shoot."

"You sure?"

"No, don't literally fucking shoot me."

"I was going to say, you really have lost your marbles." Ted squeegees his wet brow with a hairy wrist. "And the final charge is…" He skims the words. "…forgive me, this is sort of a double-charge."

"…"

"Would you like to guess?"

"…"

"No? Gotch ya."

"…"

"Should I do a drum roll maybe?"

"Ted…"

"The charge is violating a restraining order by abducting the victim."

Chuck's eyes pounce on the rearview mirror, but Orpheus has already slithered outside.

"Watch it, Ted, cop with deadly fists coming through." Chuck shakes the car with each butt-hop, but Ted plants his feet firmly at the exit and aims his taser with both trembling hands. "Stop!"

"I'm beating Orpheus' head in *with* or *without* you breathing."

"Chuck, you have a problem!"

"Oh, so being like one-percent black is suddenly a problem?"

"Not what I meant! Honestly! Wholeheartedly! I have at least one half-black friend. Does it count if we're only quarter friends? Let me guess, too much math?"

Chuck latches onto Ted's belt, reels him in and prepares a colorful quip, but can't seem to get the words out as the prong lodged in his neck pumps him full of 50,000 volts.

# Chapter 21
## $4 and Change

They dab at his soggy chin with a napkin.

They squirt sanitizer on his split lip.

They rant and rave about the accommodation—how it's been a quiet couple of days, so he'll have the cell all to his lonesome.

Ted even jests about how Chuck'll be king.

Not funny.

They shuffle along, the ankle and wrist chains rattling.

The first call doesn't count, because it's incoming. Ted holds the cell to Chuck's ear as Anderson ditches the yelling in favor of a tranquil lisp which gives the impression doctors performed a lobotomy on him.

"Everybody was right. All the goddamn signs were there. Every single one of your stunts has been a cry for help, and I've done nothing."

"Sir—"

"It's over, Chuck. You're finally safe, in jail."

"Where's Rosa? She'll explain everything."

"You two can chit-chat all you want after we bring her in."

"What for?"

"Aiding a goddamn vigilante."

Chuck erupts with laughter to keep from donkey-kicking Bruce in the gut, from sweeping Blanch's legs out from under her, from head-butting Ted in the nose and snatching the keys from his saggy belt, from executing a reverse jump rope motion to put his hands in front of him, from unlocking the padlocks and unleashing his fists in a flurry of rage, from…oh never mind. Chuck spots Casey standing prim and proper at the end of the faded, mint-colored hallway with her hand hovering over her unlatched firearm like an antsy gunslinger. By the time Chuck would reach step "head-butt-Ted-in-the-nose", Casey would have already plugged a bullet into his manhood. Besides, they don't call her Circumcision Casey for no reason.

It doesn't help that during Circumcision Casey's initial day on the force, while passing each other in the hallway, Chuck said, "Nice T & A."

"I beg your pardon?"

He said it slower. Annunciated more clearly. "Nice...T...&...A."

"Are you serious?"

"Most definitely. Nice turnip and avocado."

She was holding one of each in her hands. They were her snacks for the day. She was a health guru.

"This is a turnip," she said, bobbing the turnip, "and *this* isn't an avocado, it's a kiwi."

"Fuck," Chuck said, and not even two minutes later, Circumcision Casey filed a harassment report. To save face, Anderson traded disciplinary action for the hiring of the department's second female officer, Blanch.

"You'll serve the weekend," Anderson says.

"Listen to me!"

"With good behavior, we'll let you go Sunday morning."

Great, he'll get out just in time to scrap Mia from the pavement.

"Lieutenant, please! Lieutenant?" Chuck head-butts the cell, because any time technology doesn't work as intended, a good whacking is usually all it takes to set things straight. "Anderson!"

"He's gone, Chuck," Ted says, "not dead, obviously, he simply hung up. It's rude, I know, so I want to apologize on his behalf. I'm so sorry."

Chuck's second call matters most. She answers with, "Hello?" and he comes right out with it: "I've been arrested."

"Oh I'm sorry, this is Mia Johnson. I think you're trying to reach someone by the name of Alejandra or Rosa."

"I messed up."

"That's the understatement of the decade, Chuck—THE DECADE! I've been waiting for you all these years, waiting for your attention, waiting for an actual life, a family, and it's always one day, one day, Mia, we won't have to hide our love, yadda, yadda, yadda, blah, blah, blah, I think you're full of shit, Chuck, and I don't think you know what you want, and it's not even about me or that whore you're running around with—this is about your love for chaos above all else, which has always prevented us from having a normal life."

"Okay." Chuck clears his airways. "Do you know how you've been farting weird lately?" Of all the things to say, especially given all the things she's said. Chuck caresses the cell with his shackled hands, treating the device as though it's a beating heart, and roars, "WHAT I'M ABOUT TO SAY IS NOT A JOKE! THERE'S A BOMB INSIDE OF YOU! INSIDE YOUR LIVER, OR AROUND THAT GENERAL AREA! FUCK ANATOMY! GET TO THE NEAREST HOSPITAL, GET AN X-RAY, GET—"

"No, Chuck, no!" Ted scolds, twisting sideways and hiding the phone behind his hip. "You can't be saying those things, are you nuts?"

"SERIOUSLY, TED?"

"Sorry, so sorry, Chuck, but I had to!"

"How much did she hear?"

"Right after you mentioned passing gas, I hit mute, because it sure seems like something you'll regret saying once you get sprung from jail! Gosh golly, Chuck, you really are trying to incite panic throughout the city, aren't you? At least you're persistent with your goals. That's certainly a great character quality."

The three officers have to practically bear the brunt of Chuck's dead weight to fit him inside the barred cell and pose him upright on the wooden bench. After unshackling him, Ted tilts Chuck's chin toward the florescent rectangle of bright light. The symbolism is apparent.

"Okie dokie. Hope you're comfortable. You sure don't look so. Maybe I could get you an extra pill—"

"Fuck off, Ted, please."

"Oh gosh, certainly!"

Chuck slumps inward, his muscles and skin pushing outward, creating rolls upon rolls, giving him the appearance of a literal blob. Counting all the time he and Mia have lost makes his stomach churn.

Chuck wallows in a pit of despair. How long exactly, he's not sure. But he snaps to once a herd of officers burst through the doors, shoving a prisoner forward. With an absurd amount of chains, the inmate sounds like Santa's sleigh rigged to the teeth with bells as it's tumbling down a mountainside.

"I know I said you'd be king," Ted says, locking a tattooed beefcake inside the cage, "but I think I jinxed you, so again, I'm sorry. I'm not a liar, I just should have known better."

"Leave us be, Ted. In peace."

"Right-o. Okay, well, obviously you don't need supervision. That would defeat the purpose of a jail cell."

The officers disappear.

"Name's Danko." Free of his chains, Danko plops next to Chuck. Chuck slides away, putting a four-person gap between them.

"Good for you."

"Like my tattoos?"

"No."

Danko flexes his bicep and smooches the zombie mermaid being stretched across the lumpy bulge. One of her breasts is a hole. "I do this to her sometimes, to torture her."

"Why wouldn't you?" Chuck mumbles, wishing to resume his wallowing, but Danko insists on putting a damper on things.

"Wanna know what I'm in for? Sure ya do. Everybody always does. It's like the one question errbody's gotta ask. See this blood splatter on my wife beater? It's fresh, Baby. Ordered three cheeseburgers and a fry from Mickey Ds, and the dipshits totally botched my order, so I botched them."

"You're doing time for $4?"

"And change, Dawg. Four dollars *and* change."

"Wonderful," Chuck slides another person away.

Danko easily cuts the gap to one scrawny person in his greasy sweatpants. As he smiles big, his silver grill sparkles, and his inch-wide chinstrap highlights his second of three chins. "I tray-slapped the grub behind the register. Get it?"

"FML."

"Pussy was howling for his momma—it was so pathetic. But you think I stopped there? Hell's no. I leapt the counter and started taking errbody down. I dunked some hoe headfirst into the fries. Might not sound too dope, but them bitches were fresh outta the fryer. I even—"

Chuck finally shuts him out, prompting Danko to grin from ear to ear, putting on display his third chin. He picks at the mermaid's breast hole, but it isn't a hole at all. It's the end of a chicken bone painted black. He extracts the four-and-a-half-inch shank and raises it high. Droplets of blood dribble off the sharpened end.

*I'm going to analyze every single way I could have prevented this,* Chuck thinks, but then he's vaulted back to reality the very moment the chicken bone pierces his deltoid. However, it doesn't register that he's being attacked until he's already been stabbed eleven times over.

# THURSDAY

## Chapter 22
## Let the Bodies Hit the Floor

A text chirps.

There's a brand-new phone set on the rolling table meant for stale food and drinks with straws. As Chuck twists to reach it, a shoulder pad of soaked-through bandages pops loose, revealing rows of uneven stitches. This wouldn't be so complicated if it weren't for his right wrist being cuffed to the side railing.

The text hails from a new, preprogramed name, "Serial Killer":

*Hi!*

*Can you believe we're almost down to the final 24 hours?*

*But alas, there's simply no time to question where it's all gone, because you, my dear sir, have exactly one hour from this text's timestamp to reach the abandoned Spaghetti Factory on West Broad. Head around back and enter through the basement. From there, just follow the muffled screams.*

Chuck types furiously with one hand: *Truck you class poll*

Serial Killer instantly responds: *Autocorrect fail*

Chuck types: *GLASS MOLE*

Serial Killer: *Why're you still typing? You only have 59 minutes left.*

Chuck tightens his cuffed, black hand into a fist and screams bloody murder at the stained ceiling.

Ted pokes his head inside the room. "Knock, knock." He knocks after the fact. "Did I hear something? Was it you? Hello?"

Chuck lies on the bed, head sunken into the pillow. His chest rises and falls as words deflate from his slightly peeled lips to form gargled noise.

"Oh my, is everything okay, satisfactory even?" Ted seals himself inside and creeps forward.

"Teeeeeeeeeeeeeeeeeeeeed…"

"I'm beside you, Pal. What is it? What can I do you for?"

"No hard feelings."

"That's a funny thing to say, but yeah, definitely! No hard—"

Chuck's eyes blow open as he hooks a lefty around Ted's throat and chokes him out. From there, it's only a matter of detaching the key ring from Ted's belt, unlocking the cuffs, hoisting Ted into bed, switching clothes, angling Ted's face toward the window, tucking the rest of his body snug under the covers and securing his arm to the railing.

Problem is, as Chuck turns, every button on the slim, commandeered shirt snaps to reveal his wet and soggy wounds. This would all be moot if Chuck could hop out the window and land in a tree or on top of an ambulance, but such a move proves unrealistic given how he's currently trapped on the 9th floor. Chances are, a handful of other officers are roaming the hallways, making sure no hostiles get in, and no volatile cop gets out. Thus the 9th floor.

Chuck cracks the door and whispers to a male nurse who tries to blow by, "Pssst, over here!"

"For crying out loud, this better be good."

Well lookie here, it's Chaz, the bitchy front desk attendant from Cynthia's nursing home. Seems as though this short fuse managed to get himself hired for every position requiring the upmost patience. Perhaps in the morning, he works at an overcrowded daycare.

"What is it?" Chaz struts into the room. "Come on! What gives? Spit it out already."

Chuck doesn't feel the least bit guilty for putting him in a headlock and whispering, "Thanks for your scrubs," while Chaz goes to sleep. After switching attire, Chuck crams nearly-nude Chaz into the upright closet and slams the door shut. Chaz's head, along with a broom and dust pan, thump against the other side.

There's a harsh knock. "Chaz, it's time we talk." A second nurse waltzes in and glides across the floor, and in no time, rises over Chuck's hunched back. "I'm done with this silent treatment B.S. Why don't you face me and ask like a grown-ass man if I kissed the comatose patient in 8?"

*WTF?*

"Really? *Really?* I know you've been sucking face with this one, so don't try and play victim with me. Rumor has it you also stuck—"

Chuck's quick to throw a pointer finger up—the white one, of course, to color match Chaz's.

"What, can't handle the truth? Hurts, don't it? Hurts like a bitch."

Chuck gags.

"You see, I'm not the only sicko in this relationship. But that's why we fit together so well. You *in* me, me *in* you."

Two hands clamp over each of Chuck's tense shoulders, and a slow, long, deep massage ensues.

"Oooh," the nurse whispers, "your balls," he's referring to the shoulder kind, "are wet—are they coming? No, don't pull out, I know you want it."

As a hot, panting tongue worms its way inside Chuck's ear, he reaches behind this guy's bony head, the guy misinterprets the act as, "You thinking what I'm thinking, Doctor Meatwad? Quick 3-way with the patient?" and right before the choking is set to begin, a third unwanted guest crashes the party.

"Finally caught you two pervs red-handed," another man says confidently, his voice the softest of the lot.

The massager faces his accuser and slashes at him with a tongue dripping in cockiness, "So this is your master plan, Earl? Videotape us?"

"And post it online, exposing your sick games."

"It'd help if you actually knew what red-handed meant, Dumbass. You haven't caught us doing a *damn* thing."

"I—"

"That's right, film your own sad, pathetic—"

"Ah hem!" A woman clears her throat. "There a problem here, gentlemen?"

*It's Circumcision Casey!*

"Sure is," Earl squeaks. "How should I put this?"

"You don't," Chaz's boyfriend says, "unless you want everybody to find out about your out-of-control morphine addiction. Oops, did I say something?"

"Zip your trap," Casey says. "Earl is it?" Earl nods. "Go on, what were you saying?"

"Yawnke's raping patients."

"As if!"

"Whoa, whoa, whoa," Casey shifts, her soles squealing, "are you being serious? Don't lie to the law."

"Hey, Casey," another uninvited guest helps himself in, "you seen Ted by any chance?"

"I think we've got a bigger problem on our hands, Edward." Not "Ednerd", the grunt gunning for Anderson's job whenever the big lug finally decides to retire, which should've been three years ago.

186

"They've been raping the patients?" Edward says, kind-of smiling. "Have they gotten to Chuck yet, because we can come back? Totally joking everyone. This is as serious as serious gets." Edward wipes his grin off along the length of his forearm. "Is this true? Have you two been violating the patients?"

"Do you see me?" Yawnke spouts.

"We see you."

"Then you know I can do way better."

Ted has both great and terrible timing as he coughs himself awake.

"Look who decided to wakey-wakey. Why don't we put Chuck through a mild interrogation, see if he remembers anything?" Edward waddles over to the bed due to his heavy load (a belt sagging with tactical weapons, of course). Chuck's able to track him with peripheral vision. "Rise and shine, Chucky—there's an interesting development we need to ask you…wait a minute, hold the phone." He completes a perfect 180-degree hop. "Casey!" Casey's all *what? What the hell?* "We have a huge problem on our hands!"

Her figure appears as a shadow on the closet door. She reaches for her firearm, just in case.

Then, around her shadowy breast area, there's a knock on the other side of the fake wood.

"Whoa there, what was that?" Edward arms himself with both a pistol and taser. One can never be too careful. "I heard something inside the closet."

Both officers stare at Chuck's supposed boyfriend. They don't say his name, because they don't remember how the fuck it's pronounced.

"Yawnke, okay?" Yawnke says. "It's not that hard. Jesus Christ. And don't look at me. I don't know what's in there. Probably a bat. *Yes*, we have a bat problem. This place is a shithole. I want to quit."

"Shut it!" Casey yells while stepping toward the closet. A swift knock, however, stops everyone dead in their tracks. Then comes the muffled voice: "Hello? Where am I?"

Yawnke squints. "Chaz?"

"I've read extensively about ploys," Edward says, "this fits the very definition. Chuck could have set a trap for us in there."

"What're you talking about?"

"Ted's been cuffed to the bed, Casey, which means Chuck broke free."

They shimmy forward in unison yet take turns repeatedly shouting, "Come out with your hands held high!"

Edward suggests Casey arm her free hand with a taser. Says she could leave it to fate regarding which trigger gets pulled. She thinks that's a fine idea and joins him in dual-wielding.

Yawnke says he doesn't get paid enough for this shit while Earl snickers in the background about capturing everything on camera. He's secretly praying for bullets to increase his chances at becoming YouTube famous.

"Earl!" snaps a new voice. "What have I told you about your phone?" As both officers whip their weapons in her direction, she throws her hands out in surrender and yelps, "What in the world?"

"Who's the pretty lady?" Ted slurs, his sluggish eyes gushing invisible hearts.

"Doctor Holly," Yawnke says, clearly bored with her name and tired of her face, "she's vegan, and she hates social media. If you officers weren't pointing guns at her forgettable face, she'd break out into a lecture about how animals are mistreated and we're wasting our lives away."

"Enough already!" Casey shouts. "There're far too many people in this room!"

"Then should I perhaps come back later?" An older lady with a polka-dot face (mostly moles, most of them benign) attempts to reverse her bulky food cart, but one of the tires locks, causing the cart to windshield-wipe into the coat rack and built-in wall cabinet.

"Can you stop what you're doing, Ma'am?" Edward says. "We're kind of in the middle of an important arrest."

"Sure, I'll shut the door." She seals all nine of them inside, including Chuck.

"Where were we?" Casey takes aim at the closet and cocks her gun with her taser hand, which contains the actual taser, making the cocking rather dangerous, because the gun almost discharges.

"Casey, there's no need to go cock-crazy," Edward says, to which Casey flinches. "I've read it doesn't give us any practical advantage whatsoever."

"It makes me feel powerful."

Edward gives it a whirl. "Well I'll be damned. I think I'll always cock my gun from now on."

"Sometimes I do it when nobody's looking."

"Oh yeah, really? What do you do afterwards with your 'cocked' gun?"

"I just knew your 'cock-crazy' comment was sexual in nature, but I decided to give you the benefit of the doubt, Edward."

"I—"

"I thought you were supposed to be the chosen one."

"I am, it's just—"

"*Harassment*, and I'm filing a report first thing back at the station."

"But Casey—"

"Don't 'but Casey' me! Especially because you're probably referring to the 'butt' with two ts, you pervert!"

Earl feels his future YouTube stock skyrocketing. *Keep it coming*, he thinks, but what he thinks doesn't matter.

"I'm being serious, Casey, I—"

"Seriously," Yawnke says, "pork each other already and rid us of your awkward, sexual frustration."

While on the topic of sex, Doctor Holly leans back into the lunch lady and says, "Why's he keep staring at me like that?"

"Ted!" Casey shouts. "You, too? Women are not objects, you chauvinistic arse!"

"Arse?" Edward does a double take. "Are you British?"

"Why, are you confused since I sport a pair of perfectly symmetrical pearly whites?"

"Oh I see, you're a bigot."

"I was making an assumption that *you're* the bigot."

"You clearly made a bigoted remark, Casey. I'm filing a report first thing back at the station, and I'll definitely finish before you, because you'll get bogged down in too many details." He grins.

"How'd you know I was going to add a little fluff to my story?"

"What're you saying?"

"She's gonna do the same thing to you this little shit is doing to me." Yawnke rolls his baby blue eyes.

"Which is?"

"Say you're raping everything and everyone."

"I'd never!" Casey blurts.

"Then what'd you mean, Lady?"

"Yeah, Casey, what'd you mean?"

"I meant…you're putting words in my mouth. I forget what I meant, which makes me look guilty, but I'm not!"

Edward laughs.

Yawnke snorts.

Ted sucks in a deep breath and holds.

Doctor Holly tisk-tisks.

Chaz says, "Aaarrrrrrgggghghhmammaaalamoooma," which translates to, "Get me outta here!"

The lunch lady lets a swift yet loud fart escape but doesn't seem to take notice.

Earl captures close-ups of everybody's reactions in order to post them individually and ~~rape~~ *rake in* the ad bucks.

And Chuck confronts his timer: 48:25 to go.

"Oh, Granny," Yawnke pinches his nose shut, "whatever did you eat?"

To keep the situation from spiraling any further, Chuck's arms blossom like butterfly wings, only faster, and latch onto Bruce and Casey's tasers. Before they can fire, he jerks them across his chest, forming an X, redirecting the sights so the electric blue prongs sail Matrix-style across his face and strike each other in the abdomens. The officers convulse for a moment before dropping like fried flies.

Doctor Holly must have done this in the past, because she doesn't hesitate to sprint out of the room. Her only dilemma is the blasted cart which throws her backward into Chuck's Vice-Grip-of-an-elbow. He gently chokes her out, and as Yawnke claws blindly and wildly with his untrimmed nails, Chuck easily takes a step to the left and waits for the precise moment to hook his spare elbow around the bitchy man's throat. This is new territory for Chuck—he's never choked out two people at once. It proves to be a great stress reliever.

Through it all, Earl remains true to his mentally ill dream of achieving hollow fame by recording every possible $econd, even whilst gasping and spouting, "He's choking them…" The lunch lady's speechless despite her gaping mouth as she caresses her bosom since she can't possibly reach in and squeeze her aching heart. "…and then he's going to choke me." Yawnke hits the tile. "Oh my GOOOOOOOOOOOOOOOOOO—"

Chuck snags Earl good, then drops him on top of Yawnke and Doctor Holly. "Ma'am," Chuck says, stepping over to the lunch lady, showcasing his left and right hands, "which would you prefer?"

She's blatantly white, almost stark, so this should prove interesting. She fits her glasses back over her weathered eyes and inspects her choices.

"AASAGDGDSHDMMMTLDPPPWPP!" the closet says, meaning, "HEY MORONS, GET ME OUT OF HERE!"

"Ma'am, please hurry the F up already."

"Ew, what's wrong with this one? Why's it black?"

"Just what I needed to hear." Chuck chokes her out within seconds, then glides across the room to throw the door open. Chaz bursts out, somehow managing to propel his body airborne, which works out perfectly as Chuck places a well-timed uppercut that not only knocks him back into la-la land, but also launches him back inside the closet.

Only one last choke out remains, but as Chuck approaches the bed, Ted can't help but put on his most pathetic frown to date as he whines, "I'm so, so, so sorry, Chuck. I wasn't thinking properly. I was scared. I was terrified. I panicked."

"What're you talking about?"

Ted raises the corded, 1980s-looking bed remote without uttering a word. The red light flashes on and off. Marked below, it reads: *EMERGENCY*

It takes a solid minute and change for an out-of-breath nurse to come rushing in. He puts on the brakes rather quickly and says from the doorway, "What's the deal?"

He scans the room, doesn't notice anything out of the ordinary. The patient's tucked into his bed and out cold. The IV sways slightly but remains upright. The bathroom's shut, and according to the crack underneath the door, the light hasn't been left on by any of his slacker counterparts. Come to think about it, where is everybody, anyway? It's like he's the only one on-call.

He shrugs and goes to exit but notices the TV's been left on and muted.

"Weird," he says, extending his reach to switch it off. In the reflection of the dead screen, he notices a limp hand dangling out of a wall cabinet. His gut reaction is to slap his hands against his cheeks and scream, but that's when the hairy elbow hooks around his throat and turns his world black.

Unlike Ted, Chuck knocks, *then* pokes his head inside the tiny room. He's drawn to the wall of miniature TVs stacked from desk to ceiling, each displaying a black and white surveillance video of the hospital's innards.

"Pardon me," Chuck says to the seated security guard who rises at a speed unbefitting his pudgy character, "but would you mind—"

"What in the hell do you think you're doing, Chuck Steak?" Before the guard can unlatch his tube of pepper spray, Chuck clamps his neck inside a sweaty elbow and chokes him out.

Hold on, it was a pen and pad, not pepper spray. The poor schmuck only wanted an autograph.

Oh well.

Chuck packs the man neatly underneath the desk, then fumbles around with the monitor controls. It doesn't take long to locate the proper camera, especially since they're marked according to their respective floors. It's only a matter of rewinding the video until the stranger who deposited the new phone is located, but it proves a tad bit difficult, especially with the clock counting down inside Chuck's head. At first, he rewinds too far, missing the perp. Then he fast-forwards and goes even further. So he punches the keyboard and accidentally shuts down the entire fucking system. It takes forever to reboot. Four minutes and twenty-eight seconds to be exact, at which point the security guard jerks awake and bangs his noggin against the desk and curses quite loudly. Chuck reaches underneath with another elbow, but the man proves extremely dodgy, so a knee to the face does the trick.

Once the system's finally back up and running again, Chuck locates the exact moment the bulky, hooded stranger delivers the phone.

"Turn around," Chuck says, leaning into the screen, "you bitch."

But the bitch does something quite unexpected by placing a big, gloved paw on Chuck's unconscious forehead. From there, the paw combs through Chuck's moist hair, stroking it diligently. Back and forth, back and forth.

What happens next practically dropkicks Chuck through the wall. The stranger turns to leave, but this person is most certainly *not* a stranger. Chuck's known this person, this mother fucker, for forever.

# Chapter 23
# The Best Man

The lonely street lamp leans crookedly, the bulb cracked open like a hatched egg. The building itself, located at the end of a long, gravel parking lot, resembles a rickety haunted house with a concrete loading dock for a porch. A dumpster, parked in what would've once been considered a handicap spot, contains a chunk of the building's guts. The guts have bubbled over and spilled to the ground.

Along the side, Chuck must use his new phone's screen to light the way. The fit between buildings is virgin-tight. He can smell his raunchy breath beating off the sandy bricks, or is that the caked-on layer of slimy mold?

Chuck almost stumbles by the gap due to the cell continually entering sleep mode. The gap leads to the angled, double storm doors which are encrusted in dried earth. They're outlined in bottle caps and condom wrappers and cigarette butts and box tops and processed bits of food which never decomposed, and it's basically a fucking pigsty.

Chuck heaves the doors open, and they rain dust and dead insects, mostly the exoskeletons of stink bugs. Tiny, gagged, struggling voices reach out from deep within the abyss.

The stairs crumble as Chuck slides down them. Then, with no one to keep the doors propped open, they slam shut, shaking the exposed planks hanging overhead, making it snow. He follows the pair of voices through narrow corridors of slimy stonewalls. Lining the walls are towers of stacked and cracked barrels leaking purple wine. On the ground, there're rivers which look like the runoff of a grape massacre.

Turning the final corner, Chuck finds a single, planked door waiting for him at the end of a sinking hallway. The further he burrows, the lower he must tuck his head to avoid grazing the collapsing ceiling. There's a maze of imprinted footsteps in the soil. They disappear behind the rotted wood.

With 6:17 remaining, Chuck kneels before an out-of-place, wooden cigar box. It doesn't possess a lock, so he carefully flips the lid open. Angling the phone properly, Chuck discovers his baby, his hand cannon, The Judge, waiting inside. He hasn't seen the custom firearm since parting with it back at the temple to jam the doors shut. Plucking the barrel open, Chuck finds a single bullet lodged inside one of the six slots. With head down, he seals the barrel gently as though it were the lid of a coffin.

Then he stands and punts the door off its hinges.

Then shines his phone. Then almost drops it just as fast. Then steadies his hand, highlighting Rosa bound from the chest down to a Spaghetti Warehouse fine-dining-room chair by a worn garden hose. She screams through the used apron tied harshly around her skull, digging into her mouth. Not comprehending a word, Chuck reaches to pluck the greasy cotton free, but his phone bursts into musical chimes, making him jump and thump his head against a massive support beam.

Chuck taps the speaker button with 5:09 to go, and the killer's thick growl rumbles the dusty pocket like a snow globe of Detroit back during the pinnacle of the financial bust: "What a team you two have made. I admit, this Hispanic firecracker was meant to present you with yet another hurdle to overcome—to bog you down—to render this game brutal in difficultly—yet you've pulled shit together, Chuck. I'm impressed. Truly. Honestly. Bra-fucking-o. Yet despite your many successes, you've elected to skip perhaps the most important decision pertaining to your wedding, and we can't have that. What's the point if you cheat? An asterisk next to your big W for the rest of eternity simply won't do, which is why I've decided to hit rewind—so you can properly choose your best man. It doesn't matter if your best male friend is possibly a drug lord, and if your best female friend is only hours removed from having thrown some poor bastard off a skyscraper, which by the way was pure genius. So what I have here for you today, Chuck, is the most straightforward decision of your career. That's not to say it won't be the hardest."

3:42 left.

"Before you are three choices."

Chuck shifts the light left, hitting a wall, then to the right, highlighting Bernard. Same deal—bound and gagged by hose and apron.

"You've certainly found the present I left for you outside, so here it is, Chuck, chose a best man—Rosa or Bernard—by killing the other."

"Ha-ha, no," is Chuck's instant reaction.

"Fail to comply, and I select the third option for you."

Two muffled beeps take the room by surprise. Rosa burps. Bernard sniffs.

"I'm not too keen on the idea of blowing everybody to pieces, especially Mia," the killer, now serial, says. "We're so close to the climax. Don't you want to come, Chuck? I sure do. I couldn't imagine wallowing through the rest of my life with blue balls. What a sad, sad scenario. So be quick about it, will ya? Only a few seconds remain."

1:22 to be exact.

"Oh, and DON'T remove their gags, else it's game over. Toodles."

Click.

Bernard and Rosa go apeshit, violently shaking in their chairs, repeatedly banging into each other, perhaps attempting to knock the other unconscious—perhaps to settle this for Chuck by means of blunt force trauma. First person knocked out, dies.

58.

*Think!*

10.

What the hell, did the timer glitch?

9.

Yep!

"I'm sorry," Chuck utters. The revolver leaps to Rosa's skull with 8 seconds left, and the trigger's pulled.

Out of the corner of his eye, Chuck catches Bernard smile— or perhaps it's the angle of the apron gag. Either way, everything Bernard's ever done flashes by. The surveillance video of him dropping off a new cell and stroking Chuck's hair. The drugs they found in the rental. Bernard's previous involvement with an Asian gang of drug and people smugglers, although apparently only as an unsuspecting doorman trying to pay off his student loans, but still and all—

2.

Chuck cocks the lone bullet into alignment and pulls the trigger again. This time he looks away as Bernard's brains are blown all over the wall. Chuck drops the smoking Judge and smothers his gasping mouth in a prayer of hands, but no amount of penance can keep his soul from peeling from his body and performing a cannonball into the depths of Hell.

# Chapter 24
## Bound by the Liver

Chuck sheds a few manly tears. Bernard wouldn't have wanted it any other way.

"I can't believe you killed your best friend," Rosa says blankly at the sky.

"I didn't even know his favorite color."

"Why didn't you just shoot me? Would've saved yourself a ton of hassle."

"Want me to now?"

"There was only one bullet."

"Oh…right."

"And this is the part where you explain what in the fuck's going on."

She asked for it. Chuck's no storyteller, so the plot points seem convoluted and bogged down in unnecessary details, and there are sub-plots which make no sense and could be classified in other genres, and afterwards she has *a lot* of questions. He answers them to the best of his ability, which is half-assed.

"Can you like, I don't know, make more sense?"

He revamps his presentation and starts to redeliver, but she wraps his mouth up with her fruit-infused hand and says, "I appreciate the effort."

"Aaklfjvjlwlaladgbg."

She let's go. "What?"

"I said you're a pretty decent person." His raised eyebrows tell a different story.

"That's not what you said," Rosa snorts, "but okay, you're fairly decent, too."

They share blood-speckled smiles. Then they take turns wiping Bernard off each other's face. Then they redo the smiles, but they don't quite capture the same emotion, because something looms overhead.

Rosa clutches the bottom of her black shirt and heaves it over her six pack. There's a ragged line of stitches running like a varicose vein through her bellybutton.

"My bad," Chuck mumbles. "Were you able to figure out from my summary why that's there?"

"Because the best man is supposed to take one for the team, right?"

A lot of blushing has been omitted.

"Let's end this." Chuck hops off and lands in a puff of smoke. "Sound good, Partner?"

Rosa follows suit, and they go at each other with raised, flexed arms and lock hands to kick off a new, non-sexist tradition of midair arm-wrestling.

Nobody wins, because everybody's equal.

"I'm all in," Rosa says, squeezing harder. "What time are the guests arriving tomorrow?"

. . .

. . .

. . .

. . .

. . .

"That's your queue to tell me when all of the guests are arriving."

"Ooooooooooh," Chuck mumbles, "about that…"

"No."

Chuck paces.

"Tell me you didn't forget to invite your fucking guests."

"Since we're not lying to each other anymore, I probably shouldn't."

"Is there supposed to be a wedding tomorrow?"

"Yes."

"You mentioned something about a diary."

"Uh huh."

"And that mentions something about how many guests are supposed to be in attendance, which is?"

"Two-hundred-and-fifty."

"And you didn't invite a single one?!?!"

"Would it be better if I remain silent?"

"CHUCK."

"All right, all right, I'll figure it out!"

"How!?!"

"I always do."

# Chapter 25
## You Work for Me Now

The electronic billboards display Chuck's lovely 1080p mug high above the city streets, flashing the text: *WANTED FOR QUESTIONING IN MULTIPLE INVESTIGATIONS.* One's visible from the tree branch Chuck's perched on. He uses an absurdly long thumbnail to pry open a second-story bedroom window and slip inside. A drip, drip comes from the bathroom's slightly ajar door. As Chuck eases it open, causing a long, metallic squeal, Anderson flops inside the porcelain bowl whale-like, causing little tsunamis which soak the tiled floor.

"CHUCK!?!" Anderson didn't use bubbles, and there's a lot of flesh to take in. "FOR THE LOVE OF—"

Chuck clamps his mouth shut.

*Look away,* he tells himself, but part of him can't help steal a glance. Why would Chuck do such a thing? The water's crystal clear, and he sees everything.

*Everything.*

"I will never be able to unsee this."

"AAUGHAUNNNNTHSSSPSSST!" Anderson spouts.

Chuck catches himself staring. "I don't mean to, seriously. No homo."

"PPPPPPPUPPPPPPPPPPSSSSSSSSS!"

"You wanna put me away for a long time, I get it, and I'm willing to give you what you want." He peels his hand from Anderson's salivating mouth, and for the first time in forever, the big boss man is at a loss.

"Earth to Anderson," Chuck snaps his fingers, "you're gonna give me what I want first."

Anderson gulps, worried this could get extremely kinky *and* hazardous to his health. "And what's that?"

"A wedding."

"You want *us* to get married?"

"*Me* and *my girlfriend*, Sir, and I'm not giving you any privacy until the manhunt's called off."

"You think because I'm in and out of the hospital that I've lost my goddamn mind?"

"Here's how this works: I fill the tub and drown you." He laughs. "Just kidding. But seriously, I'm gonna let you set a trap for me. You call everybody on this guest list," he takes a paper towel from his pocket and waves it around, the names are scribbled in crayon, some have phone numbers, "and you explain the details— that the only way to catch me is to make me think my wedding's still happening. Don't worry, when you tell a few, they'll tell all the rest."

"And then you'll magically give yourself up without a fight?"

"The moment my fiancée says, 'I do,' I'm all yours."

"You think I believe this?"

"Then how about this? There's a bomb hidden within city limits, and if you don't do exactly what I say, when it goes off, a shit-ton of innocent people will die."

"You wouldn't!"

Chuck pauses briefly at the door to say, "Every time you've ever said that, I've went ahead and done it." He leaps from the bedroom window, not to the sound of an explosion, but to, "CHUUUUUUUUUUUUUUUUUUUUUK!"

# FRIDAY

## Chapter 26
## Recreating the Magic

They wiped Chuck clean from all the billboards overnight and replaced him with run-of-the-mill dental offices professing they care and activists protesting animal hair. And other shit, too.

Just before noon, Mia answers what amounts to his 11th call. He had a good feeling about the 11th but had never once heard anyone say, "The 11th time's a charm," so he began to sweat bullets.

Then he took a shower.

He urinated into the drain.

He laughed at this, because if Mia had caught him like she had multiple times in the past, she would've made two observations:

1. You're clearly dehydrated...*again.*
2. And that's sick, Chuck. When are you going to grow up?

Once, she had pushed him against the glass, so he pushed her against the tile, so she pushed him harder, right out the door. He stumbled into his closet, soaking the carpet. He was quick to hop back inside with a belt, at which she shouted, "Don't you dare!" He gave her tosh a light smackin', which prompted her to wrestle the fat piece of leather out of his fist, at which she pelted red lines into his hairy ass, all whilst shouting, "You like that? Huh? Feel good?" He dodged the rest of her incoming attacks and pretended to tackle her with a mighty bear hug, but he accidentally applied the inappropriate amount of force, thrusting his shoulder into her bosom, and ping-ponged her torso into the wall, resulting in the soap dish stabbing her in the mid-back, giving her a bruise the size of a baseball which she wouldn't let him live down for weeks.

A serious lecture ensued about safety and chivalry, which ended with her thrown on the bed, drenching his sheets in water and love, or maybe it was conditioner.

"Hi," Mia says.

"Hi," Chuck says, staring googly-eyed.

"Chuck?"

"Yeah?"

"Who's hiding behind you?"

A head sprouts over each of Chuck's shoulders. "You ever heard of Tinder?"

"What do you think?"

"Ha, ha," he cranes his neck, addressing each head, "she's not very tech-savvy, but whateves. Anyway, Mia, it's a place where you meet like-minded peeps who feel you."

She gives him the "okay-what's-this-got-to-do-with-anything?" look followed by the "and-why-are-you-talking-all-ghetto?" look capped by the "you-only-act-like-this-when-you're-trying-to-impress-younger-guys" look.

"Listen, Babe, I created a free profile for you and got a bunch of messages, so I totes selected the top two dudes I thought were purrrfect matches." He bobs a finger at the screen suspended from the ceiling. All their names are already punched in, awaiting the first ball to be thrown. This is Chuck's attempt to recreate how they first met and fell in love all those long years ago—at a bowling alley on a quadruple blind date. It's a long story. Be sure to read about it in the second installment of DLC dedicated to all the flashbacks which would've kept this story from moving at a decent pace.

"LumberJACK and Carl?" Mia says, squinting.

The burly white guy in the denim shirt strokes his upside-down mountain of a beard and says, "I'm Jack, pleasure to meet you. I work in a lumberyard."

"I'm Carl, and by God, you're breathtaking! Girl, your profile pic doesn't nearly do you justice."

"I know what you're thinking," Chuck says, nudging both guys into the background, "Carl's name sucks. Not very imaginative, but he graduated from Harvard, and look," he leans into Mia and whispers, "he's one of you!"

She tilts her head. "You serious?"

"Oops," he flashes his black hand like a badge, "I mean *us*—he's one of *us*."

"I'm going to kill you."

"Yo, broskis," Chuck faces the broskis in question, "mind dishing us out a few minutoes?" They don't understand him nor recognize the language. Is it English or Spanish or a mishmash of both? "BRB," he says and chaperons Mia over to their lane's private table.

"You've got precisely three seconds."

"Why's there always a time—"

She knees him in the crotch. Luckily he wore his best jeans, which also happen to be the stiffest since they haven't been used and abused and aren't littered in holes and worn patches. Still, the knee registered—he can feel the sharp pain in his abdomen, which begs the question—why do testicles always deflect their pain upwards? Testicles should just take it like a man occasionally.

"Chuck!"

"Okay, okay." He gropes his crotch. "I thought this would rekindle our fire."

She laughs. "You're serious?"

"I think so."

She doesn't mention how Anderson rang her late last night and explained the situation, but not before saying, "Hi, we've never met." After a brief introduction and summarization of events involving Chuck, Anderson yapped, "And then he let me know there's a goddamn bomb hidden somewhere within the city."

At the thought of more chaos, which seems like Chuck's true love as of late, Mia's eyes gloss over.

"Everything all right?"

"Oooh yeah." She steps past Chuck and fits herself between the Tinder dates. "So, Harvard?"

Carl snuggles into her. "I don't like to brag, but I'm sort of a big-time lawyer. I've actually sued the police department over Chuck too many times to count. And won easily I may add." He winks, but Chuck doesn't remember this man. Perhaps next time he appears in court, he'll skip nap time.

"Once," Carl says, easing his sly hand around the small (or rather medium) of Mia's back, "Chuck's lawyer had to slap him awake because I forced him to take the stand."

"That was you?" Chuck chirps.

Carl laughs. "Chuck's hair was so matted, and his face was covered in drool from nose to chin, and he had these big, oval sweet stains rounding his pits, and to top it all off, he had an absurd erection."

Mia and LumberJACK shoot Chuck a look of amazement, and embarrassment, and something like, *no—no you didn't.*

"True story," Carl says. "They made him take the stand, and everybody was hootin' and hollerin'. Finally, when Chuck got things under control, he turned to me with these blazing, hate-filled eyes and said, 'WHAT?'

"I turned, threw my hands in the air and said, 'No further questions, your honor.'"

It appears exaggerated, but Mia hunches over and howls at the floor, pushing her rump backwards.

"Damn, Girl, you've got quite the booty! You work out much?"

"No," Chuck spits, cutting between the two to grab his ball, "she fucking doesn't, Carl."

"Why don't you let the lady speak for herself?"

"Can I say something?" LumberJACK says.

Nobody acknowledges him.

Chuck heaves a flaming purple ball into the air. "How about I let my game do all the talking?" He sprints forward, pretending the pins are Carl's teeth, and hurls the ball through a rave of lasers. It rebounds off the gutter and skips several lanes over, interrupting a competitive game in progress.

"Real smooth," Carl says, clapping to draw attention, then he points at Chuck and mouths to the crowd, "He did it."

Chuck goes in for a second ball but bumps arms with a stranger. Looking up, fully prepared to yell something snarky, Chuck realizes it's not a stranger at all. It's, "Ted?"

"The one and only." Ted's sporting khakis and a tucked-in Hawaiian polo. None of this matters. "Bet you never, ever in a million, trillion years would've guessed it was me."

Chuck smacks Ted's manicured hand out of the way, causing his loose-fitting, shiny Rolex to spin around and around his furry wrist, and fingers the bowling ball quite forcefully. "Don't flatter yourself," Chuck says, striking a runner's stance, "I know Anderson's got most of the force tailing me. I spotted Casey driving an empty taxi and Edward pushing a doll in a brand-new stroller. If it were me, I would've had them switch roles."

"Not what I me—"

"Plus you're obviously a professional bowler."

"Wow, thanks, but—"

"Because aren't all nerds?" Chuck pitches his ball directly into the gutter. It bounces out at the last possible second and clips a pin. The pin wobbles, flirting with kissing the lane, but then the rack drops down and snags it, slapping a big, fat zero on the scoreboard.

LumberJACK hops around in circles, shouting, "BOOOOOOOOO!" He only calms his horses when Mia slides out of Carl's butt-grip and moves within hugging range. "You're funny," she says, batting her thickly-coated eyelashes at him.

Sensing Ted's smug lips peeling apart, Chuck flicks him the bird while passing by and says, "You know where to stick your advice."

Not what Ted was going to say, but okay. He takes hold of his ball, and while nobody pays him any attention, drifts forward and lobs. The ball strikes the right-most three pins at 9mph, which isn't impressive, and in total, five fall. After his second bowl, Ted earns himself a grand total of six.

Luck would have it Carl's the real professional. He nails a strike, kisses his pointer finger, points it at God and whispers, "Thank you." Upon his return, Mia gravitates under his arm and gushes about the way he rocked those "naughty, naughty pins." Carl bobs his head, unsurprised, and says, "I'm far better at rocking *other* things."

Chuck goes to put Carl in a headlock and pop his brains out, but then LumberJACK nails a strike with a 27mph hurl and gets Mia to gravitate underneath his pit.

"Pssst, Chuck!"

"Ted, for the love of everything, I'm in the middle of something here."

"But—"

"Hey, Mia!" Chuck snatches her by the wrist and tries to take off.

"Why don't you pick on someone your own size," Carl says, shoving from behind.

Chuck swipes for Carl's throat, but the lawyer's quick to bolt behind LumberJACK who's had a hard time keeping up with the action.

"You know, Chuck," Carl shouts, sounding like he's tucked snuggly inside LumberJACK's back pocket, "after this fellow puts you in the hospital, I plan on wheeling you into court and suing all your bandages and casts off."

"The F you will." Chuck readies both fists to take on the entire lot, but Mia wrestles him over to the vending machine. He punches the slab of glass, and a bag of Teddy Grahams falls.

"You know," she beats on his chest with hammers for fists, "I've sacrificed so much for so long hoping you'd get your shit together. I once dreamed of us having four or five kids. But by the time you got around to entertaining the idea, I didn't even know if you'd be capable of caring for a single one. After our first real talk, I went home and cried myself to sleep, because I wondered if we were truly meant to be. Obviously my love for you outweighed my desire for children or else I wouldn't be in this predicament. When you proposed the other night, I thought the tides had turned. But then I wound up crying myself to sleep again, but not because you ruined my family—because for once, despite all the stupid things you've ever done, I dreamt of our future—of you leaving the force—of us having kids—of a happy ending."

Chuck swipes the Teddy Grahams and tears them open. He pours about 65% into his mouth and offers the rest to her. She swats them to the floor and grinds the Teddy heads into dust.

"You know what?" she barks, "*I'm* the idiot." She turns to leave.

"I'm not good," he chews, "with words, Mia." He spits crumbs. "I've been having something of a third-life crisis." Pause for a swallow. "I don't know. I think I woke up one morning and realized what really mattered. You, not my stupid legacy. Once I started thinking about everything, how I've treated you, how I've acted—like some big hotshot who mattered in the grand scheme of things—it freaked me out, because I had pushed you away for so long when all I've ever wanted was you, only you. That's why I've been so weird lately. Talking isn't my forty."

"It's *forte*," Carl says as he purchases a pack of Trident Layers.

"Thanks, Carl."

"Any time!" He unwraps the plastic packaging and opens the flap. "Care for a piece?"

Chuck bats the pack fourteen lanes over.

"I thought this," Chuck makes an encapsulating motion, "would rekindle our fire or something. I know, I suck." He slaps himself across the face, lightly, so it doesn't hurt one bit. "I've sucked for a long time. But guess what? I've grown up. I'm locked and loaded, ready to blast you with my love. Sorry, that sounds *wrong*. I mean I love you more than…the moon loves, um, when the sun goes away, you know, so it can shine brightly?

"No? Bad analogy? Mia? What kind of look is this?"

"Mind getting me some Swedish Fish?"

"Oh, sure." He socks the glass, and an oatmeal cookie drops. "That's disappointing."

"What else is new?" She swipes it and struts away, and upon noticing her escape, the Tinder men break to intercept her at the exit.

Chuck'll get there before them, he always—

Ted stumbles into the way, and Chuck nearly tramples him to death.

"The fuck, Ted!"

"Let's try this again." Ted taps Chuck directly on-the-nose. "Never imagined it was me, did ya?"

This time, something feels different.

"You're having a revelation, aren't you?"

Chuck shakes his head, even laughs. "I almost thought—"

"—*I* was the killer? Oh, snap, will ya look at that! I finally, FINALLY, after all these longs years, have your full attention. I'm no longer 'Ted the loser'. 'Ted the doorstop'. 'Ted, the—'"

In one motion, Chuck puts Ted's head through the glass.

"Sir!" A smokestack of a woman with a butch cut slinks out from behind her counter. "I didn't say a word the entire time you were bangin' that there machine, but you cannot, I repeat, CAN-NOT, put a man's head through it!"

"Yeah, Chuck, you can't—"

Ted gets plucked, his face cut up with jagged, red lines, and flung onto lane 3, interrupting a toddler's birthday party. It's game over, though, as Ted draws his firearm, and the crowd disperses.

"No more Mister Nice Ted! What're you doing? Can't you see I'm pointing a frickin' gun at you?" He shoots. Chuck halts and performs a quick scan. "Missed, now you die."

Ted unloads, sticking Chuck in the throat, white thumb (of all places) and left kneecap with miniature syringes. The Novocain spreads fast, bringing Chuck to his knees.

"That's right, bow before me!"

"Teeeeeed. Youuuuuuuuu? Theeeeeeee—"

"I know, I'm just as shocked! 'Ted the killer'? Or rather, 'Ted the-only-person-to-have-ever-defeated-the-undefeatable-Chuck-Steak'? Yup, that was me who beat you in our foot race! I'm not sure if you're aware, but I used to be a track star. Kids called me "Runner", how cool is that? But then bullies broke my caps and ruined my future, but no biggie. Back to my point, which is, out of all the baddies you've ever faced, you fall to TED!"

"Embaaaaaaaaaresssssssssin—"

Ted pistol-whips him, but since the gun's made of hard plastic, it doesn't hurt too much. "You will RESPECT me! Everybody will RESPECT me, you understand? Chuck?" Ted drops flat on his stomach and matches Chuck's planted-to-the-floor face. "You're paralyzed, hell yeah! But you can still see me—you can still feel." He stands and drops his pants and performs a squat to lower his ball sack. Chuck tries to scream, but it's no use. "I've always wanted to do this. Why, you may ask? Because once, when I was in high school, somebody finally invited me to a sleepover. Long story short, three bullies tea-bagged me while the rest snapped a bunch of pictures. One of them worked on the yearbook committee, so there I found myself, tea-bagged in print. In case you're wondering, all of this is revenge for that, and of course many other things!"

Without further ado, Ted teabags Chuck. Nine dunks later, which seems like overkill, Ted thumps Chuck in the forehead with the butt of his plastic tranquilizer. Ted's been trained by movies to believe one wallop does the job, but five thumps in does nothing more than give Chuck a handful of what looks like mosquito bites.

"Gosh, I'm sorry," Ted says, staring into Chuck's fully exposed, bloodshot eyes as he delivers another good wallop, "this is unbefitting a villain, I know." Another wallop. "What in the heck? Really?" Wallop, wallop. "Chuck?" Wallop. "Oh, crap, your eyelids probably don't work." He closes them manually. "You've been out this entire time, haven't you?"

Now the world will never know how many wallops it takes to knock Chuck Steak unconscious.

**FLASHBACK ALERT!**

*It all started in the '90s. Action heroes had taken over the big screen and were strolling through city blocks with their true loves, exotic guns, and leaving trails of rubble along with henchmen body parts in their wake. These heroes could hardly find clothes to hide their veiny, bulky muscles, so most of the time they wore tank tops or wife beaters. This was before wife beaters became offensive, or perhaps they were always offensive, nobody knows.*

*Fact is, Ted was trying to figure out high school. The coolest kids played on the football team. They worked as one, even wore their lettermen jackets to signify unity, and they lifted weights and showered immediately afterwards together. They measured their wieners in both length and girth and kept a mental list of how many "chicks" they had "porked". This was their off-the-field game, and most times, it grew nastier than helmets clashing and bones breaking. The game caused many unintended pregnancies, accusations of rape, and the basic demoralization of the human spirit.*

*Ted is a fine example. He was a junior and virgin, both in sex and football. He tried out for the team. Since it was a small school, there were no cuts. He rode the pine and passed out water bottles to the players, no biggie. He was always the squatter and wiped the other boys' sweaty bodies off with towels, no biggie. He was pee shy and showered in swimming trunks and took a little shit for it, but still, no biggie. Things played out as they usually did—not even a week into the routine, and everybody forgot about Ted. He became oxygen.*

*Then, after a bitter loss in the State finals, one of the team's captains decided to cheer everybody up by yanking Ted's trunks to the floor. Before a single thought could register, the captain pointed and laughed his ass off. But then everybody gasped, and the captain almost passed out, because Ted had a huge cock. By looks alone, it was easily the biggest of the lot. The revelation didn't help team morale any—in fact, it put everybody in a worse mood, and*

*Ted earned himself the attention he had always desired. Only, this was the bad kind. His jealous comrades would go on to ridicule him and spread rumors of a wiener covered in warts.*

*Shamed, Ted turned to his only source of hope—the movies. In his free time, he worked tirelessly to complete chores around the household and mow neighbors' lawns and shovel their sidewalks, all to earn enough dough to feed his out-of-control theater addiction. On average, Ted would watch no less than eleven action flicks per week. He'd go alone, sit alone, and to get the most bang out of his buck, sometimes, when the opportunities presented themselves, he'd take cover behind a curtain to catch the next showing, and he'd watch the same movie twice. Or he'd leave during the credits and slip into another theater.*

*His only rule was to avoid the following:*

- *Romcoms*
- *Teeny bopper movies*
- *Everything Disney*
- *Oscar-nominated films*
- *Subtitles*

*Ted's addiction eventually peeked at twenty-three flicks in a single week. This was when the epiphany hit. What did Ted truly love? Weiner size? "Porking" "chicks"? No, he loved action heroes, and his greatest love of all was Arnold Schwarzenegger. His body was the very definition of perfection, so too his chiseled-from-stone jawline. His one-liners made Ted swoon, and the way Arnold blew shit up got Ted's juices flowing.*

*Ted's attempts at fading from society were thwarted by a football player who had also been shunned. The player's name was Jimmy. His wiener was two inches long while limp and five-and-a-half inches long while erect. The girth was debatable.*

*However, this didn't matter. Jimmy just wanted to be friends. He wanted to come over and hang out, and when Ted finally granted him access to his bedroom, Jimmy discovered the eerie monument dedicated to Arnold. The walls were covered in his oily, bare-chested posters and printouts of his famous one-liners like, "Get to the choppa!" only "the choppa" was crossed out and replaced with "Ted's room". And then Jimmy spotted a teddy bear with Arnold's face*

Chuck Steak

*sewn on—it was tucked neatly underneath some Arnold-print sheets and blankets.*

*"Whaddya think?" Ted said, brimming with passion. It felt euphoric to finally have someone to share his passion with.*

*"You're fuckin' gay!" shouted Jimmy, and he ran from the room, from the house, and he told the team he had successfully infiltrated Ted's life, and through word of mouth, by going door to door when phone lines were busy, the football team got the entire school to believe Ted was a homosexual. And back in the '90s, that was a big no-no.*

*His reply to such an accusation?*

*"Maybe I am gay," Ted said, not exactly sure himself, as the team slapped his face with ball sack after ball sack. That's when Ted switched sports from football to track—to run away from his fears. After he won his one and only State championship, the bullies treated him to ice cream and then proceeded to break his knee caps.*

*Fast forward.*

*After Arnold left the big screen for the beat government, Ted endured the emotional and crushing blow of a first breakup.*

*He cried.*

*He wrote poetry.*

*He even considered becoming a priest.*

*But then he switched over to a news story in-progress about an up-and-coming cop who saved a rollerblading gal only after crashing a cruise ship, and Ted fell instantly in love.*

216

Chuck blinks and traces Rosa's herculean outline. She has Ted splayed across her lap. His abdomen gushes life down her legs. "Help!"

Chuck's painfully confused.

"I don't know what I'm doing!" Rosa barks.

They've taken shelter inside a huge sewer pipe.

"I clipped him in the gut," she presses hard on the hole, but the blood won't stop. "Who the hell thought it'd be this bad?"

Chuck manages to crawl through a puddle of toxic sludge, which contrary to popular belief, isn't neon green—it's dark blue, closer to navy. Chuck takes Ted's head in his hands and aligns the bleached face with his own.

"Why, Ted? Why'd you do it?"

Ted's purple lips curl upwards.

"What does that even mean?"

"He's—" Rosa says, dropping her head and mumbling into her chest, "—he's dead, Chuck."

"Confess!" Chuck grinds his rigid fingernails into Ted's cheeks and pulls, tearing his lips at the corners. He peels the skin completely off Ted's jaw, revealing the bone mandible. At this sight, Chuck falls back into the sludge, and with patches of skin caught in both fists, utters, "How're we supposed to stop the bomb now?" He glances at her stomach. "*Bombs.*"

A shrug's the best she can muster. "I told him to freeze."

"Jesus, nobody ever listens to that."

"No kidding. Bastard pulled *this* on me." She pries the plastic gun from his cold, dead hand. "It's not even loaded."

None of them say it, none of them say a word for quite a while, but what's implied is this: of course Ted would die the lamest death ever. Fucking poser.

# Chapter 29
# True Love

"There was someone else?" Chuck snaps. "Seriously?"

"You think Ted could lug you around all by himself?"

"Christ, Rosa, you should've led with that."

"Oh, I'm sorry, I might'a been a little distracted trying to save our only suspect's life so we could possibly get some real answers. Like hey, Ted, why'd you put a bomb inside me? When'd you even do it? Or hey, Ted, why's this wedding so goddamn important, and why such the hard-on for Chuck?"

*Several months ago, maybe three:*

*Ted backtracked and bent over to fetch a newspaper. He jogged up the porch stairs and presented it kindly to the balding woman clutching her walker. "As always, Ted—"*

*"Nope, you never have to thank me, Miss Applewood." He held such a radiant smile. "It's the very least I can do." He hopped off the porch, seemingly energized from the encounter.*

*Further along, Ted crossed paths with June Moore. They paused to chat. He scooped her infant from the stroller and cuddled the girl close to his chest. He smiled at the babe, and June smiled at him, and then the mother of three said, "You're so good with children, it'd be a shame if you never had one of your own."*

*"Gosh, you're too kind." He pecked the babe on the nose and tucked her back under the fleece blanket.*

*After they said their goodbyes, Ted continued skipping along. Children were always adorable in small doses, so he didn't know how he'd feel with one in his life 24/7. Would parenthood ruin his perception?*

*There was a stranger parked on his front porch, ringing the doorbell as he rounded the corner. At the bottom of the stairs, he said with a gust of friendliness, "Why hello there, what can I do you for today?"*

*The kid in the ball cap turned and smiled and produced a clipboard and said, "I'm selling cookie dough for—"*

*"Say no more, I'll take four. Hey, that rhymed!"*

*They both giggled.*

*Inside, Ted flung his police cap across the room. It bounced off the wall after barely missing a wall hook and flopped to the floor. Ted snorted as he strolled over and swept it up in one motion—reminiscent of how he snagged Miss Applewood's newspaper. He marched ten paces across his living room's freshly steamed hardwood, turned at the kitchen and flung again. This time, the cap missed wide right.*

*"Okay," he said, grinning as he waltzed over and snagged the cap. After another ten paces, he twisted and flung, and the blasted thing struck the ceiling and fell short of its mark by a good three feet.*

*"You're getting worse, Ted." He laughed, but not in a good way. And then he marched over, swiped the cap, marched back ten paces and jolted around. This time he took his time—threw with precision. The cap floated across the air like he imagined an alien's saucer would. And then it snagged the hook, and he closed his eyes and threw his fists into the air, and just as he was about to shout hallelujah, he made the mistake of peeking and found the cap lying upside down on the gleaming floorboards.*

*"I don't understand. How is this even possible? Answer me!" He stomped over and raised the cap to eye-level. "Why'd you fall? I threw you perfectly! What do you have to say for yourself? Huh? Well? Are you listening? Are you deaf?"*

*He chucked the cap again, and this time it veered far right and struck the TV. Ted was under the impression the cap thought everything simply hilarious, so he hoisted his flat screen off the stand and hurled it, screen-down, to the floor. It shattered. He pried the cap from Shard Mountain and said, "How'd that feel? Yeah, not too good, huh? Maybe this time you won't cheat me out of certain victory."*

*He flung the cap once more, and it bounced off the glass of his fireplace. "Holey moley!" He reached right for the iron poker and gave the cap a good golf club whacking. When it hardly moved, Ted entered a whacking frenzy which saw him shatter a lamp, gut several pillows, prod a constellation of holes into his popcorn ceiling and gash the living daylights out of his hardwood.*

*Through it all, the cap remained unharmed, sitting smug in the recliner.*

*"Mark my words," Ted's stomping shook the house, "I am going to tear you apart and spread your fabric all over the house!"*

*"Bad time?" came a distorted voice which was neither man nor woman.*

*"Huh, who's there?"*

*The knock on the wooden bannister drew Ted's full attention. The stranger had been waiting upstairs.*

"What'd the other one look like?" Chuck says.

"They were wearing a hoodie."

"What kind?"

"Something from The Gap? How the Hell should I know?"

"What was the jacket made of? What'd it look like?"

"Black, maybe leather or that fake stuff."

"Pleather."

"And the hood was gray, made of sweatshirt material."

"Man or woman or both?"

Her burning eyes state the obvious.

"What were you even doing here?"

"Heard the commotion on the scanner and rushed right over. Saw two sketchy fuckers cartin' you down the alley. Ted had you by the rear—"

"Please choose your words wisely."

"—and I could barely make out the other person. When I dropped down into the sewer, Ted drew his gun on me."

"You said *barely*."

"The dude or chick," Rosa gives him the funny eye, "or *both* as you call it, was dark-skinned."

Chuck feels the blood rush to his head—not that one. "You're certain?"

"I know my minorities."

Chuck puts his hands on display, the left A., the right B. "Can you point at the correct color?"

"They're both drenched in blood."

"Sorry." He wipes them clean. "How about now?"

She slaps his black hand the way a scolding nun would, then rolls Ted's corpse off her lap, but can't manage to bring her folded, dead legs back to life.

"Random question time," Chuck says, "but what do you suppose Ted's sexual preference is…*was*?"

"Gay." No hesitation there.

"And why's that?"

"Sometimes you can just tell, okay? Besides, he sure seemed to have a hard-on for you. What's this got to do with anything anyway?"

"Nothing," Chuck says, but what he means is *everything*.

*Ted climbed the stairs and followed the voice into his bedroom. The three windows' blinds were intentionally shut. The figure stood admiring the mural of clippings framed above Ted's monstrous headboard. On the center shelf was*

*a smorgasbord of Chuck Steak memorabilia, including a bobble head doll and a 1:1 scale replica of "The Judge".*

*The entire room was an altar of sorts—this was where Ted prayed to Chuck Steak.*

*"Can I help you?" Ted said more embarrassed about his little outburst in the living room than spooked about someone having broken into his home. But then again, Ted didn't lock his doors.*

*"No, no, no, the real question is," the person didn't budge—they were wearing matching sweatpants and a hoodie and looked terribly comfortable, "can I help you?"*

*Twas the same question, only asked by a different person. Ted was rightfully baffled.*

*"You know you're never going to be an action hero, don't you, Ted?"*

*Ted's legs felt weak. His body swayed. He almost passed out but didn't. This wasn't necessarily news to him, but somewhere deep within his soul, Ted still clutched the dream close to his heart.*

*"You lack the psychical tools. It's not your fault, and you shouldn't hate yourself. You can thrive in your fantasies, but here, in the real world, the hero's already been chosen, so you need to pick a different role."*

*"The villain?"*

*"Yes, exactly! You've got great wits about you."*

*Ted blushed.*

*"Feel free to stop me whenever I make a false accusation." Ted nodded. "You grew up a loner. You were bullied, sometimes cruel and unusually. Society has always pushed you to the backburner even when you've tried your damnedest to scratch and claw your way to the forefront. You are currently, at best, average. It's a struggle to remain there. Your fear is that you'll sink and never float majesty above the sea of life. Am I wrong yet?"*

*Ted hesitantly shook his head, the tears welling behind his lids.*

*"That is no way to live, especially when you dream so big. It's heartbreaking, Ted, and I feel immense pain for your current state, which is why I've come. Think of me as the angel of opportunity. Once I present you my offer, understand this: if you reject it, I will walk out that door, and you will never, ever see me again. But if you accept, you'll become more than somebody—*

*you will become the man. The one opposite the hero. And what will separate you from your idol Chuck Steak, a bully who treats you worse than a dog, worse than the shit caked on the bottom of a shoe, is the fact that when you two clash, only you, Ted, will arise victorious."*

*The killer suddenly had Ted's full, weeping attention.*

*"I have already prepared a game, one which ends with Chuck Steak in ruins. All you have to do is act as my inside man. When the dust settles, you will take full credit. You will be studied and talked about for ages to come. Who knows, perhaps in a thousand years, aliens will stumble upon your story and spread it amongst the stars."*

*"Do I have to—"*

*"Kill anyone?"*

*"Uh huh."*

*"Never, Ted. Never in a million years. Unless you want to, of course, at which point I can't stop you. I've already done a majority of the work. As for the glory, I'm gifting it to you, Ted, because there's nobody more deserving, and I don't want to see your dream die. I want to see you rise above your worth. I want to see you mature into a man. So what say you? Do you want to become a legend, or would you rather fade away with time?"*

*"I used to be really good at running away, especially from bullies. Those were the days."*

*"Okay…"*

*"I was known as 'Runner'."*

*"Okay…"*

*"But my caps."*

*"Okay…"*

*"I want, I mean really, really want to, no I need, really, really need to run away from Chuck just once. Don't believe the bullies who found and friended me on Headbook, maybe I shouldn't have accepted, and maybe I should unfriend them, sometimes I'm too nice, I know, but one thing I'm not is washed up. I know I can win! I need to best Chuck at something. Would you grant me such a wish?"*

*The stranger shrugged. "I guess."*

*Ted grabbed the edge of a poster and tore a harsh line across Chuck's oily heart. To the stranger, he said, "I think I love you."*

"Can you hide the body?" Chuck asks in a hurry, and this seems like a growing trend—first Bernard, now Ted.

"Sooner or later they're gonna find these corpses, and then they'll trace them back to us. Then what? Will someone sit us both down in a fancy room, fetch us some lattes and listen as we babble on about this completely ridiculous tale?"

"We just need to make it through tomorrow in one piece—"

"Not funny."

"—and then take things step by step, day by day."

"Even less funny." As she curls Ted, her biceps balloon. Nice form! "And while I'm doing all the heavy lifting," pun intended, "what will you be doing?"

"What I always do." He winks and begins to jog away.

"Let me guess, catching the bad guy?"

"'Killing', but close enough." He's pretty far away now, so he has to yell, "Meet back at my place later, and we'll celebrate!"

# Chapter 30
## The Many-Faced Man

With no way to investigate the apartment from afar, not with only two windows, both of which are concealed by thick blinds, Chuck rides the elevator to the 8th floor. He suctions his ear to room 813's door and listens to the ominous groan of violins beyond the pine.

The door's locked, and Chuck's got nothing of use, so he heads down the hall and around the corner and knocks on room 835. He asks the paranoid pothead for a paperclip, stating he needs it to keep a resume bound together.

"What's the resume for?" the kid says, poking his head out into the hall. "You a cop?"

Before Chuck can answer, the door's slammed shut.

*You bastard.*

He contemplates beating his way inside the apartment, but he'd most likely blow his cover. As Chuck turns with 836 in his sights, he spots a paperclip glide across the carpet and flick his boot.

The straightened piece of steel wire does the trick, and as Chuck twists the knob to 813 and eases the door open ever-so-gently, razor blades on strings welcome him to this harmonic torture chamber. In enters the beat of horsehair against cymbal as the door snags on a golden chain. Chuck waits for the electric cellos' violent entrance, for the song to mimic the sound of a garbage disposal, to tuck and ram, snapping the chain and throwing the door wide open. He makes the catch before it slams against the wall, a moment before every string instrument abruptly cuts out, and a hammer smashes a crash cymbal. As the metallic chime fades, the occupant can be heard mumbling in their study.

The first step Chuck takes is accompanied by a razor blade slicing across chords. The second as well. The third, which isn't a charm by any means, makes the floor squeak as if there's a giant dog toy trapped underneath.

A tuba makes its presence known with a thick, constipated fart.

"Huh? Who's there?"

The contrabassoon begins its soft, lighthearted honking. As the apartment owner rises, the cellos and violins ease their way back into the picture. The bass drum's quick to follow suit, as to is the horsehair as it beats against multiple cymbals. The music culminates with Chet pouncing into the living room with his arm raised, fist clutching a letter opener.

The tuba blares a WAH, WAH, WAH sound as Chet finds himself alone with the front door properly secured. He waltzes over to the record player, the tempo matching his pace, and plucks the needle off. The eerie skip of static fills the room as Chet stretches his reach for the closet door while his armed hand remains cocked and ready to stab.

As the doorknob squeals pig-like, Chuck can't help but squeeze his eyes shut and tuck himself into a tighter ball.

"Die!" Chet screams at the top of his lungs as he throws the door open and repeatedly stabs into the shadowy wall of hanging jackets. "Die, die, die!" He furiously hacks apart chunks of skin until the intruder drops at his feet. Using both hands, he parts the see of jackets, pulls the chain to switch the light on, and discovers that the pile of skin on the floor belongs to none other than his favorite leopard print jacket. He checks the letter opener for blood, finds none.

Chuck rests his head against the wall behind the TV stand and monitors his racing pulse with two fingers to the neck.

"I must be losing it again," Chet says, laughing at the pile of twice-slain leopard.

The resident who lives directly above stomps their ceiling and shouts, "Do I have to call the cops again?"

*Again?*

Chet flicks his ceiling the bird before tearing a coat off the hanger, sliding his arms into the sleeves and thrusting the hood over his head. The jacket's made of black pleather with a stitched-on, gray, cloth hoodie.

There's a moment of dread as Chet unlocks the door. The next natural step is to unlatch the chain which currently dangles from having been snapped in half, but since Chet clearly has many thoughts clouding his judgement, he hurries out into the hallway, forgetting to lock up, and scurries off.

Chuck shimmies out from behind the industrialized metal stand and crawls across the long, oriental carpet, by the waist-high Greek columns displaying the marble statues of Beethoven, Bach and Will Smith.

By the purple futon.

By a pirate-themed treasure chest.

And finally, into the snug study where there's a fat oak desk sandwiched between two gargantuan wall units. There're clusters of books spread amongst the shelves. Encyclopedias. Text books on accounting, calculus and physics. Here's one for the police exam and another about Ohio laws and regulations. Oh, and look, a nonfiction title about America's most famous serial killers. The fiction titles prove even more telling: *American Psycho*, *Mr. Mercedes*, *Misery*, *Carrie* (Christ, we get it, you like King), and *And Then There Were None*.

Seems Chet was in the middle of handwriting a letter. The quill's dunked inside a tar-pit ink jar with gooey, black lines running down the sides. Chuck snags the letter and reads what's written:

~~Dear~~ *Mom, Dad and Mia,*

*You probably have a lot of questions. Good, you should. All of you.*
*I'll be a doll and address the most obvious: why have I done this horrible thing?*

*Well, I'm tired. Fed up. And frankly, I don't possess any other outlets for my rage.*

*Have you ever felt a stampede of emotions building inside of you? Have you ever sliced apart your skin for some release? It doesn't work. The pressure's always there.*

*What am I talking about?*

*I'm rambling, I know.*

*Think back, far back, to our lives together. What do you remember? Because when I look back, all I remember are Mom, Dad, Mia. I don't see me. Sure, I'm there in pictures, but when Mom had her mental breakdown, didn't the family rally behind her? When Dad gave himself to God, didn't we rally? And when Mia totaled her car in high school and killed her best friend, wasn't that the first time we actually rallied? Isn't that what later caused Mom's mental break down? Why Dad turned to God?*

*The funny thing is, as far back as I can remember, most of my memories play out more of the same. Rally behind Mom's stupid business idea to make yarn teddy bears and sell them on eBay. Rally behind Dad's self-righteous hunger strike to make himself seem holier than thou. Rally behind Mia's pregnancy scare. News to you, huh, Dad? Yup, your perfect angel found out she was pregnant a few years ago and went and had it killed. She came to me and Mom bawling her eyes out. She wanted the baby more than anything but feared for its safety. I've always wondered what you would've told her. I know how much hatred you harbor for Chuck regardless of how righteous you perceive yourself to be. Would you have gone against your God's wishes and told her to take a life? Well guess what, Dad, I told her to go with her gut, to have that baby, but Mom talked her into the abortion. Mia tried to get Chuck to leave the force, but we all know how that worked out.*

*After the procedure, Mia wasn't Mia anymore.*

*I'm curious, when you read this letter, or when someone mentions this fact to you, how will you view your sweet, precious baby? Will you treat her like you've treated me after discovering my homosexuality?*

*I am not a plague. I am, however, a person. But when I look back, I don't see Chet. I see Mom...Dad...Mia. Where was I? Where was my rallying family?*

*Is this not the time when we need unity the most?*
*Whatever. We've made our beds. Time to sleep.*
*I am who I am.*
*Fuck th*

The rest trails off. Chuck slaps the letter against the desk. He punches the air. He spits and grinds his teeth. How could she? They used to talk about everything under the sun. It's been years? That means most of their children-related discussions happened post-abortion.

*Abortion.*

He never thought there'd be a word more vile than the C word, but there it is: *abortion*.

And he never thought he'd endure pain worse than the time he plunged head-first into a vat filled with three tons of hot-off-the-press tacks.

But here it is: *abortion*.

Chuck's bound to the apartment, not able to leave until Chet gets back so he can rip the punk's head off and proceed to run with it over to Mia's condo to use as a door knocker. When she answers, he'll scream, "How could you?" and she'll scream back, "How could *you*?" He'll finish with, "Your brother was a serial killer, what's your fucking excuse?"

Within three minutes, the pacing begins.

In five, Chuck's already rooting around the pantry and fridge, hunting for anything to smother his feelings, but everything's fat-fucking-free.

After fifteen minutes of sucking on saliva, Chuck's back to pacing, this time at a breakneck pace.

Where in the hell did Chet go, on vacation?

He should be back by now.

At the half hour mark, Chuck threatens to leave. He pops out into the hallway, and then as fast, pops back in.

It's too stuffy in the apartment, what with it being filled with death and lies, so Chuck rushes to open a window. He draws the blind and catches the sun setting in the west. He didn't realize how late it had gotten.

Tomorrow's supposed to be the big day, but tonight is the real showdown.

Shy of the hour mark, Chuck can't control his emotions any longer. He barrels out of the building and sprints wildly through the streets, proving the theory that Mia *has* and *always will* matter more than Chet.

By the time he reaches her storm door, he no longer feels the urge to smash it open with her mailbox. A nearly five-mile run will have that effect on anyone. Chuck does, however, let himself in. He doesn't remove his grimy boots according to one of the house rules. He *does* extend her some amount of common courtesy by long-stepping onto a fluffy throw at the bottom of the landing to wipe some of the gunk off, but it's currently being occupied by a wide array of footwear. Everything from penny loafers to high heels to sneakers to flats. And then they call out to him, wondering who's arrived to join their rebooted dinner party.

Chuck sidesteps into the hallway, and there they are: Mom, Dad, Mia, Chet—all huddled together at the intimate kitchen table meant for four, gasping at his presence.

Mia immediately intercepts him before he can take another step forward. "I can't even ask if you've lost your mind, because we're far beyond that."

"I could say the same about you."

She gives him the look. "What'd *I* do?"

There won't be an easier lead-in than this, but the nosy audience injects Chuck with stage fright.

"What's going on here?"

"We're having dinner," she says, "you know, like normal people?"

"Hope you made extras." He blows by.

"This is a pri—"

"I'll just grab the rocking chair Nana gave ya." As he rounds the table of three, Chuck winks and waves. They're hesitant to return the gesture, even more so when this uninvited guest drags a heaping pile of wood across the linoleum and wedges himself in-between Henriette and Orpheus at the round tabletop. At this position, he's seated directly across from Chet.

Mia puts on her best Suzy Homemaker smile and serves up dinner, a full-size aluminum foil tray filled with gluten free lasagna drowning in red sauce, a big, badass bowl of tossed salad, and of course sliced garlic bread, also gluten free.

Once everybody's seated, they stare at the rising steam—it symbolizes the fog which has always prevented them from seeing eye to eye to eye to eye to eye.

And cue grace.

Nothing.

How about now?

Nada.

Out of all the people to break this silence, Henriette reaches for the spatula and slaps a corner slice of lasagna onto her doubled-up paper plates. "You could have served meat, Dear."

The table's too shocked to address this, along with the fact that Orpheus, too, fills his plate without uttering a word of graciousness to God.

During the chewing, so much noisy chewing (they sound like cattle), Chet eats through more of his fingernails than the pitiful servings of food oozing across his plate.

"We shouldn't beat around the bush any longer," Henriette says, swallowing a tiny gulp. She points her spork twice, once at Mia and once at Chuck. "The wedding is happening, no?"

Mia reluctantly nods, Chuck shrugs.

"For future reference, you typically grant your guests several weeks' notice, not one day." Why have Orpheus and Henriette suddenly switched bodies?

"What are you implying?" Mia says. "That this won't work?"

"I'm not implying."

"You're implying I'll marry again."

"Eat." She leads by example.

"Since you're no longer a mute, Mom, why don't you tell me how you really feel?"

"Mia!" is the first word to catapult off Orpheus' tongue.

Henriette sticks the spork in his face. "No, we shouldn't hold back."

Chet slaps his hands against the table and laughs mockingly. "You finally going to stick up for me?"

"Don't be selfish—this isn't about you, Chet."

Staring directly at Chuck, he throws his hands in the air as if to say, "See this bullshit?"

Chuck tosses him another shrug.

"Your father and I are getting a divorce. Don't look at me like that. This wasn't a spur of the moment type decision—it's been in the making for many years. If you must know, I have a boyfriend. We're taking things slow, out of respect for your father."

It's Orpheus' turn to shrug as everybody looks his way.

"Be certain you're not settling, Mia."

"Wait a minute." Orpheus twists in his chair to face her head-on and say, "Did you settle for me?"

"In retrospect, yes."

"I saved you."

"Oh please, you haven't been able to save anyone."

Orpheus twists back, clamps his hands on the edge of the table as if holding on for dear life and says, "Would you like to know how your mother and father actually met?"

The children look to their mother. She says, "Go ahead. Like I said, hold nothing back."

"Your mother was a whore."

"And your father was a John."

"Let me finish."

"As if you haven't talked enough for us both to last an eternity."

He goes to smack her but scrounges together the strength to hold back. "I'm not proud of my younger self, but if it weren't for my misguided youth, I wouldn't have found your mother. She had been brought here from overseas. She was stolen as a baby and forced into sex slavery. By the time I met her—"

"Paid."

"'Met'. By the time I 'met' her, she was broken and lost. I had never done what you're thinking, and I didn't with your mother. I was shy, so was she. When my time was up, I asked the man what it would take to release her. He gave me a dollar amount, and after seven or so odd months, I scrounged together the money, and the rest is history."

Everybody remains shocked and silent.

"I've always felt indebted."

"You loved me, don't lie."

"I honestly don't know."

"Do you love Victor?"

"It's too soon to tell, but I feel different."

"And what did you mean about me not saving anyone? I've dedicated my life to saving people."

"What about those who matter most? Have you saved your own daughter?"

"What about me!" Chet knees the table, nearly overturning it. Lasagna spills everywhere.

"Chet," Mia places a hand on his shoulder, "calm down, okay? Don't lose your cool."

"Easy for you to say, Sis. You've never felt hatred like this. Everybody's always loved you to death, including me. Truth is, you're spoiled. Maybe it's about time you get spoon-fed a dose of reality."

She gives him the "who-even-are-you" look. "Why're you acting like this?"

"Especially the day before her wedding?" Orpheus adds.

"You fucking people." Chet shoots to his cream socks. "For a bunch of goody-two-shoes who claim to be sooo enlightened, you're all the blindest bastards I've ever met."

"Not me, Chet." Chuck rises, both in body and spirit.

"What secret are you going to blurt out now, Mr. Tattletale?"

"I know what you're doing."

"Oh, well this should be interesting." Chet shuffles his sweaty hands. "Come on, let's hear what you've got to say."

The heads swing from side to side, Meerkat-like. The anticipation for what Chuck has to say couldn't possibly be any higher.

"Um—"

"Um what? If you've got something to say, now's the time."

"How about we step outside?"

"*Or* you could say it in front of everybody like a real man."

Is this a game of chicken to Chet?

"Liver," Chuck says.

Chet waits for him to finish, but it appears Chuck's stopped working. "Liver what?"

"Liv—er."

"You could say it a hundred different ways, but I have no damn clue what you're getting at."

Judging by looks alone, it seems true. Chet hasn't flinched, hasn't given a single indication of understanding the word's significance, but then again, he *is* the many-faced man.

Chuck leans over his plate, dipping his crotch in sauce. "*Bomb.*"

"Is this even real life?" Chet shoots a glance to each of his family members. "Are you people robots?"

"Nice jacket, Chet."

"See," he looks around, "what's that even mean?"

Chuck fists the table. "Stop playing games!"

"Me? How about you, Psycho!"

Orpheus catches Chuck's fist in a net of hands. "I won't stand for violence tonight." This coming from the man who almost smacked his wife into next week. "Let's step out back, I'd like to have a word."

235

The door's located a foot behind Chet's chair. On their stroll around the table, the two stare each other down. And before Chuck steps out onto the square patio, he jabs the door, which in turn jabs Chet's chair, which in turn jabs Chet in the rear, which in turn pisses Chet off and brings some much-needed joy to Chuck.

Both doors slam shut.

"Can I help you?"

"You certainly can," Orpheus says. "Look."

"Where?"

"At me I guess."

"And?"

"I know we haven't seen eye to eye, but what you said the other night has really stuck with me."

"You mean right before you had me arrested?"

"If it matters, I almost called them off."

"It doesn't."

"Very well, but per your suggestion, I have decided to reconcile the situation between Chet and I."

"You're timing couldn't be any worse."

"I'm going to go in there, sit Chet down and talk to him man to woman."

"He's still a guy, you know?"

"Right. Man to man, then."

"What, pray tell, are you going to say?"

"If it makes no difference to you, I plan to say something similar to what you did the other night. 'Chet, you are my son, and I love you. I will go to Hell with you if this is what it takes.'"

"Are *you* a robot? Never mind, it doesn't matter. But seriously," Chuck pats Orpheus' back, "maybe you were right— maybe you should disown your son."

"This isn't the place for your inane humor, Chuck." He climbs the three concrete, patio stairs. "Please, take my wife and Mia for a stroll. Do you think you can handle such a task?" Orpheus pushes into the kitchen. "Where'd he go?"

Henriette and Mia both point at the front door and how it's been blown wide open.

# SATURDAY

## Chapter 32
## Until Death

Chuck jolts upright. The motion causes a sharp stab in his genital direction, so he throws the breakfast-inspired quilt Nana made him off and pries open his tighty-whities. Praise be, all is well…endowed.

Yet, he's not alone in bed. Resting on the neighboring pillow is a brand-new bottle of half-empty American Honey. Or maybe it's half full. Who the F wants to get into such a fickle debate, especially with a crushing headache which feels like it could tip into a full-blown migraine at a moment's notice?

There's ringing, could be in his ears. Searching the area, his nightstand's been kicked over, and his cherished lava lamp from the mid '90s has erupted green ooze all over his winter-green-painted wall and pools into his creamy shag carpet.

Chuck slides off the bed, which proves to be quite a literal pain in the ass, and finds his closet blown open. The clothes which were once ironed and color-coordinated and hung properly on hangers are spewed across the floor. He digs deep to locate the cell.

*Serial Killer calling…*

"Chuck," the serial killer says, "I'm soooooooooo excited for today, so much so, that'll I'll be attending today's festivities in the flesh. Maybe you'll spot me. Here's a hint, I'll be dawning black and white, the attire of a referee."

"As long as you bring a gift, whatever." Does Chet know Chuck knows?

"I think you'll be *floored* by my surprise. Perhaps even marvel at how *big* and *long* it is. At the *load* it can carry. Speaking of, I better get to *warming* it up. See ya in an hour!"

Click.

An hour? Checking the time, Chuck discovers it's already 8:03am. Even though the wedding's not until 9:00am, he vaguely remembers sharing a glass or two or three of wine with Orpheus along with a half-hug, at which Orpheus whispered into his ear, "Nooo hooomoo," and then later, much later, before Chuck stumbled over to his neighbor's condo, then to another's, then finally to his, he remembers saying to Orpheus, "Pick you eight sharp, ya heard?" at which Orpheus thrashed his head, trying to nod, but fell head-first into a China cabinet, prompting Mia to barrel down the stairs, and Chuck to wave and smile and say, "Care, take it," as he reversed down the condo stairs.

Chuck must hurry, which has become the story of this story. While hunting through the closet's spilled guts for his tuxedo which Rosa went and fetched last night, he witnesses a burst of light, then this:

<<<<<<<<

*Buck-naked Chuck ripped the closet door open. He gave his wardrobe a bear hug and hurled it to the carpet. Then he reached forward and clenched the iron rod and slurred, "Hi...hit you...me...your breast shot!"*

*Rosa bounced off his rear, wobbled to and fro, tripped on the pile, yelled incoherent words at a gray, wrinkled-into-an-accordion tank top, then swooped back in with the cucumber Duct taped to her hairless pelvis.*

239

"Whaaaaaaaaat?" Chuck slurs, kneeling inside the mess. "Ha-ha, yeah right."

<<<<<<<<<

*Buck-naked Rosa towered over Chuck, and in-between hard rams, boomed, "Who your mommy?"*

Chuck rams, no, jams, no, *puts* two fingers down his throat and hurls inside a trench coat. There's an immense release of pressure inside his head.

*I banged Rosa?*

He peeks inside his underwear and locates the brownish-red stain.

*No, she banged me!*

8:09am.

There's no time to hunt for the tux, so Chuck tears an outfit from the pile at random. Of course he'd select the one pair of desert camouflage cargo shorts he pondered tossing out last week along with the navy-blue polo he's always regretted keeping handy.

Rosa's unconscious downstairs, stuffed inside a carpet. As Chuck unrolls the tequila-scented burrito, she thumps across the floor. This doesn't wake Rosa from her rather loud snorefest, which is good, because she's still sporting that barbaric contraption. Chuck plucks the cucumber off in one motion, then flings the damp vegetable behind his couch. It leaves a brown splat on the wall, but whatever. It's not until the tearing of Duct tape that Rosa jolts awake.

"Kelly Osborne!" Noticing her state, she instantly shields her breasts and vagina, leaving her exposed, flawless set of abs to taunt him. "Where're my clothes? What happened?"

Chuck balls the tape behind his back. "We got wasted." He gulps. "Remember?"

She wags her head. "We didn't, *you know?*"

"Ha-ha, fuck no! I stayed strictly in *my* room, in *my* bed, *all night, alone*, while you did whatever down here."

"You sure I was by myself?"

"I wouldn't lie to you, Rosa, not since we started not lying to each other."

She lets out an enormous, liquor-filled sigh of relief. "Alcohol almost cut my life short once. I used to abuse it to escape. While sober, people would recount all the bizarre things I did. They'd laugh at me, mock me, so I'd turn around and drink some more to forget. Then I'd go do even crazier shit."

"Mind laying off the cursing today?"

"Did you find God or something last night?"

"It's deterring from a rather fine story is all."

"Well then, how's this to plug you back in?"

*No, no, no.*

"I know I've been riding you pretty damn hard lately."

*Seriously?*

"Even though I don't show it, you mean a lot to me. Hell, I'd be back in prison if you hadn't taken one for the team."

"I think that's quite enough. It's 8:11, sooo—"

"Hold on."

"…"

"I've had a hard time fitting into this world, Chuck. I've always felt like a square peg trying to drill its way into a round hole. Everywhere I'd go, I'd try to force myself in, but I never fit. But it's different with you. It's like my peg fits your hole perfectly, and I'm able to slide right into place. What I'm saying is we make a great pair."

Chuck muzzles her mouth with a ball of her filthy, unwashed clothes, and before he can rush out the front door, she spits out her stank underwear and screams, "Who crammed the stick up *your* ass?"

It doesn't get any better in the minivan he commandeered from his neighbor. Halfway down the block, there's a Labrador seated on the welcome mat of a door stoop licking its butthole clean.

A mile later, there's a kid sucking on a fat fudge bar. The fudge is smeared across his lips, cheeks and chin.

"Chuck!" Rosa smacks the dash, drawing his rubbernecking attention to the stopped SUV. Chuck slams on the brakes to avoid collision, but the tailgater in the Audi rear-ends them.

As the flamboyant man springs out of his car and approaches with hands thrown high in the air, the suspended TV screen in the SUV plays a movie where the quarterback reaches between the center's legs and clamps his hands around the ball. The camera zooms in on the snap which happens in super slow-motion. The shot plays out like the birth of a football, or the quarterback removing the first of a series of anal beads.

Audi man raps his knuckles against the window and speaks through the glass, "Hey, Man, you—"

"Better have insurance?" Chuck hops out, thumps him in the nose with a forehead and catches him mid-fall, but the guy's still conscious. He slurs his words: "—safe and sound?"

"Fuck, I'm sorry, Guy, I had no idea you'd be kind."

"I was texting."

"I knew it!" Chuck readies a fist.

"Texting my sister who's at the hospital."

"Oh, damn."

"That's my father's Audi, not mine. I didn't have any other means to get there. Not at the speed required."

"Death in the family?"

"As if. My sister tweaked her ankle. I dropped them off forever ago and am running hella late. Smoked too much bud at a bud's house. I said 'bud' twice!"

Their foreheads connect again, this time knocking Audi man down for the count. After Chuck tosses the body in the backseat of the minivan, Rosa says, "And you're doing what exactly?"

"Upgrading us. Let's go."

They go, and the Audi gets them there by 8:20am. It's record time, but Orpheus isn't in the celebrating mood. After sliding into the back, he confesses: "Henriette went with *him*."

"Sucks to be you."

"Just reunite me with Chet, Chuck. He's all I've got left in this pathetic world."

Until Chuck puts a bullet through his head.

"I hope it's not too late."

*Okay, stop laying it on so thick.*

"Hey, look," Orpheus points, "those two fellows are fencing with bananas, how odd."

"SILENCE!" Chuck blasts the radio for the next fifteen minutes. At 8:35am, they skid to a halt outside Chet's apartment. Orpheus reaches for his door's handle, but Chuck hits lock and says, "I got him! I mean, I'll bring him down. He's mine?"

Everybody stares.

"Wait here." He flies out of the car and into the building and doesn't even bother with the elevator because the thrill of making a premature bust grants him an adrenaline boost which whisks him up the eight flights of stairs faster than any mechanical box ever could.

At room 813, he boots the door off its hinges. With The Judge drawn and aimed, Chuck glides into the living room, chanting, "Knock, knock, mother fucker."

Unfortunately, the mother fucker is suspended in midair by a bungee cord quadruple-wrapped around his neck and knotted to a ceiling rafter. Chet gift-wrapped his body, up to his chest, in a plastic, black bag covered in smiley faces. There's an extravagant red bow tied around his waist. Tucked into it is a vanilla envelope.

Chuck swipes the letter opener and cuts the rope. Chet's body thuds against the floor. The neighbor below pounds the ceiling with a broom handle and tells Chet to die already! After finding neither a heartbeat nor pulse, Chuck mumbles, "Too soon."

He slides the letter out. It's the same version from last night, only it's been completed. The newly penned paragraph reads:

*Fuck the God who hates me. I plan on spending eternity with the one who will love and cherish me for the person I was born. Too bad none of you will ever have the opportunity to meet him, because he sure is a great guy—you just never gave him a chance to show it.*

*Your mistake,*

*Chet*

*P.S. – I lied about Mia having an abortion. She was never pregnant. There, I'm dying the bigger, better man. Fuck ya'll.*

"We've got a problem," Chuck says with his head dunked inside the Audi. "Chet isn't coming."

Orpheus leans forward and wipes the sweat from his brow. "For the first time ever, I hope you're joking."

"He needs time."

"If he's not going, I'm certainly not. Now let me out of here."

"Whoa, hold on, he's still coming. It's just—"

"Just what?"

"Damnit, Orpheus, if you must know, he's freaking out about his makeup, okay? And he was wondering if Rosa," he flicks her in the arm, "could assist him in painting it on perfectly."

The partners step out and speak over the roof.

"No," Rosa says, "no way."

"Chet's dead."

"You killed him?"

"He fucking hung himself!"

"Then why're you telling me this?"

"You ever see *Weekend at Bernie's?*"

"I'm not bringing a corpse to the wedding as my plus one."

"If Chet's not there and Orpheus skips out, Mia's not going to marry me."

Rosa sighs. "Then how am I supposed to get him there?"

He explains how to commandeer a vehicle.

"You're sick."

8:41am.

"Chet's in room 813. Push on the door, and it'll fall right off."

She scatters, and he hops behind the wheel.

"I should tell you something," Orpheus says at 8:49am, four miles from the temple.

"Probably not."

"This is a sting, Chuck. The entire wedding. Your own blue bloods are going to arrest you. I don't know if they'll wait for your 'I dos', but I thought you deserved to know."

"I appreciate the heads up," Chuck says, "but your daughter's worth it."

Orpheus smiles.

Upon arrival, Chuck parks in the fire lane, and a bearded homeless man packed inside a potato sack says, "Yo, Sonny, you can't be a parkin' there!"

"How you doing, Greg?"

"Good, how're—" The undercover officer wags a dirty fist. "Damn it!"

Chuck hurdles the temple's cement stairs. To the lady in hot pink on step number nineteen, choking on a joint, Chuck says, "Really, Blanch, black face?"

At the tippy top, on step twenty-four, Aaban Hossain greets Chuck with a handshake, a hug, a peck on the cheek, and a forehead snuggle. "Welcome, Chuck Steak, and congratulations my good sir!" He hugs again, and pecks the other cheek, and maintains an excruciatingly long forehead snuggle. "The entire Muslim community has come together and gone to great lengths to accommodate you and your bride! We simply cannot wait to watch this special event unfold!"

Chuck's cell dings:

*ATTENTION, ATTENTION! Change of plans! I couldn't contain my excitement any longer and decided to park your wedding gift out back. "Park?" you say? Yes, if you must know, it's a bus, Chuck. There, surprise ruined. You probably thought it was a giant dildo by the way I was describing it, LOL! Let me go ahead and blow the rest of the surprise as well☺ You're getting married on this bus. That's right. I don't care how you do it, but you need to cram no less than fifty people, including your lovely bride-to-be, inside. You have twenty minutes to get it done. By then, if you're not traveling at least 55mph, Mia dies. If successful, you'll be given an additional five minutes to tie the knot, and if you don't, Mia dies. If at any time the bus's speed falls below 55mph, Mia dies. And if you even think of accusing me of stealing this concept, Mia dies. "Speed" is one of my favorite movies of all time—if anything, I'm paying homage to it.*

Aaban Hossain stares at Chuck with a heavenly grin.

"Ummm, about the accommodations…"

"Yes?"

It's better to show than tell, so Chuck runs inside.

A tiny hole in the wall on the far side of the temple leads to an equally tiny hallway. There's a door two-thirds the way in with a piece of printed paper reading *BRIDES' ROOM* tacked into the wood. Chuck wonders how many brides are beyond the solid mahogany as he pounds a fist which barely registers.

A Native American man slips out and seals the door shut. He's very broad, and every inch of his rough skin is covered in tribal tattoos, even parts of his face. His slick, jet-black hair is pulled into a fine ponytail, and his earrings look like miniature daggers. Which throws Chuck for a loop when the man extends a tiny hand and says, "How," then pauses, then says, "can I help you?"

Chuck's thrilled for this man since it's the second Native American he's seen this week, which is a good indication that they're starting to reclaim their land, but that is neither here nor there. Especially when Chuck goes to nudge him out of the way, but he remains stationary like a seven-headed totem pole.

"But I'm the groom," Chuck barks.

"I was told to keep you out."

"And who the F are you again?"

"Ummm—"

"Okay, Ummm, who gave you this order?"

"Ummm—"

"You ordered yourself?"

"My girlfriend did."

"So *you're* the guy." Orpheus' commanding voice strikes like a sniper rifle, each word a resounding, well-placed CRACK! "You're my Henriette's play thing?"

"Ummm—"

Despite his thirteen-inch disadvantage, Orpheus doesn't hesitate to place his chin on Ummm's pounding chest and speak upwind: "Do you know how I know why you're going straight to Hell?"

"I, ummm—"

"Because I'm going to send you there."

With 17:03 left, Chuck wedges in-between the two. "Guys, how would Mia feel if she overheard this? Why don't you both take your nonsense outside?"

"Ummm—"

"You're making the most sense ever, Chuck. Has Hell since frozen over?"

"Tell me when you get there." Chuck shovels them both out of the hole. "Preferably by postcard."

Orpheus waves frantically at the entrance, where Chet leans awkwardly against a candelabra. There's an orange scarf wrapped thrice around his neck to conceal the deep, pale indentations, and reflective Aviators to hide his glazed-over eyeballs.

Chet doesn't wave, because he's dead, but Orpheus seizes this opportunity to sway his son—to prove he's not merely a man of words. Orpheus reaches for a chalice set on a foldout TV stand and cocks it way back. Wine splashes and douses the carpet. But Ummm has since retreated back to the *BRIDES' ROOM* to barricade the door.

"Congratulations, Ummm," Chuck says, "you've officially become a nuisance." Chuck cocks his leg way, way back, but Ummm crosses his thick thighs to shield his stallion. Perhaps it's a pony, nobody knows. Point is, Ummm believes he's figured Americans out. Little was he expecting Chuck to come at his neck with two pairs of timid ticklers.

Ummm's brought to his knees, shouting, "Come on, ha, ha, ha, stop it!"

Chuck drives Ummm into the ground with a double-fisted, ten-finger volley of stomach-stabbing silliness.

The chalice thuds against the back of Ummm's head. Orpheus stands there, dumbfounded. He burps, because he engulfed whatever wine remained to stop it from sloshing about and staining the carpet. "He okay?"

"Gee, I don't know, let me check." Chuck places a hand on Ummm's chest. "Great, he's dead," Chuck kicks to his feet and shakes his head, "and there's no way I'm fixing it. Your turn." He stabs Orpheus in the chest.

Orpheus asks how, so Chuck explains.

"I'm not 'making out' with my wife's lover! How dare you suggest such?"

*Whatever.*

With 15:42 to go, Henriette answers the mahogany door sporting her classic dead-inside stare.

248

"Wow, you sure look lovely today, Mrs. Johnson. Or is it Miss Johnson now?"

The joke doesn't register anywhere on her scowl.

"You do know this isn't a funeral, right?" She's decided to wear all black, save for the white belt and high heels.

Still nothing.

Chuck places his hands on the door and applies a generous amount of force, but Henriette, that clever girl, releases her hold, causing him to flail into the quaint room and tackle the table containing a vast array of essential cosmetics, including the rest of Mia's face.

Half-faced Mia shrieks to the high Heavens. Chuck springs from the pile of spilled containers and vials and bottles, their once bright colors pooling together to form a nasty gray, surely a sign of the cloud which will follow him from this moment forward, and says to his nearly naked bride-to-be, "No reason for alarm, it's just me."

She stabs a purple fingernail at the extra-large dress pinned underneath the bleeding table.

"I've got some exciting news which might liven the mood."

She taps her bare foot.

"We're getting married on a bus, so you can dress casual."

"GET—"

Chuck backs away.

"—OUT!"

While maneuvering around bronco-riding Orpheus, Chuck doesn't have the heart to tell him *less tongue, more blowing*.

Out in the temple, where Johnsons stand disjointed on one side and Muslims kneel in harmony on the other (they're occupying the space reserved for Chuck's family since he doesn't have any), Chuck whistles, but nobody hears over the raucous gossiping and an organ player's subpar melody.

Chuck swipes a golden saucer from the TV stand and flings it across the room. It smashes through the stained-glass window of an ornate tabernacle which was transported from Mia's church and set in the corner where it belongs. Suddenly he's got everybody's jaw-dropped attention.

An elderly woman pumps her cane into the air and shouts, "He killed Jesus!"

Too many people agree.

"Yeah, okay," Chuck says, "just like how I supposedly killed Santa Claus last year when that stray missile struck his hut in the mall?"

"What's he saying?" some guy shouts.

"That Jesus ain't real!" some woman shouts back.

"Let's teach 'em a lesson!" a whole handful holler.

As a few rash souls scramble forward, Chuck attempts to get ahead of this with only 11:16 left: "Hold on! You people are being completely selfish!"

"'You people'? What's he mean 'you people'?"

"Whaddya think he means?"

"Excuse me," Chuck raises his black hand and twists and turns it Miss America style, "but I can say that!"

They gasp.

"Enough already! I need fifty guests to head out back and hop on a bus."

"This guy tryin' to make an ill-timed Rosa Parks joke or somethin'?"

Chuck's getting nowhere fast, especially when Henriette materializes in front of his face and spits, "What sort of stunt are you trying to pull now?"

"It feels like," he wipes the slobber from his lips, "we just French-kissed." Before she can smack him, he says, "You gotta have faith."

She mimics a buzzer. "Wrong. I've had faith for many years and look where it's gotten me. And I've married a man I wasn't in love with and look how that's turned out." She bobs a thumb at the tiny hole where Ummm's regained consciousness and is engaging Orpheus in a rolling, all-out tickle war. "I've kept my opinion to myself for far too many years, but you're toxic, Chuck Steak, and my Mia doesn't love you, and I'll be damned if I stand idly by a second longer. This wedding's officially over."

He snags her shoulder. "Henriette, please, give me one last chance!"

"I won't let you turn my daughter into me."

As she tears free, Chuck withdraws The Judge and clobbers her over the back of the head with it, sending her unconscious body to the carpet.

"Okay," an unnerving amount of Johnsons drift toward him, "so that looked way worse than it is."

They're done listening, which is great, because Chuck's done talking. He cocks the gun and takes aim.

"Whoa there," says the nearest Johnson, frozen in his tracks, "now you're actually trying to offend us, right?"

He's referring to the way Chuck aims the gun sideways in his black hand.

"That's not how we shoot, partially because it looks stupid, but mainly because it's impractical."

Chuck turns the gun straight.

"Gee, thanks."

"Don't mention it."

Rosa appears. She's dawning a sleek, black and white tuxedo. Chuck wonders if it's *his*. He stops wondering as they bump rumps. Tis a painful reminder.

"What's the plan?" she says with her dukes raised.

"Put those down," he bats them away, "and here, take this." He hands off his cannon. "I need you to gather fifty guests and load them onto the bus parked out back." He explains how to use force. She explains how she's getting tired of running all these side errands. He laughs, because she's funny, and this is *his* story, so a side-character is all she'll ever be, unless, of course, she gets a spin-off, but they suck, so best of luck. Chuck hurries off.

In the tiny hallway, Orpheus tries to clog the way through with both his person and questions. What's going on out there? Does what transpired make him gay? Will Chet appreciate such? If so, he won't suddenly find his son attractive, will he? He had always thought Chet was handsome, but not like that, Orpheus assures him.

"For fuck's sake, do you ever listen to yourself?" Chuck barges by, straight into the *BRIDES' ROOM* to the sound of, "I SAID GET OUT, **GET OUT!**"

4:03 left according to the cell he drops back into his pocket, so Chuck scoops Mia into his arms and sprints out of there with her kicking and screaming. It's not like such a reaction isn't warranted. Mia is, in fact, stripped down to the bare minimum. She's sporting a tight, white bra which can hardly contain her breasts, and a black thong which hardly leaves anything to the imagination, especially the tampon string which sails in the wind.

"You bastard!" she screams, latching onto a patch of hair behind his ear. Chuck's quick to warn, "Don't you even—" but she yanks anyway, prompting this: "I should just let you die!"

"Excuse me?"

2:59 left.

"I didn't say anything."

"I just heard you."

"No, *you* said it."

As Chuck staggers out of the temple's entrance, Edward (who's been dreaming of rearranging Anderson's office to accommodate his physical and cultural lifestyles) releases a clump of balloons into the atmosphere in favor of performing a spontaneous yet heroic tactical maneuver. He plucks the shiny, red ball attached to his nose off and speaks directly into the nostrils, "I'm going in. I repeat, Mister Bonkers is taking Chuck Steak down once and for all!"

However, Chuck accidentally collides with Edward, knocking him down the stairs. At the bottom, Edward cracks his broken nose into place and waits for the red ball to bounce within reach. He clutches it with a twisted hand and strains to pull it to his busted lips. "Don't worry, Houston, I'm going to make it."

"Goddamn it, you're fired!"

With 1:48 to go, Chuck slides down the iron railing on his tosh. Poor idea, because the bar digs into his crack, forcing out a guttural scream: "AHHHHHHHHHHHHHHHHHHHHHHH!"

"Jesus," Mia says, "why're you screaming? *I'm* the hostage!"

They have so much to talk about, but with 1:41 remaining, Chuck stumbles through the landing and hightails it around the temple.

With 59 seconds and counting, they'd have to be clinically blind to miss the hot-pink school bus illuminating the blacktop. Along the side, instead of stating which school district this bus hails from, it reads in enormous, white, capitalized letters: *WHY AM I MARRYING THIS BITCH?*

Luckily Chuck needn't explain as they've arrived onboard. He drops Mia with a much-needed yet terribly timed sigh of relief, and before she can lash out, they discover a mob of fuming Johnsons staring at them. Mia uses her arms to try and conceal as much of her own flesh as possible.

"I'll explain later?"

Okay, she decides to get one, good smack in.

Chuck can't help but snicker and say, "I saw a titty." His humor is lost on all but Rosa who cuts to the front of the bus and plops into the driver's seat. The keys have been left in the ignition, purposely. "Now what?"

"What the fuck is *she* doing here?" Mia swings, doesn't even come close to Rosa, but almost clips Chuck's ducking head. "Chuck, you dumb asshole, she—"

"MIA!" He's in her face, hasn't brushed, so it takes her breath away. He lowers his voice, sneaks it inside her ear. "In about ten minutes, when everybody is safe, I'll explain everything. I'll answer every question you have. But until then, just trust me this one last time."

Chuck turns to Rosa, would love to relay the synopsis to her, but a log line is all they have time for.

Rosa floors it, and the bus blows out of the parking lot. Well, not exactly. The bus more or less crawls forth and scrapes its undercarriage on the curb. It's quite pathetic from Chester the ice cream vendor's perspective. Which is why Chester the ice cream vendor is able to hop onto the rear bumper and rap his knuckles against the glass and shout, "Police, open up!"

With 31 seconds left, nobody raises a finger to aid Chester. Little do they know this is a black man disguised as a white man (using white face) disguised as an ice cream vendor. If they did, this would be a totally different story, but it's not, because they don't, so...

At 49mph and with 22 seconds to go, they blaze over a spike trap and blow out three tires, shedding several precious mphs. The police roadblock consisting of two parallel, unmarked vehicles (both "borrowed" from Avis) cost them a few more as the bus smashes through. Immediately after impact, an entire fleet of cruisers and tactical trucks converge on them from every angle imaginable.

With 18 seconds remaining, Rosa downshifts, and Chuck yells at the incoming world through the theater-screen-sized windshield, "Go, Bitch, go!"

Great, he gave it a gender. Next he'll probably give it a name.

Probably Betsy.

With 15 seconds and counting, the bus's odometer stretches its reach for 55. Only, a Mercedes blows through a red light, and the bus obliterates its entire left side. With the vehicle snagged under the bus's frontend, smoke and sparks douse the windshield, yet the odometer and its reading of 43mph remain visible.

12 seconds remain.

A head pokes out from within the smog. It's Edward! He surfs the convertible while drawing his firearm and pumps three well-placed bullets into the windshield, carving out a big enough chunk to toss a grenade through.

If a superior with any sense were present, or plugged into Edward's ear, they'd scream, "WHAT HAVE YOU DONE?"

The live grenade bounces down the aisle with 5 seconds left whilst the bus drudges along at 50mph.

Chuck takes off and dives under a seat to snag the grenade before it rolls one row yonder, then fists open the rear floor hatch, and with 2.5 seconds left, chip-shots the grenade against the street. The resulting explosion sets fire to their backend, but the force alone grants them the equivalent of a nitro boost, pushing them well over 58mph as the old timer expires.

A new one has since begun.

Overtime.

T-minus 2:59 and counting to perform a wedding.

T-minus 2:58 to get Mia to say, "I do."

"Chuck!" Rosa hollers.

Edward's fumbling around with his second grenade's pin.

With T-minus 2:51, Chuck puts his boot through the jagged hole, knocking Edward into the passenger seat and sending the grenade airborne. On its downhill trajectory, with T-minus 2:47, Chuck closes his eyes and kicks sideways, and even though his leg's since gone numb from the shards of glass eating through his flesh, he can feel the grenade connect with the side of his boot. The explosion happens somewhere else. No telling if there were any causalities.

That, dear friends, is the real Chuck Steak at work.

He turns toward his horrified hostages. "Where's Father Dennis?"

Everybody shrugs.

With T-minus 2:29, he needs a priest, pronto. Typically, they're a dime a dozen, but he only spots one in the far back. "Orpheus!"

But Orpheus only acknowledges the dead son splayed out across his lap. "You're safe with me, Ole buddy, Ole pal, I promise. I might've never been there for you when you needed me the most, but I'm here now, better late than never, right?" He halts his weeping to laugh. "I'm never going to leave your side again. You hear me, Buddy? Can you ever forgive me? Please, say something, anything."

He has yet to pluck those sunglasses off and peer into those lifeless, white orbs.

T-minus 2:20.

"Okay," Chuck claps his hands, "any ordained ministers hanging around?"

T-minus 2:15.

"*Really?* Nobody? That's impossible."

"And that's racist," someone shouts.

"Ma'am, you're ordained, aren't you?"

"Motha fucka, how'd you know?"

Chuck retrieves The Judge from Rosa's pants pocket and takes aim. "Congratulations—you're marrying me and Mia."

"Mia and I!" someone calls out.

"Whatever." He snags Mia from the 4th row.

She flails. "Not happening, Psycho!"

"Mia, we don't have—"

"NO!"

"Fine." He plucks an elderly woman from her seat and presses the gun against her temple. "I'll just have to shoot this sweet, little, old lady."

Mia crosses her arms. "She's from your side of the family."

"You serious?"

"Cynthia's friend from the home."

"Oh, how embarrassing." With T-minus 2:01, he helps the woman back into her seat and snags the flower girl instead.

Mia gasps. "That's just wrong."

"So, will you marry me?"

"Only to save this little girl's life."

"Okay, Lady, front and center!"

The ordained minister throws her hands up as she squeezes passed her hefty husband. "The name's Bernadette, Asshole."

"Very well, Bernadette, *go*."

She doesn't go.

"You need batteries or something?"

"I need a Bible, Smartass."

"Of course you do." With T-minus 1:52, he spots someone peculiar. Back in row 9, on the left-hand side, the seat meant for three kids is being occupied by a single, overtly large woman. Her rolls are wrapped tight in a black, ready-to-burst spandex dress, and her hairy arms are concealed up to the elbows in white gloves, and her bosoms are the worst bosoms Chuck's ever seen, because her obscene cleavage is a product of two rainbow-colored beach balls. And her profuse sweating has given her a dripping crown of white, because the black makeup is washing away, and underneath that ridiculously absurd afro hides Lieutenant Anderson.

*Mother fucker.*

Chuck pushes through Bernadette and Mia, and as he approaches row 9, Anderson stares harder at the purse in his lap. With one row separating them, Anderson unbuttons the purse, flips the flap, and his fingers crawl inside, reaching for the handle of a baby pistol. But with T-minus 1:43, Chuck blows by Anderson and swipes the golden bible Duct taped to the back window. It was blotting out part of the Emergency Exit sign. Written below the word *BIBLE*, it reads in pen, *Use for an express marriage.*

Surprisingly, the ice cream vendor has still managed to hang on. The fire has since dwindled on its own accord, mainly due to the wind, but it's left a memento—the vendor's charred overalls. He thumps his head against the dusty glass and yells, "Come on, help a brother out! I'm tired, and I'm cold, and I'm—"

With 1:38 remaining, there's no time to tell what else he *is*. And there's no time to push the sliding glasses back up the length of

Chet's nose. And there's certainly no time to tear Anderson's afro off and ask him what the F he's doing on this bus.

Chuck slaps the bible against Bernadette's chest. "Use this."

"Sexual harassment."

He cocks The Judge, twice.

Bernadette parts the book like Moses once parted the sea. Or so they say. As she clears her throat, Chuck massages both of Mia's hands within his unarmed paw and says, "Try to enjoy this. I know these aren't the greatest of circumstances, but—"

With T-minus 1:32, the bus scrapes against the bottom of the Hilltop's hill, and the people on the bus go up and down, up and down. Their speed steadily decreases from a comfortable 72mph by a rate of 1 mile every 22 feet. Based on this information, what is the slope of the hill if drag is unknown?

"Let's get this show on the road, Bernadette, literally." Chuck chuckles alone. "Tough crowd."

Her husband holds her by the waist so she doesn't go tumbling backward as she squints at the text. "Dearly beloved, we are gathered on this bus to witness the union between Chuck and Mia. Love is a four letter word, like wife and died."

Chuck swipes the book, flips it over and finds text scribbled on the backside: *If you opened this, the priest must read every single word or POP goes the Mia! LOL.*

Chuck slaps the bible back into Bernadette's hands, and with T-minus 1:15, says, "Read every single word."

She tugs at her tight neckline. "Chuck, Mia—please, stare deep into each other's eyes."

They do, but Mia's trying to murder him.

"Mia, do you promise to love Chuck? To not switch sexual sides even when pressured? To keep loving the D no matter what?"

Both Bernadette and Mia seem baffled with T-minus 1:02, so Chuck rests his firearm on the flower girl's shoulder and says, "Say you do."

"Fine, I do," she mumbles, "you fuckin' happy?"

"Language, there are children present." Rosa taught him that.

"Chet!" Orpheus shouts. "Why aren't you answering me?"

"Bernadette, focus."

"And Chuck, do you promise to…oh, this is good…do you promise to delete all of those photos you took of Mia's bare feet while she was sleeping because you have a foot fetish?"

"That's so not true."

"And do you promise to quit telling anybody who will listen, including complete strangers, that Mia's entire family are a bunch of conceited heretics who are going to Hell no matter how much good they think they're doing?"

"Is there much more?"

"Just a bit."

T-minus 52 seconds.

"Chuck, do you promise to stop telling Mia that the weird smell on her freshly dried clothes isn't mold, but you wiping them with your ass when she does something to anger you? Do you promise to come clean about how you accidentally shot Mia's ten-year-old dog dead a few years ago because you were trying out a new gun?"

Chuck whispers, "To be fair, the dog was like super old and—"

"Chuck, do you take Mia to be your lawfully awful wife?"

"I do, I do, I do!"

"Go ahead and—"

A S.W.A.T. truck rear-ends them, and all the people on the bus jerk back and forth, back and forth.

55mph with T-minus 43 seconds left. Another rear-ram knocks them up to 56mph with 40 left, and finally, the Hilltop flattens out. They have arrived at the pinnacle. But as someone famous once said, everything which goes up must come…

"Hold onto something!" Rosa shouts as their speed increases at an uncontrollable rate, and everybody on the bus goes flying forward, flying forward. At a near nosedive, the bus pushes 86mph, and two large brothers who only came for the reception's buffet clog the aisle, causing a buildup of guests.

Through the blockage, Chuck shouts, "Bernadette, finish your sentence!"

With T-minus 22 seconds, she pops her head out from someone's side roll and says, "You may now kiss the, AHHHHHHHHH!"

Anderson rolled out of his seat and squashed her flat. Who knows how many bones are broken. "You lose!" He takes aim, but before he can extend his arm fully and align the pistol with Chuck's throat, Anderson seizes as a series of vine-like veins reach out of his dress, up his neck and clench his reddened face tight. His mouth hangs wide open as the gun discharges, missing a dozen heads and instead piercing Rosa. As she's thrown into the window, her body spins the wheel, flipping the bus onto its side as it sparks downhill at a speed of 76mph.

With T-minus 11 seconds, Orpheus roars monstrously from inside the pile, "Chet, come back to me!"

Their speed drops to 59mph.

"Bernadette!"

She mumbles into his back, so he arches it, granting her enough breathing room to mutter, "Kiss her already, fuckhead!"

And with T-minus 3 seconds left, Chuck dives forward, his nose the tip of a rocket, and collides with Mia's face, shattering her nose in order to connect their lips.

The bus cries in mechanical agony as it hops a curb and taps against a general store's brick wall.

T-minus 0.

No explosion, no nothing. Chuck's either achieved success, or there was never a bomb in Mia's liver to begin with. Only an x-ray will tell, and it'll have to wait, because the S.W.A.T. truck skids to a halt outside the roof, and within seconds, a small team covered from head to toe in tactical gear rush the bus and sort through the clump of flesh. As the tumorous ball dwindles in size, several discoveries are made:

Chet's dead, so Orpheus begs for a gun—he even scratches and claws at a S.W.A.T. member's holstered sidearm to blow his brains out and follow his son into the depths of Hell. Orpheus is eventually dragged away kicking and screaming and pelvis thrusting.

It takes five S.W.A.T. members to heave Anderson's stiff body an inch off the glass-riddled floor and begin their journey outside. Without a doubt, he's dead, having endured an actual heart attack this time around.

Once the path is cleared, Mia flees on her own accord. She hurries to the other side of the street where a local woman hands her the jacket straight off her back. Mia says, "Thank you," in-between sobs.

Two S.W.A.T. members pin Chuck's arms behind his back and push him to the front, avoiding the wall of seats on their right, since they're walking and crunching through a path of fragmented windows. Before Chuck's nudged out the flaps of exposed windshield, he notices the blood dripping off the steering wheel.

He gulps.

They force Chuck down onto the sidewalk's edge, zip-tie his wrists together, then, as if it's completely necessary, draw their machineguns and place the silencers against his temples. The cool steel gives him chills as the three-lane road ahead seems like an endless ocean, and over there on the other side, on a deserted island he has no chance at reaching, awaits the love of his life. He's seen her exact expression countless times before, that of the emotionally wrecked victim. Another timer has begun, because soon, the adrenaline will wear off, and she'll find herself in a pit of despair, and she'll need Chuck to help pull her out.

He ponders what he could possibly tell the two gunmen, or gunwomen, or gunpeople, so they'll let him cross and be with her.

"Excuse me, but—"

"Shut up," one of them says.

"—I know how this looks, but—"

Chuck gets clobbered in the back of the head by a clip, prompting the machinegun to accidentally fire.

All goes black.

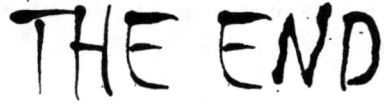

The bullet ricocheted off the asphalt and disappeared into the sky. Case closed.

Chuck spots Rosa splayed out on the concrete steps of a pawn shop. Her leaky shoulder's being stuffed with cloth by a woman from S.W.A.T. who tossed her helmet off and got right to work. While her bandage is zip-locked into place, Rosa eeks out a smile through her inflamed lips, then winces, to which Chuck mouths, "Pussy," which makes Rosa smile wider and wince so hard she hisses.

The five S.W.A.T. members have finally crammed Anderson's round body through the rectangular exit. One of them shouts, "My back, my back!" and drops Anderson's left shoulder, and the rest shout about not being able to bear the load. As the members wobble across the street, something in Anderson's back pocket slides out and catches the reflection of the sun. After another member drops out, Anderson's mid-section twists and droops closer toward the street, casting a shadow upon the mysterious object. It's some sort of silver rod tipped with a ruby red button.

*Button!*

As Chuck shoots to his boots, the pair guarding him stab their machinegun handles into his delts and scream, "On your knees!"

Anderson sways wildly like a hammock during a hurricane as the S.W.A.T. member clutching his kankles struggles to maintain grip.

Chuck makes fists and pries apart the zip-tie like it's taffy. Then he sweeps the S.W.A.T. members' legs out from under them, and they smack the pavement. He then takes off toward slumping Anderson with arms flailing like propeller blades, screaming, "Don't let go!"

But the kankle-bearer's given it his all, and his hands slip open like the mechanical claws in those stuffed animal games, so Chuck turns to his love and screams, "Mi—" but Anderson's dropped, and his rear flattens the button, and Mia's waist explodes, and two chunks of body rocket through the sky, raining blood and smoke upon the horrified masses. The civilians scamper off, screaming about terrorism in the Hilltop of all places, while the S.W.A.T. members draw their machineguns and take aim at the barbershop's fiery hole. Thankfully, nobody was getting a new hairdo. Unfortunately, the coat loaner was broiled and died of internal injuries suffered from being pelted against a telephone pole.

Chuck crashes several feet shy of Anderson and lets his body violently tumble across gravel and glass and shrapnel. He paints an uneven line of blood across the asphalt, not caring in the least if he bleeds out and dies. This is the first time he's never made it, and it feels like the end of the world.

He eventually flops to a stop and stares into the burning sun as the raging fire sizzles and crackles. There are cries and shrieks and frantic shouts sprinkled throughout. And sirens, too many to pinpoint. And it reeks of roasted flesh and burnt rubber. And the sky quickly fades to black from the smoldering smoke. And Chuck finally thinks there's some credibility to religion, because it feels like he's burning alive in Hell.

But then the hands of an angel, large and crimson-tinted, swoop in from the blackening clouds to caress his cheeks and pull his head into a cool lap—that of Rosa's. She peers down at Chuck with glistening eyes and whispers, "It's okay, you're not alone," and Chuck lets it all out—the reservoir of tears he's been accumulating since age 10.

Oops

# 2 Years Later...

## Chapter 34
## The Goddamn Epilogue

The bomb's detonator found on Anderson pretty much resolved the entire serial killer fiasco. No one came forward about the suicidal jumper. Bernard's remains were never found, because they were buried in the vacant lot next to the convent where all the nuns were forced to abort and bury their priest-produced babies. Henriette decided to remain with Orpheus, mainly to keep him from joining his children in the afterlife.

All in all, everything seemed to come to a rather depressing yet convenient end.

Rosa leads Chuck, paw in paw, skipping down the shady block. In this part of town, instead of valet, every shoddy business has a beggar parked out front offering to not harass customers in exchange for some loose change.

As a soot-covered hand springs forward and smacks Chuck on the tight ass, he feels like his transformation into a woman is finally complete.

No, not like that.

You see, following the death of his beloved Mia, Chuck lost the will to fight. And the few bad guys who surfaced, looking for an epic battle, couldn't find it in themselves to pick on such a sorry sack of shit, so most of them retired, or found God.

Anyway, Rosa moved Chuck into her brand-new home after he accidentally torched his condo after falling asleep on his sectional with a lit joint. Chuck didn't even know where the joint had come from, or that he even smoked, but he had been drinking quite a bit, and he spent that evening with Rosa at the Cock and Bull bar, drowning his sorrows, so it was what it was. Besides, everybody knew what happened at the Cock and Bull stayed at the Cock and Bull.

Besides, besides, if Rosa had acquired the doobie from a sketchy associate, so be it—she was merely trying to see Chuck through this rough patch. Which was why she moved him into her two-story home located in the suburbs and bought him an entirely new wardrobe (one she handpicked due to his lack of style) and urged him to retire because rumor had it the new lieutenant, an esteemed woman with a partial mustache, wasn't going to put up with his shit for much longer. So after they kissed, and eventually snuggled, and stared deep into each other's eyes and saw a sparkle neither of them ever thought would come back, they did it, but not like fucking, more like an hour-and-a-half long love massage, then Chuck retired and Rosa was promoted into his position, and with the pay increase, she was like, "Thank God, I'll finally be able to afford my mortgage," which was weird, but whatever—with the end of his watch came immense relief. And happiness. Chuck took over the stereotypical womanly duties and cleaned the house and cooked breakfast and served hot dinner and even eased himself back into renovating. Each time Rosa stumbled home from a long day of whooping ass, she'd find another new project furthered, or completed, and before long, her home started looking a lot like *their* home.

This was the life Chuck had always been meant to lead. The only problem was, Rosa kept putting off her doctor appointments regarding the very serious removal of the bomb lodged inside her.

On the x-ray, it appeared as a liver tumor, but whoever surgically planted the thing didn't slip it *inside* the liver, but *alongside* it, and over the course of a few months, the liver grew over the thumb-drive-sized device like moss, engulfing it.

Chuck left little reminders scattered around the house, like when he would write on the fridge's dry erase board: *Good morning! I packed you that Cooking Light salad you've been drooling over. Please get your fucking tumor removed! Love you, but not if you die☺*

"Attention to Chuck," Rosa yaps, her smiley face turned back toward him as they race, skip, whatever, "we're almost there, pay attention!"

Attention to Rosa, he's sort of reliving the birth of their family, which reminds him: "Watch out!" She turns in time to hurdle a homeless woman packed tight inside a tattered trash bag lying in the middle of the sidewalk. "Be more careful!" he barks, to which she barks back, "and you focus—we hardly ever have time to hang out. I want your full attention today."

He'll give her that, especially since the last thing he wants is for her to trip and crush the five-month-old baby she's lugging around in that still-hard-yet-bubbled stomach of hers.

But before he can give her 100%, here's the rest of their tale in a nutshell:

By the time Rosa finally got around to seeing the specialist, they discovered she was a month pregnant and wouldn't be able to have the operation until after the birth.

And so it went, and so it goes.

They zig-zag through the slum, which begs the question why did they park so far away in the first place? Perhaps so Rosa's still brand-new-looking Camaro wouldn't get put on blocks and stripped of its shiny wheels?

In any case, this certainly feels like Deja vu. Like Rosa's got something sneaky up her sleeve, perhaps another one of her lesson-teaching moments, or perhaps...perhaps she's going to propose!

*Jesus, Chuck, grow your goddamn balls back.*

"Ta-da." Rosa drops Chucks hand and motions at a shitty ice cream parlor which reads in once-red, now-faded, pink lettering: *Ice Cre m.*

This is it, the place she had been talking up the past few weeks. It looks like a tight squeeze, like the limit is three people, which would be their entire family, but it's hard to tell what exactly awaits what with the warped yellow, plaque-like storefront windows and everything.

"Wait right here, I'm going to surprise you," Rosa says, plucking her fat wallet out of her ass pocket. She hands him over three worn fivers. "Why don't you feed the homeless?" She hops the stairs in one go and whips herself inside.

The homeless man valeting this joint sports a blue Snuggie with a bikini model graphic stretching from neck to ankle. Too bad his head, which rests on a juicy trash bag, tarnishes the image. He looks to be in his late fifties, but it's hard to tell with that face full of gray and tattered fedora. And those beaten down eyes. And that scarred forehead. And those—

"Didn't your mother ever teach you not to stare?" the man rasps through a tiny black hole.

"My mom was killed when I was young." It's the only unclosed case of his career. Well, that and when his first love vanished.

"Oh I'm sorry, Sonny." He stares at Chuck while Chuck stares off into space for quite some time. "Ah-hem. You know the drill. Got any spare cash?"

Chuck hands over the $15, and he's not an expert on these encounters, but in the very least, he expects the needy man to leap to his dirty socks with some newfound energy and squeeze Chuck tight against his will and perform an awful song and dance and tail him back to the Camaro, all the while pointing and shouting, "This gentleman's the best! You hear me? He's a Godsend! An Angel! I'll never forget him for as short as I live!"

But the guy shoves the cash inside his bikini breast pocket and gives this look like he's been shorted. "Come on, Son, that the best you can do?"

"Seriously?"

"Seriously." He takes his right hand, which has remained concealed this entire time, and showcases how it's not there. There's only a ragged stump which looks as though it was never properly attended to and forced to heal on its own after being cauterized by a hot iron. "Help an amputee out, will ya?"

Chuck slides his glove off and fits his black hand over the stub—it's a perfect match. The two stare at each other, dumbfounded, confused, angry, and a lot of other adjectives, too.

The *Ice Cre m* joint's door swooshes open, and out hops Rosa, from the top of the stairs to the bottom. She hasn't purchased any ice cre m, yet she's just as giddy as if she had. "Surprise!" she shouts, and with one good look at her face, the homeless man shoots to his dirty socks like Chuck had imagined and takes off running. He begs for his life to be spared, even after he skids around a corner, granting the two lovebirds some much needed privacy.

"Rosa," Chuck's shaking, sweating, peeing, "what the fu—"

"I bested you," Rosa says all proud-momish, "and I bested the system."

"Tell me you didn't—"

"I killed Mia. I had the detonator in my hand the entire time they were fumbling around with Anderson's fat ass. You should've seen your face when you looked over at me—all I could think was, this dumb bitch doesn't even have a clue."

"But," Chuck mutters, "but I won."

"No, *I* won! I was always going to kill your girlfriend, fiancée, whatever you wanna call her. Haven't you figured it out by now that this entire story has been about proving a point? That it's not about you? Didn't you listen to a word I said? To my clues? The only way you were ever going to stop me was by literally stopping me. I gave you a used wedding planner. I made you get married. I ruined your happily ever after. I made my hatred for the law clear, told you straight away that my wife had been taken from me by a man in blue. For Christ's sake, you met me at a protest. All my associates have professions which make this entire scheme possible. And then there's Mia, the love of your life, the woman you're supposed to trust the most—she warned you about me. I even confessed to coming onto her. What I didn't tell you was at first, this entire game with you wasn't the plan. I had tried to lure Mia away from you, to get her to be my lover. When she resisted, I drugged her protein shakes. She caught on during our last session, but I still managed to seal the deal. That's right, Chuck—I fucked you, and I fucked your girlfriend, too. The only difference is, she fought back, you didn't. You like being dominated."

Chuck vomits down his chin, inside his coat.

"Listen, I've never done this before, so I'm pretty sure my execution wasn't the greatest, but goddamn, Chuck, I feel like I gave you enough to go on and plenty of time to thwart my master plan."

"I, I—"

"Jesus, get up." She saves him from falling. "No, you know what? Sit down." She sits him down, then kneels before him. "Open your mouth, because here comes my backstory."

# Chapter 35
# The Goddamn Epilogue Continues

Rosa's real name is Alejandra, no real shocker there, but for a period of six years, she lived under a different alias: *Mateo*

*Alejandra's story began and ended in a small town somewhere in Texas.*

*Alejandra was considered a Tomboy. Sure, she had jerked off a few boys, just to try it, but they claimed she was too rough, and that, if they thought deep and hard enough about it, it didn't feel like her head was totally in the game—like she wasn't giving those hand jobs her all.*

*Nor would she, so the hand jobs stopped coming her way. In an odd twist of fate, the boys accepted her as part of their gang, and they played football together, and watched '90s action flicks together, and they even slept over each other's houses and jerked off under the same blankets to their parents' smutty Cinemax flicks like* In the Garden of Eva. *The girl on girl action got them all hot and bothered, and one time, one kid had to muzzle Alejandra's mouth shut with his sticky hand.*

*If Alejandra hadn't been so riled up, she would've broken his hand, but instead, she finished herself off in silence, and never once did it occur to her that she might have been a lesbian.*

*She wouldn't discover her sexuality until weeks later after the girl gang had an epiphany. Since Alejandra was a girl, and she had been welcomed into the boys' pack and treated as one of their own, what if they befriended her and used the tomboy as a mole?*

*One would think this the part of the story where everything went to Hell, but quite the contrary. The girls invited Alejandra to join their ranks, and the boys urged her to try it.*

*Alejandra gave the girls a whirl. No, she didn't invade their pink and purple sleepover with a strap-on and go to town—she didn't partake in a massive, topless pillow fight either—the girls let Alejandra dictate their night, so they arm-wrestled, played hide-and-go seek and even held a tag-team style royal rumble. Surprisingly, the girls had a blast, as did Alejandra. It wouldn't be until later, after they had turned in, that the topic of boys arose.*

*Alejandra knew everything—which guy had a crush on which girl, and through this connection, she ranked up in the world from tomboy to matchmaker. The title fit her well, and she became friends with everyone. And these weren't ungrateful kids—after they found their happiness, they wished to return the favor—they wanted Alejandra to find "the one". But for all intents and purposes, since neither boy nor girl seemed to tickle her fancy, she figured herself to be asexual.*

*Then, a year and a half later, Angel entered the picture. She was the new girl in town. She was as white as her name suggested and hailed from a fancy place in California. The reason for her family's plight could be seen painted around her sunken-in eyes, around her cracked, painted-black lips, on her swollen nose. Angel had been bullied. She used her long, black hair like picket fences to cover her tiny, innocent face. And she wore oversized Korn hoodies and sweatpants to conceal her true frame, which when later discovered, turned out to be thin and bony. For all intents and purposes, Angel was the equivalent of a Chihuahua monk.*

*Which is funny only for the simple fact that her only pet was a Chihuahua named Monk.*

*But that little tidbit has no actual significance in this sub-story.*

*So, what does?*

*Well, the two girls finished their junior and senior years of high school without meeting. Alejandra tried, her friends tried, but Angel had social anxiety problems which put a gulf between them.*

*And after high school, when most of the kids moved on with college, Angel stayed behind, because her job as a waitress at the local diner seemed safe, so Alejandra stayed behind, too, because she had never once over the years gotten Angel out of her mind—and even then, faced with either pursuing a career or a young woman who never gave her the time of day, Alejandra swung for the fences at love.*

*With this new direction in life, Alejandra decided to fully embrace her tomboy nature. She renamed herself Mateo (God's gift) and began anew.*

*It took months for the cook position at the diner to become available, but when it did, Mateo applied and didn't land the job. It would take nearly four years for the grunt who won the position to get fired for stumbling in too drunk, and then, finally, Mateo got the call she had been waiting for: "Hey, you still desperate?"*

*Yes, she was.*

*On the first day of the job, Mateo arrived with an amount of pep none of the locals had ever seen before. Her boss even said, "Wipe that shit off your face and cut these potatoes."*

*"Yeah, sure, Boss! By the way, is Angel working today?"*

*The boss laughed. "You just missed her."*

*"She working tomorrow?"*

*"You fuckin' with me?"*

*"Um, no?"*

*"'Cause that bitch up and quit last night."*

*Nobody called the love of her life a bitch, so Mateo overturned the bucket, dumping twenty pounds of slimy potatoes all over the floor, tore off her apron and tossed it on the grill, and after saying, "I quit, too, Asshole," she swiped a bag of BBQ chips for the road and dinged through the door.*

*Not even an hour later, two cops arrived on her mom's doorstep asking for Mateo by name. The mom wanted to know what was going on, and the cops wanted to know which of her seven kids was Mateo. The mom insisted she didn't know who this Mateo was, and only one of her kids fit the bill, her name was Alejandra, and she was sobbing in the basement. The cops bullied their way inside and insisted they'd give Alejandra a real reason to cry as they cuffed and prodded her out to the squad car. Mateo's mom stood there on the porch with a bottle in hand, shaking her head, balling. The mom had been banking on Alejandra or Mateo or whoever she was to fill her ex-husband's shoes. But Mateo and her mother had had this fight many times before. Mateo made it quite clear that it wasn't her fault her mother couldn't keep her legs closed, and the mother made it quite clear that if she closed shop, how would they pay for the bills? Those men who came and "came" and went were the only sure thing in their lives.*

*Mateo found herself locked in a slammer for 24 hours. Her crime on paper? Stealing potato chips. Her crime in theory? Being Latino.*

*The real injustice occurred when Mateo was released and wandered home to find it flooding. Several holes had opened in the popcorn ceiling and were gushing waterfalls.*

*"Mom?" Nobody. "Pedro?" Nobody. "Carlos?" Nobody. "Jasmine?" Nobody.*

*This went on and on as she hiked the stairs. Only the rumbling of water talked back. And then, barging into the bathroom, she saw the overflowing tub filled with half her submerged siblings. The others were piled up next to the toilet. And as for the mother, that mother fucker, Mateo sought her out, screaming, "Where are you? Show yourself!" She was lying in her bed, tucked snug under the covers. Mateo hopped on top and began to choke her to death, but the mother was already blue. The pill bottle she usually binged on was completely empty. The white residue outlined her navy lips.*

*The mother had finally checked out.*

*In a state of shock, Mateo did what any rational person would have done and called the police. The entire force swarmed the scene, all six of them, and initially arrested her. Police threw Mateo back in the same slammer and swore she'd be charged with murder, but later that night, the coroner's by-the-books report saved her hide.*

*Quite a few of Mateo's friends drove back and flew in from their colleges and threw together enough cash from their odd jobs to pay for the mass funeral. Only the mother was cremated. After the funeral, after Mateo took cover behind a rather large statue for some fancy dead person, she filled her mother's urn with American Honey and pounded the morbid cocktail. She vowed, right there and then, to absorb those who would try to wrong her.*

*Angel slid into view—she wore her same ole black sweatshirt and matching sweatpants. "Who're you talking to?"*

*Mateo was quite drunk and emotional, but even so, she seized like a dried-out engine.*

"Sorry," Angel said, "about what happened. Are you okay?"

Mateo didn't speak, didn't look away from the withered grounds.

"This is a bad time." Angel went to leave, and she got nine epitaphs away before Mateo finally shouted, "Wait!" She stumbled over to Angel and said, "Ever see Minority Report?"

"Isn't Tom Cruise in that one?"

"Exactly!"

"I've wanted to."

"Let's go."

"Right now?"

"Right now."

"What about the rest of the funeral? Isn't there food or something?"

"I can't eat."

"Of course."

They both smiled.

"I'd rather see the movie—let it take me away."

"All right, I'll go."

Mateo couldn't find the courage to say it, but only Angel could take her away.

Half-way through the movie, they held hands.

And a week later, during the next flick, they finally ended with a kiss during the credits.

Stereotypical lesbians would have fucked each other raw during the trailers for the first movie, but this wasn't the case with Mateo and Angel.

# Chapter 36
# The Goddamn Epilogue Will Never End

"Chuck," Rosa says an inch removed from his good ear, "for once in your life, focus. I'm almost finished."

*The donations for Mateo's dead family eventually sputtered, amounting to the equivalent of chopped liver. "Chopped liver" was a popular comparison back in the early '00s. So was "a pot to piss in", and with nothing but "chopped liver" to her name, Mateo literally did not have "a pot to piss in" and was given a swift "kick in the pants" eviction for her troubles.*

*Angel arrived at the dubbed "suicide home" with the FOR RENT sign taped to the storm door. She insisted on being the one to pick Mateo up for their ritualistic Friday movie date. She arrived with a box of Dots and two juice cartons as a surprise. They'd smuggle these into the movie, because snacks were always double the price of admission.*

*Mateo had been running late. She found it troublesome cutting through the neighbor's yard. She was coming from the alley where she slept. She pissed in a tin coffee can. Then she wiped with some used paper towels from the dumpster. Then she spritzed juice from a half-eaten orange onto her neck. Then she got a move on, but the move wasn't fast enough. She hopped the fence six minutes later than expected and found herself out-of-breath while trying to intercept Angel. But Angel had already discovered that her girlfriend was now her homeless girlfriend—which didn't change her feelings, not like Mateo thought it would.*

*Angel threw open her arms, her heart, and seconds later, her apartment. She was adamant as she said, "You're moving in with me. No ifs, ands or buts."*

*That week, the two finally made love. There were no ifs, ands, but there were definitely butts.*

*Months later, with Angel working 60 odd hours a week to maintain the roof over their heads, Mateo vowed to get a job to alleviate pressure. But Angel insisted she relieve stress by way of her tongue.*

*"My tongue's not gonna pay any bills, Angel."*

*"It will."*

*"I'm not whoring myself out like my mother, so don't even try."*

*"I'd never!"*

*"Then whaddya mean?"*

*"I took another job."*

*"What? Why would you do that?"*

*"To pay for your education. Like it or not, you're going to college. You're going to work your ass off to become that big-shot lawyer you've always talked about, and you're not only going to let me retire from rundown diners and bowling alleys and gas stations, but you're also going to help those like us— women, minorities, and anybody classified as 'different'. Hey, chin up. Don't be scared. You can do this. Besides, you know what my favorite Korn song always says: 'Fuck all that bullshit!'"*

*While Mateo commuted to and fro a community college exactly 18.9 miles away, she came home exhausted only to turn around and work her tail off at Brewster's, the local sports bar. The move allowed her to see Angel for longer than a brief hello, kiss, sometimes screw, before they went their separate ways, because she, too, worked as a waitress.*

*The tips were great, especially since precisely 62% of their patrons were alcoholics—it took them a handful of drinks, sometimes a dozen, to even get buzzed, but once they hit such a state, their wallets burst open and money shot out. The problem was, the drinks were dirt cheap. The other problem was, 100% of the six police officers fell into that 62%.*

*One day, four of those officers happened to be seated in Angel's section. There were at least a half-dozen different games playing on the TVs lining the bar. The officers chatted and drank and watched these games with their top shirt buttons blown open. There was plenty to do.*

*But shortly after round five, Officer Riley flicked Officer Bubba in the shoulder and said, "You fucking see that?"*

*Bubba saw a quadruple bacon cheeseburger and licked his chops.*

*"Not that, Dipshit. The fucking spic."*

*The spic in question was Mateo.*

*"And you see what she just did?"*

*Now the officers twisted and turned, trying to see.*

*"That spic kissed our waitress."*

*"On the mouth?" Officer Pete had popped a semi.*

*"Of course not," Officer Riley said. "On the cheek."*

*"You fucking kidding me?"*

*"I'm not fucking kidding you."*

*"Can't even be hot lesbians?"*

*"Can't even be hot lesbians."*

*Officer Riley begun the tipping of glasses which culminated with Officer Bubba smacking his barely touched draft to the floor and belching, and ended with Angel dashing over with a rag which wasn't nearly large enough and saying, "Oh my gosh, what happened?"*

*She and Mateo happened.*

*After Angel hurried back with a bundle of towels and got on her hands and knees to clean the deliberate mess, Officer Riley ducked underneath the table and said, "So that your partner or something?"*

*She sensed the bitterness in his bite and knew well enough to shake her head and say, "Of course not."*

*"Of course not?" He laughed, then pulled his body upright, then let the tablecloth fall. "We'll see about that."*

*"See about what?" Officer Thomson said.*

*"Oh, nothing."*

*But it wasn't nothing.*

*It was something.*

*It was everything.*

*Even more so because after that night, after those officers gave Angel all sorts of shit, and she insisted she had endured the worst night of her life, Mateo couldn't wait any longer, so after their shower, Angel reached for a towel and*

*Mateo reached for a ring, and in the seconds following, the big question was popped, and Angel said, balling her eyes out, "I do!"*

# Chapter 37
## Looks like the Goddamn Epilogue is Here to Stay

"Are you even paying attention?" Rosa pinches the tip of Chuck's dick. She must have eased it out of his pants while he was in la-la land. "Fight the A.D.D."

"A.D.H.D."

"Because here's the real reason I ruined your life."

*Mateo took on a second job, not out of necessity, but to earn a few extra bucks to splurge on certain things. One of those things was a wedding planner. It helped her not only keep track of their very busy lives, but also count down the days leading up to the day she had always dreamt of but never thought would come true.*

*It was going to be amazing.*

*Wonderful.*

*Out of this world!*

*But the very next week, while Rosa was off learning, Officer Riley stopped by Brewster's in the middle of the day. Angel met him at the greeting stand with her usual, "How many today?" Then she recognized this man to be Riley, only in civilian clothes. He tapped the oak and said, "I'm not staying. Gotta be at the office in a few."*

*"Oh." She noticed the butt of his firearm peering out the crotch of his jeans. The rest of his short-sleeved button-down shirt was tucked in around it, like he wanted all the attention there on his big, gleaming gun.*

*"I wanna take you out on Friday."*

*But she already had plans with Mateo to see* The Matrix Reloaded. *Not to mention Angel wasn't into men, especially fascist pigs.*

"Oh."

"You say anything other than oh?" He pumped his pelvis just enough for the silver to catch light from the Tiffany's lamp hanging overhead.

"Yeah."

"Great." He slapped the stand, shaking both it and her. "Pick you up at six sharp."

That was around the time Mateo typically arrived home with their only car, a Ford Focus hatchback.

"Actually—"

"There a problem?"

"No, none at all. Six will work."

"Act happy," he said, smacking his paws together and turning to leave, "because we're going somewhere awesome." The somewhere awesome was the strip club across town where Angel had almost taken a position if it hadn't been for Mateo taking on multiple jobs.

How could Angel do this? She felt instantly nauseous, and as Riley left, it was now or never to stop this, whatever this was.

"Excuse me!"

He turned on a dime. Maybe it was that black ponytail. Those dark, slanted eyes. Those thin lips surrounded by all that rough, prickly hair. That gun. The way he said, "What?"

"Don't you need my address?"

He laughed. "Already know it."

Mateo made it home twenty minutes before six with a smile on her face and a poem snug in her hand. She read the poem, which she had written during one of her more boring classes. Angel told her she shouldn't have, and Mateo said, "I know, I know—I'm supposed to be learning, but I just love you so, so much," and Angel said, "No—you shouldn't have, period." She felt *terrible, especially after the poem's emotional recital, and especially, especially after lying about something having come up last minute.*

*What could've been so important?*

*"My dad contacted me." But her dad had abandoned her as a toddler. Dropped her off at an orphanage after her mother died. "He wants to talk. I've decided to hear him out."*

*"Of course, you should definitely go," Mateo said, both happy and scared. "If and when you need me—"*

*"I know where you'll be."*

*And ten minutes later, Officer Riley honked. Angel was relieved to see him driving an unmarked car with tinted windows.*

*They rolled away and didn't talk much, especially not at the start of the strip club, because it was incredibly loud with the thumping music and all the men hooting and hollering. But after Riley pressured enough drinks down her throat, she eased open.*

*He asked what she enjoyed, and she went on and on about movies and music and—*

*"No, no, no," he said, snaking his arm around her neck, reaching into her blouse to fondle her nipples, "come on, stop playing princess."*

*"Okay."*

*What was she to do? He hoisted her to a stand and chaperoned the trip to the back where a dank hallway awaited. They passed the filthy, stinking restrooms, passed the utility closets and dressing rooms, and once around the far corner, a woman with her tits hanging out loud and proud asked if they wanted a private one on one on one.*

*Officer Riley's badge had a sobering effect.*

*"Oh, hey Mr. Riley."*

*"Officer Riley."*

*"Officer Riley, duh. Just one on one then?"*

*"Just one on one."*

*She pushed open a door on her right, and Officer Riley led his victim into the green room with the purple, low-rider bed. Angel knew exactly where this road led, but there were no turn arounds.*

*After the door was pulled shut, Riley unbuckled his jeans and dropped his pants and underwear. He tugged Angel over to the bed and plopped down on the edge. He jerked himself hard and said, "Now I know you aren't no fucking lesbo, right, Missy?"*

*She shook to her core. "Yeah, right."*

*"Well?" He removed his firm grip from his dick and clenched the bed. It towered between those hairy, pale thighs a good five inches and change.*

*Angel hesitantly settled onto her knees as if confused at church and tied her hair into a bun. Before she could swallow her pride and his penis, he pushed her head back and said, "You're fully clothed. Where's the fun in that?"*

*He talked her out of every piece, even her socks, and after she went down on him for a solid nine minutes, he pulled her up by her chin onto the bed and mounted her from behind. He didn't use protection, and he made it a point to switch from her anus to her vagina for the final shot.*

# Chapter 38
## The Goddamn Epilogue Finally Gets Interesting, Then Ends

"That's why I fucked you in the ass with a cucumber," Rosa says, chuckling while Chuck upchucks.

*After the strip club debacle, Angel wept herself to sleep in Mateo's arms.*

*Of course, after such a tense meeting with her fake father, this was to be expected. So too were the following late-night rendezvouses where Rosa spent that time planning every little detail to ensure their wedding was one neither of them would ever forget.*

*Angel found out a month and a half later she was pregnant.*

*Another two months afterwards, during a night spent binge-snorting coke and tackling as many pages from a Karma Sutra book as humanly possible, Officer Riley laid flat on his back and said to the slow-moving ceiling fan, "So, you finally converted?"*

*"What's that mean?"*

*He smacked her. "Don't fucking talk to me like that."*

*"I didn't mean to."*

*"Damn straight." He smacked her again. "You gonna continue to fuck that spic or what?"*

*Her heart wouldn't allow her to say no, so she said nothing, but this infuriated him to no end. He called all five of his officer buddies over, and they stripped down to nothing in the living room of his two-bedroom home. He said, "Any problem with this?"*

*Resistance was futile, so she wagged her head dog-like, just as he had trained her to do. And then the buddies took their turns, one after the other after the other, and so on and so forth. At one point, all five of the buddies were involved. They high-fived over her soggy face, and at the end, when everybody felt drained, and Officer Bubba said, "I gotta jet, wife'll be expecting me," Officer Riley made the big announcement: "I'm gonna be a father!" and they all high-fived one last time.*

*The announcement didn't end there. With the drugs still kicking in his veins, Officer Riley got the bright idea to chaperon Angel back to her place, make her ring the doorbell a dozen times, and after Mateo answered with fists digging crust out of her eyeballs, he made Angel confess to how she wasn't gay anymore, that she had been seeing a guy for months, that her dad hadn't come back—her boyfriend, in fact, had been wining and dining and swining her this entire time, and she loved this man, and they did things—a lot of things— and, oh yeah, Angel was pregnant with his son...or daughter...they'd be finding out at their next ultrasound.*

*"Wait, what the fuck?" Mateo couldn't have been any more alert. "What're you talking about?"*

*Angel's sobbing brought a reality to her words.*

*"But our wedding's in exactly one week."*

*More sobbing.*

*"No." Mateo stumbled back with hands damming her mouth. "Angel, stop this."*

*"You stop this," Officer Riley said, stepping forward, pushing Angel into her submissive role, "you fucking scoundrel." He dawned his police attire.*

*"She brought protection?"*

*"She brought her lover, Fag."*

*"You?"*

*"She doesn't want a sicko like you in her life anymore, so get the fuck out."*

*It all came so very fast. "But—"*

*Riley gripped the gun shoved into his crotch and said, "Easy, Bitch—this here is private property, which means you're trespassing."*

*"Angel!" She got up high on her tippy-toes and jerked from side to side to find that familiar, yet foreign face she had come to dream of every night before snuggling underneath the covers.*

*Officer Riley shoved her, and the landing's pole gouged her in the lower back. She recovered quickly and leapt forward, swinging at Officer Riley's blotchy cheek but catching him in the Adam's apple instead. She'd serve two years for this, but not just yet.*

*With Officer Riley rolling on the carpet, gasping for air, Mateo wrapped her Angel in the mightiest of all bear hugs, hoisted her into the air and shouted in her ear, "You're safe, I'll protect you," but Angel knew, given their predicament, that this entire clusterfuck was out of their control, which was why before Officer Riley tackled Mateo and pummeled her skull with his bare fists, Angel whispered back, "I never loved you." She knew such a crushing blow would make the path to recovery easier on Mateo, but she didn't know it would result in her own murder exactly eight years later during her and Officer Riley's seven-year-old son's school play. All the other five officers were in attendance that day to cheer on their comrade's leading son.*

*Mateo posed as a background tree on stage. Nobody knew a person was even in the cardboard cutout until Mateo's eyes popped open. Nobody knew the branches could move until they reached behind the 2D bushes and withdrew glocks and opened fire on the crowd.*

*All but one officer lived to recount the horror. Officer Lewis. And as Angel bled out, her bloody trail leading from her seat to the stage, she cradled her dead son in her arms, close to her stomach, attempting to force him back in so she could perform a rebirth, but such a thing, as you know, isn't humanly possible.*

*The play was Peter Pan, not The Resurrection, and it was little, lifeless Pan in her arms, not Jesus.*

*And the tree was not a tree, it was Mateo.*

*And Mateo was no longer a timid tomboy brimming with love. That skin had been shed, revealing Rosa, a chiseled body fueled by hatred and revenge.*

*And Rosa's mission would not end on that day—not after her story, her struggle, was overlooked on every news channel, ditched to paint her as the sole, cowardly villain of this story, and eventually dropped weeks later in favor of bigger, juicer events.*

*Rosa would not fade so quietly.*

*Her voice would be heard.*

*To force the masses into hearing her silenced voice, Mateo knew she had to aim higher. Much higher. The target needn't be some no-name, once gay slut with one kid, but a hero, or better yet, an idol—and not an American Idol. A real fucking idol. One people had painted on their mugs and knitted into their shirts.*

*The masses, whether they knew it or not, lived alternate lives through this man.*

*When they weren't boring, ordinary citizens, they pretended to be Chuck Steak. In the shower, men made the spitting sound of bullets and saw the water raining down on them as blood. Outside, kids revved their bicycles and jumped over explosions. And in the bedroom, women saw his square face on their husbands as it went downtown.*

*For all intents and purposes, the masses were Chuck Steak clones. They felt his triumphs, so Rosa would make them feel his heartbreak—her heartbreak.*

*And so it goes.*

"Six dead siblings," Rosa sings, "six evil officers, and Mateo who only lived to age six."

Chuck swipes Rosa's firearm (which is always buried barrel-first inside her crotch) and takes aim at her teary, bleeding eyes.

"6-6-6, I'm the devil." Rosa dangles the silver pendant once slung around her neck in front of his face. It's been opened to reveal a ruby. "And this isn't a ruby," she says, "it's another detonator. It blows the tumorous bomb situated next to our baby."

Chuck beats the gun against air and blows steam out his nostrils. "What the fuck do you want from me!?!"

"Cool down, Man," some random passerby says, and then the young lad pauses and puts out his mitten and says, "Say, can ya spare—"

Chuck puts a bullet through his palm, then points the smoking barrel at Rosa's forehead.

"Don't play chicken with me," Rosa says, "I know you won't let your child die." She's right. "Now give me back my goddamn gun." He drops his head and hands it over. "For the next four months, you're gonna follow my every command. I'll toy with you the same way Riley toyed with my Angel, and after the birth, you're going to finally fight me, no weapons, just fists, and after I easily win, I'm going to fuckin' strangle you to death with the umbilical cord hanging out of my vagina."

www.ingramcontent.com/pod-product-compliance
Lightning Source LLC
Chambersburg PA
CBHW051413170626
46809CB00006B/2145